Dreaming of Darkness

Book Two Of Monster in the Darkness Series
Bella Reves

Contents

Dedication

Unclassifiable castoffs, misfits, marginal cases:
when you're one yourself, or close to it, there's
a reassurance in proving you haven't quite gone
under by taking up with somebody odder than you are.

– Amy Clampitt, *A Hedge of Rubber Trees*

Trigger warnings

List of trigger warnings:

Mentions of Suicide Attempts

Suicidal Ideation

Cigarettes

Snakes

Spiders

Knife Play

Nipple Piercing

Anal

Biting

Accidental Pregnancy

PTSD Nightmares

Kidnapping

Torture

Mentions of Exorcism

Graphic Violence

Dismemberment

Chapter One

Addison

In the aftermath of a traumatic event, there are several ways that people might cope. After what happened with Jake in the warehouse, we all agreed that one way for us to cope was to get a fresh start.

My lab was closed after the "break-in" and "vandalism", so I applied for stress leave, using the murder of my study subjects as the excuse. After everything that happened, I had no pushback from the dean. I spent my newfound free time searching for properties for sale near all the universities with acceptable biology departments who would allow my transfer. As it turned out, finding a building that could host our eclectic job requirements as well as house five people was harder than it sounded.

Shockingly, this left us with very few options. After close to a week with no success, I finally asked Piper if he could do… whatever it was he did to help find us a place. He'd done it before. At least that was what Cain said when I asked how he discovered this building. Piper was game, but he had no idea how he found this place either, so it was the blind leading the blind.

In the end, Wyatt suggested that we'd get drunk, give Piper a map, and see what happens. Not exactly the well thought out process I'd been hoping for, but I'd seen the man throw up a spider, so we were well past sanity at that point. We shared a bottle of whiskey and I sat in Piper's lap - he claimed that was to guide the intention but I thought it was just an excuse for him to be handsy - and we all stared at a map and watched Piper work.

Even though it was deliberate this time, it was still a little terrifying when Piper's eyes clouded over and he started mumbling under his breath. One of his arms was wrapped around me, his palm flattened against my stomach to prevent me from moving. We gave him a sharpie, which he clutched, almost forgotten, in his other hand, leaning over toward the map spread out over the coffee table. His breath tickled my ear as he mumbled, communicating with unseen forces, as the sharpie hovered over the map. Nobody moved for fear of breaking the spell, and I saw Cain scowl as a sudden chill dropped down over us. When I exhaled, my breath was visible and Austin shivered, shifting closer to Cain for warmth. I heard whispering, but when I glanced at Piper, his lips were no longer moving, instead he was listening intently to the words that were just out of reach for my normal ears.

We all flinched when Piper's hand jerked and slammed down on the table, hard enough to break the pen. Ink stained his hand, and he dropped the broken pieces on the floor, leaning forward and pressing one blackened finger onto the map, leaving a single fingerprint behind. The frost in the air abruptly dissipated, and I stroked Piper's cheek soothingly as the haze over his eyes began to clear, the blue of his irises visible once more. He clutched me tighter, exhaling a shaky breath and pressing his face into my neck. My skin felt damp, and when I turned to check on him, I noticed tears staining his face.

The next day, Piper had assured me it was nothing, just the stress of the prophecy mixed with too much whiskey.

I'd taken a look at the map, searching online for the area covered by Piper's black fingerprint. It was halfway across the country, and, unfortunately, the map we'd used wasn't overly precise, so his thumb print covered nearly half of the city it had landed on. It took me another day to search the entire area online, but I finally managed to find a building for sale that fit our needs... well, oddly perfectly. The main floor was designed for a business. It had an open-floor concept with plenty of space for both Wyatt and Austin to see clients simultaneously. There was no basement in this place, which was fine with me. I wasn't going to miss that alley stairwell one bit. The second floor had a kitchen, a living room space, and one smaller bedroom off to the side, and the floor above it had the master bedroom and two additional bedrooms. When I pointed out the math problem of five people and four bedrooms to Cain, he just shrugged and pointed out the ridiculously cheap asking price. I guess for that sort of steal, we could afford to just build another fucking room if we had to.

Cain had called the realtor that afternoon and signed the paperwork that very evening. The next week was a messy blur. Wyatt had to contact his existing clients and give them the news that he was moving and he shut down their website, opting to start from scratch with a whole new one. I applied for a transfer to the university two blocks away from the new place. When they asked why, I lied and told them I was moving to be closer to family, after all that had happened. I knew none of it was actually their fault, but the guilt-trip was enough to get them to push through the transfer so I'd be all set up there once my stress leave was up.

Packing up the current house was easy enough. Most of the furniture was fine to leave behind. A lot of it had been found or stolen over the years and held no sentimental value. Cain was able to find a buyer who agreed to take the place furnished, although I think he was mainly excited about the pool table, which was too heavy to take with us, anyway. We rented one of those moving vans, and I boxed up everyone's clothing while Cain and Wyatt loaded up the tattoo benches and all their equipment. Going through everyone's clothes was an eye-opening experience, and I made a mental note to go shopping and get everyone some new things.

One thing we had to problem-solve was Austin's... pets. Wyatt had mentioned that when I had been abducted, they'd gotten a rough estimate of just how many snakes were actually living in Austin's room. None of us were trained in animal transport, and I knew leaving them behind was absolutely not an option. In the end, I rounded up a bunch of boxes and stuffed the bottoms with Austin's clothes, and he coaxed them into their temporary transport homes. We loaded them up last, first thing in the morning while it was still dark and the street was relatively empty. It took all of us to pack the boxes into the van, and they took up more room than the rest of our stuff combined. Once the last of them were loaded up, Austin climbed inside and we locked the door. It wasn't the safest, but Austin figured they'd be calmer if he stayed with them. I thought that was a better option than having venomous snakes loose and angry in a moving vehicle.

We took one last look at the building that had housed them for so many years, and had welcomed me in so recently. My gut clenched when I saw the smiley-face painted on the side, fading now after a couple of rainy days. I didn't think anyone was particularly sad to leave, not after everything that had happened. A fresh start was exactly what we needed. I hopped in the van with Cain. Wyatt and Piper followed behind in Cain's car. We had GPS'd the route, and the drive was doable in one shot, as long as everyone was comfortable with an eighteen hour drive. With a van full of what I can only assume were very illegal snakes, we were all willing to risk a little bit of exhaustion to get this done as quickly as possible.

The ride was long, but blissfully uneventful. After the last month, we were all content with a little boredom. Cain was as taciturn as usual, and I kept an eye on him as he drove, making sure he didn't nod off or close his eyes for too long. I could've sworn he didn't sleep anymore, even though Jake was long gone. All I could do was hope that the new place would give him the sense of security we were all missing. We only stopped for caffeine and the occasional bathroom break. Cain refused to let anyone take over driving the van, so I didn't press the issue, sticking to giving him directions and checking on Wyatt and Piper in the mirror.

We arrived at our new place just after midnight. Cain fished the keys out of the lockbox, and we got the door open. He and Wyatt went in ahead of us and checked the place out, making sure no one had gotten inside and was waiting to surprise us. After everything, I was okay with them being overcautious, even if it meant sitting outside in the chilly van while nursing stiff legs from the long drive. As soon as we got the all-clear from them, I unlocked the van and woke Austin up. He was curled up with his boxes of snakes, tucked in a pile of blankets we'd left out for him to be comfortable. All I wanted to do was find a relatively clean space inside and fall asleep, but we didn't know the area well enough to leave all of our possessions in the van.

Starting with the boxes of snakes, we unloaded our things into the new space. We chose a room on the third floor for Austin and brought his snakes and his heaters directly up there. It was the smaller of the rooms, but it was directly over the kitchen and would stay the warmest, which was exactly what the cold-blooded reptiles needed.

I left Austin to sort out his friends and started bringing in the boxes of clothes and toiletries while Wyatt and Cain brought the tattoo benches inside. On my seventh trip up the stairs, I found Piper sitting alone on the kitchen floor, mumbling to himself with his eyes closed. I left him alone since he didn't seem to be in any immediate danger and continued dropping off boxes in everyone's rooms. Just like in the old place, Cain wanted the room off the kitchen/living area, preferring the privacy. I dropped off his boxes and brought Piper's upstairs, leaving his meager box of personal effects in the room next to Austin's.

Mine and Wyatt's boxes went into the master bedroom for now since we still hadn't quite figured out the bedroom arrangements. It would matter a little more when the furniture Cain ordered was delivered, but at least there was a walk-in closet in the room that would store our things while we sorted it out. It was after 3 a.m. by the time the van and the car were emptied out, which meant we'd been up nearly twenty-four hours straight. I could barely form a coherent sentence, and Piper seemed to have passed out on the kitchen floor after his... meditation?

Gathering up some blankets from one of the boxes, I draped one over him to keep him warm. I found Cain and Wyatt down in the shop area, sprawled out on the tattoo benches in the middle of the room. I checked to make sure the vehicles were locked up, and locked the front doors, making sure that the key was accounted for. Wyatt was passed out already, snoring softly as he lay on his stomach across the bench. I tossed a blanket over him and brought the last one over to Cain, who was laying down but still awake, watching me silently.

"How are you not asleep already?" I murmured, unfolding the blanket. I moved to throw it over him, but his hand shot out, catching my hip and pulling me on top of him. He must have been beyond exhausted, he wasn't normally a snuggly guy. I relaxed in his arms, stretching out my body half on top of him, half on the tattoo bench. It wasn't the most efficient bed, but at this point I was just happy it wasn't the floor. I closed my eyes and buried my face against his neck, already warming up as the heat oozed off his skin. Cain's hands idly trailed up my back as I dozed off in his arms, listening to Wyatt's soft breathing next to us.

CHAPTER TWO

Addison

I t felt like I'd only closed my eyes for a second when some god-awful noise echoed through the room. I groaned as Cain shifted underneath me, pulling the offending cell phone out of his pocket.

"What?" he snapped into the phone, and I bit his shoulder to show my displeasure as my eyes blinked open. The sun was in full force, light streaming through all the windows in the studio. *Well then, I guess I'd been asleep for a little longer than a few seconds.*

"Who the fuck is calling you? You have no friends," Wyatt grumbled, pulling his hood down to cover his face, and rolling over onto his back.

"Shut up, it's the furniture guys," Cain replied, and I sighed and rolled off of him, rubbing my hand over my face.

I left Cain to organize the drop-off and went upstairs to check on the other guys. Austin would stay in his room while the movers brought things inside, and we'd set up his furniture ourselves. When I peeked in on him, all I could see was a pile of blankets surrounded by heaters and the odd flash of a scaly body. He'd been much more withdrawn recently. His skin was now mottled with green-blue scales where he scratched through his skin during my... absence. Every time I looked at his torn-up body, I couldn't help but feel guilty. He had been hurting so badly while I'd been gone. I slipped back out and shut the door, making sure not to disturb him.

I woke up Piper and got him off the kitchen floor. He seemed very confused about where we were, and I reminded him that we had moved. I stroked his cheek until his eyes cleared up, and he smiled wanly. Piper's face still had a gaunt, pinched look, having yet to recover from everything that had happened. He gave me a gentle kiss and wandered off, and I just hoped he wasn't planning on heading outside. All I needed was him getting lost on our first day here.

The door opened, and I heard Cain speaking with someone, likely the delivery guys from the furniture company. I headed upstairs and got a blanket, settling myself in a spot where I could watch Austin's door. I felt grimy. My long black hair was up in a messy bun, desperate for a wash. The leggings I'd worn for the car ride had a hole in the knee that I picked at idly while I watched the movers bring their first load of furniture past. They leered at me as they huffed and puffed, carrying boxes and mattresses up the two flights of stairs.

Wyatt got us coffees from a nearby coffee shop, making the day a tad more bearable. He sat with me for a few minutes, stroking the back of my neck as I rested my head on his shoulder. Wyatt still had a haunted look on his face, the dark circles under his eyes like bruises against his pale skin. Healing me had taken its toll on him, and he refused to talk about what had happened when he'd absorbed all of that pain and fear into himself. I missed his smile. It was a rare occurrence now. Cain shouted for him and he reluctantly stood up, kissing the top of my head before disappearing back down the stairs.

Sipping my red-eye coffee, I smiled thinly as one of the large, burly men strode past, having just deposited my new Alaskan King bed in the master bedroom. It was enormous and all thanks to me teasing Cain that I'd need a big enough bed to fit all five of us. According to him, this was the biggest mattress on the market, and it barely fit through the door-way.

"You really need that big of a bed?" the mover commented, and I raised my eyebrows at him as I lifted my cup to my lips.

"I have a lot of pillows," I replied blandly, staring back at him. He blinked in confusion before scoffing and shaking his head, trudging back down the stairs. Once they were finished with the boxes in the master bedroom, Cain headed inside and shut the door behind him, leaving Wyatt to supervise downstairs. I heard the violent slamming noises and muffled curses and decided to stay out of whatever war he'd decided to wage on the furniture in there. When the movers were finished upstairs, I finally drifted into Piper's new room and started unboxing the new dresser and the bedframe we'd ordered for him, leaving the door open in case any of the movers decided to wander back upstairs.

I stripped off my hoodie, sweating already as I struggled to assemble the furniture using the dinky little Allen Wrench they provided. Now I understood why Cain was cursing so much. By the time I was finished building the main body of the dresser, I was muttering profanities under my breath. At least the drawers were smaller. Once it was finished, I took a break from building and started taking Piper's meager collection of clothes out of the boxes and got them settled inside their new home. I set his odd assortment of keepsakes on top of the dresser. I was sure he'd rearrange them later more to his liking. Folding up the now empty boxes, I turned to the bed frame reluctantly.

Look, I was a strong, independent woman. I was fully comfortable admitting that I wanted a nap, and I didn't want to build a fucking bed frame with an Allen Wrench. Movement by my feet startled me, and I looked down to see a little red-bellied snake begin to wind her way up my leg. I knew this one. Austin called her Little Red. She was usually wrapped around his wrist like a bracelet. I held out my hand and let her twist herself around my hand, coiling and hissing. "Are you a slithery text-message?" I murmured, smiling. Austin still preferred to send one of his friends to get me.

I abandoned my construction and headed back toward Austin's room, slipping inside with my tag-along wrapped around my wrist. The entire room was more alive than it had been earlier, and I stepped inside nervously, overwhelmed by the sheer amount of scales covering the floor. Austin was sitting in the middle of the room on one of his blankets, his blond hair messed up from sleep.

"You called?" I asked, smiling as I held up Little Red. He grinned at me, beckoning me forward. I was a spider kinda gal, and I could admit without shame that wading into a pile of somewhat venomous snakes made me a little more than nervous. Barely lifting my feet off the floor, I shuffled toward him, trying to avoid stepping on anyone's tail. As soon as I was within striking range, Austin snagged my snake-less wrist. I tumbled to the floor, caught in his wiry arms, and he lowered me down on the blanket, hovering over me.

"Are you nervous?" he asked, cocking his head to the side. A rattlesnake passed by my ear, the telltale sound sending a shiver down my spine.

"I can't talk to them like you can," I teased, and he smiled, flashing his fang-like canines.

"They would never hurt you. You're my mate," he murmured, nuzzling his nose into the hollow of my throat. His hands slid underneath my thin tank top, kneading my breasts through my bra. The word mate made my cheeks burn. He'd used the word before, and it rang differently from plain old girlfriend, that's for sure.

"Austin, the movers are still here," I reminded him gently, shivering as a scaly body brushed against my stomach. I could feel something tickling my ear, and my hair tugged as something else coiled through the mess of a bun on the top of my head. Maybe it was the new environment, but I'd never seen the snakes this... agitated while I was in the room. Austin's teeth grazed my collarbone as he moved between my thighs, oblivious or uncaring of the frantic energy around us.

"The new den smells like strangers," he rasped, tugging down my leggings. "I need it to smell like home." I arched into him as his hand slid between my thighs, two fingers dipping into my already slick entrance. Whimpering, I wrapped my arms around his neck, pleasure building in my stomach as he fucked me with his fingers, hitting the spot that made me see stars.

"Austin..." I moaned, biting my lip to muffle the sounds as I jerked my hips. His fangs sank into my shoulder as I came, the sting barely noticeable compared to the bliss of the orgasm that tore through me. Gasping, I watched as Austin slipped his fingers out and licked them clean, staring at me with a fierce intensity. "Did you… fucking bite me?" I asked, touching my shoulder gingerly. That was a new one.

"You're mine," he murmured, his eyes flashing gold. Leaning down to capture my lips, he kissed me until I was breathless, and I tasted myself on his tongue. When he finally pulled away, he dropped his face back to my shoulder, his tongue brushing against the small punctures in my skin. I felt a little lightheaded as I sat up, tugging my leggings back up my legs as snakes slithered around us, some of them climbing brazenly over my legs. I propped myself up and immediately Austin's twin vipers coiled themselves up my arms, their glistening jet-black scales captivating to watch, but also a little unnerving.

"Alright Mr. Possessive, we should finish building the furniture so we don't have to sleep on the floor again tonight." I smirked at him, and he hopped to his feet, holding out a hand to help me up. The vipers twisted around my neck, coiling together so tightly I worried they'd tie themselves in knots.

I peeked outside, and from the sounds of things the movers were just finishing up downstairs. I could hear Wyatt chatting with them by the door. They wouldn't be able to see up the stairs from there, so I stepped into the hallway and showed Austin where his furniture was set aside, the dresser and the bedframe in boxes just like Piper's. He dragged them back into his room and then helped me get the snakes untangled from around my neck. He claimed they wouldn't bite me, but I wasn't sure if they extended the same courtesy to the other guys.

I found Piper in his room, busying himself with the bed frame I'd abandoned. Leaving him to it, I figured I should probably check on Cain and dig out all the bedsheets so

I could start a few loads of laundry. I found him shirtless on the floor, surrounded by disassembled furniture, looking absolutely murderous. A singed set of instructions was lying on the floor near my feet, and I picked it up, looking at him incredulously. "Need help?" I asked.

"I hate this," he snarled, raking his hand through his hair. I laughed and tossed the little paper booklet at him.

"It's easier if you follow the instructions," I told him, earning myself a glare. I stepped over the strewn out pieces of the bed frame and grabbed my box full of linens.

"If it's so easy, why don't you make it?" Cain growled, and apparently my stubbornness overrode my exhaustion. I tossed the sheets at him and stepped over the wreckage.

"Wash, dry, and fold," I smirked at him as he moved out of my way. I waited until he closed the door before groaning and smacking myself in the forehead. Okay, so this would be a lot easier if I was stronger, and if I had proper tools. Oh, and if some buffoon hadn't thrown the pieces all over the goddamn place. I was sweaty and furious an hour later, having managed to get half the damn thing put together. Honestly, did we even need a bed frame? Couldn't we just stick the mattress against one wall and call it a day? It turned out Cain had been hiding a screwdriver, so that made it slightly less excruciating, but I was still very unsure about the sturdiness of this. I went to the bathroom to get some water from the tap, sticking my head under the faucet like a cat because we didn't have any cups unpacked.

It took another hour, but I finished building the damn thing. The caffeine had exited my bloodstream a long time ago, and my muscles shook as I tried to shove the bed frame over against the far wall. There was no way I was going to move the mattress on my own, so I left it leaning against the wall, cleaning up the bits of cardboard and foam still floating around.

We'd left the garbage bags in the kitchen, so I headed down to grab one, and found all four boys clustered around our new kitchen table, a case of beer sitting on top of it, as well as a large pizza box. I dropped the garbage and nearly dove for the pizza, ignoring Cain's smirk. "You'd better put that mattress on that frame," I told him, swallowing my mouthful of pizza.

Wyatt pulled me down onto his lap, cracking open another beer as I devoured my slice. We were all unnaturally quiet, all of us just busy chewing and fighting to keep our eyes open. Cain finished his pizza and he and Austin disappeared upstairs. I listened to the loud thumps coming from the master bedroom and prayed that my shitty construction job wouldn't crumple under the weight of the enormous mattress. It took another two pieces of pizza before I was finally satiated; the food making me even sleepier than I had been earlier. I snuggled in Wyatt's arms, letting my eyes drift shut as he chatted with Piper about the businesses nearby.

I jolted awake in a confused panic, unable to see in the darkness of the room. I felt a hand on my hip radiating heat, which was strangely bare, even though I had been wearing leggings earlier. My skin prickled with anxiety since the last time I'd woken up naked hadn't ended so well. I shifted and found Cain laying behind me, fast asleep. A shape moved in the darkness in front of me, drawing my gaze, and I was able to make out Wyatt's dark mop of hair on the pillow next to me. Sitting up a bit, I could just make out two more shapes further down the bed – Austin and Piper curled up side by side.

Sighing happily, I settled back down on the bed, leaning into Cain's warmth. Already, I could feel the wounds beginning to heal.

CHAPTER THREE

Piper

I didn't remember how I got here. There was been a bus, I think... and maybe a truck? I'd been aimless for too long, stealing my way across the country, searching for... something. *Someone*? They appeared in my dreams as a faceless being made of smoke and rage. Sometimes I would almost see them out of the corner of my eye and end up following them onto a bus, or through a crowd. The tug was tethered in the center of my chest, pulling me toward something I didn't understand.

Where was I now? I looked around, blinking back into the present. I was holding a glass, a pint? That meant a bar. Finishing the last of the beer in the glass, I set in on the nearby table, glancing around me, looking for a mark. My hands had minds of their own, probably more functional than the one in my skull. As a couple of men passed by, I slipped my fingers in the nearest one's pocket and snatched his wallet, quickly tucking it into my own pocket. Not one to linger with stolen goods, I headed for the exit, stumbling into a table on my way out. *I guess I had more than one drink here.*

The fresh night air greeted me as I stepped outside, the moon casting a glow across the parking lot. I had no clue where I was, and I rarely did anyway. A pang of warning twinged in my chest right as a fist connected with the back of my head. I landed on my knees and dropped into a clumsy roll, popping up further away and whirling around to face my attacker. The face shifted as I tried to focus on it, aging decades as I blinked, trying to stay in the moment. "Give me my fucking wallet, you hippie prick!" he snarled. *Oh, shit.*

I smiled at him, holding up my hands in defense. "There's been a misunderstanding," I offered, and he swung at me again, catching me in the chin and knocking me back. Arms caught me from behind, pinning me down. I laughed and slammed my head back, feeling something crunch as my skull connected with my attacker's friend. My victory was short-lived as a fist connected with my chest, knocking the air out of my lungs. I doubled over and the man slammed me down onto the sidewalk. Pain exploded through my body as two - or maybe three? - of them attacked me ruthlessly.

I rolled over and curled up, protecting the back of my head. As a boot tip caught me in the ribs, I watched a red glow flare up from the shadows beside the bar. "Hey!" someone shouted, and I saw a terrifying demon of a man emerge from the darkness. Smoke pooled off of him, or maybe just off of his cigarette, and the men attacking me were so surprised they actually stopped kicking me for a moment.

"Mind your fucking business and go back inside!" my attacker shouted back. I took this opportunity to shift up to my hands and knees, trying to stand. One of his friends caught me in the back with his boot, dropping me back to the pavement. With my face pressed into the ground, I could only hear the sounds of a bone snapping and a high-pitched shriek. There was some yelling, and a lot of scrambling, and then someone's hand was pulling on my shoulder.

"Come on, can you stand up or what?" the demon barked, yanking me to my feet. The world tilted uncomfortably, and he held me steady as I regained my bearings. I finally caught sight of his face under his ragged gray hood, and his eyes glowed red as time shifted, making me dizzy once more.

He is death; he is fire; he is home.

The whispers surrounded me, showing me a future where the burning man kept me in the present. I saw warmth; I saw pain, and worst, I saw my death. But the tug wouldn't lie. This was the someone I'd been tethered to, I'd been looking for him all along.

"Did they scramble your brains that much, or were you like this before?" he asked coolly, and his hand radiated heat through my shoulder, warming me in the freezing night air.

"I finally found you." I smiled, feeling my lip split. He grimaced, and his hand dropped away from me, leaving me in the cold once again.

"Alright dude, get yourself to a hospital. They fucked you up pretty good," he muttered, and stalked away, heading down the street. I followed him like a puppy, stumbling forward as my body ached from the beating I'd just received. He didn't seem to notice me for the first few blocks, but after a while, he seemed to sense my presence. Spinning around, I saw his eyes flash red in the darkness, like embers flaring in a dying fire.

"Leave me the fuck alone, man, or I'll beat you worse than they did," he snarled, and I hung back, tucking my hands into my thin hoodie to keep them warm. I waited until I nearly lost sight of him before trailing after him once more, letting the tug in my chest lead me forward. I followed him to a rundown apartment building and slipped inside behind him. His apartment was the last one on the third floor. I watched him slip inside and slam the door behind him. When he didn't come back out, I curled up on the floor in front of the stairwell next to a creaky radiator, drifting off to sleep.

A foot connected with my leg, jarring me back into consciousness. I blinked up at the man in front of me, who had smoking holes where his eyes should be. I rubbed a hand over my face and his eyes returned, no longer smoking, but furious. He was in a suit, looking completely different from last night.

"Are you fucking kidding me? You must have a fucking death wish," he snapped, nudging me harder. I groaned and tried to roll over, but my battered body seized up on the hard floor and refused to obey me. I saw his face soften imperceptibly, looking me over carefully. "You don't have anywhere else to go... do you?" He sighed, running a hand through his hair. "Look... you can't fucking stay here, man. I have to go meet a potential client. It's really fucking important, alright?" He shifted uncomfortably and swore under his breath.

Hands were under my armpits, hauling me up to my feet, and I lurched forward, letting him guide me to his apartment door. He jimmied the door open and shoved me inside, toward the sad-looking couch along the far wall. "I have nothing worth stealing, so don't fucking try it. Sleep here, don't move, and I'll be back soon," he snapped, tossing me down onto the worn out cushions. I grabbed his wrist, listening as the whispers grew louder, more insistent.

"Mention fishing," I blurted out, feeling fresh blood dripping from my damaged lip. He turned, looking down at me with a scowl.

"What?" he growled, wrenching his hand away from me. I teetered and sagged back onto the couch, watching him shrink into a small, cowering child in front of me.

"Mention fishing to your client. Lie, say it's your favorite thing. Pike, you like pike," I told him, wishing the cowering child would stop staring at me. I couldn't help him. No one could... *no one had.*

"Get some sleep," he sighed, shaking his head. My eyes were already closing as the door slammed shut, the whispers drowning me as my consciousness fractured and time slipped away from me completely.

Pain woke me up sometime later, and I couldn't tell what kind. Was it the beating I took, or was it hunger? My stomach ached fiercely, and I blinked open my eyes, not recognizing where I was. That was nothing new, though. I rarely knew where I was anymore. I stood up gingerly with my hand out to brace myself against the wall. This building was old. It practically screamed at me with its ghosts. Cain hadn't been living here long, it seems. *Wait, who was Cain? Oh right, the demon, the voices named him for me.* I limped further into the apartment, finally finding the bathroom.

I didn't recognize the person in the mirror. No really, I didn't. The image in front of me rippled and shifted, my features fading in and out like crappy reception on a TV. I tried to focus harder, to ground myself, but I was too weak and in too much pain. Ignoring the shifting image in front of me, I washed my face and scrubbed some of the dirt and blood off. When I was finished, I dared a glance back up and was finally able to glimpse the pale and bedraggled person I'd become after weeks - *was it months?* - of wandering. Limping back outside, I tried to make it to the couch, but my foot caught the edge of the coffee table and I landed just short, hitting the floor with a dull thud.

"Jesus Christ, you'd better not have died in my fucking apartment." A voice floated toward me and I groaned, shifting my head to the side to see who was talking. Cain was hovering over me, his tie undone and hanging loosely around his neck. He hauled me up effortlessly and dropped me on the couch, sighing heavily. "When was the last time you ate something?" he asked sharply. I shrugged. I honestly couldn't remember.

"Unbelievable," he muttered, storming off toward the kitchen. I heard cabinets slamming as he rifled around, and I rubbed my face, trying to clear away the cobwebs that were filling my vision. He returned with a glass of water and a protein bar and I took them with shaky hands. He stood in front of me, crossing his arms over his chest, waiting for me to do something. I took a sip of water and tore open the wrapper of the bar with my teeth, biting off an enormous piece. My stomach clenched, and I realized that I must have been pretty hungry. Cain continued to watch me with a scowl, his eyes dark and stormy.

"How'd you know about the fishing?" he asked suddenly. I swallowed and sipped some more water to wash down the bar.

"I..." I frowned, trying to figure out a way to explain that wouldn't get me thrown out of the warm apartment. "I see... things?" I offered weakly, and he glared at me.

"Like, you've been following me?" he snapped, and I took another bite, thinking quickly.

"No, well, yes. But no, not like that." I sighed, my head ached, and I couldn't think clearly. "I *see* things." Wiggling my fingers in an attempt at humor, I could hear his teeth grinding together. The whispers around me grew louder, offering me the help only they could.

"Look, I saved you from that ass-kicking because three on one isn't fair, but I swear to god if you jerk me around any more I wi-" he snarled, but I cut him off.

"You're made of fire, Cain. And you don't know why. Your parents worried it was demonic possession until you learned to hide it. You hate water though, it makes you feel weak. That's why he liked to hold your head under water, because he knew it hu-" Cain lifted me fully off the couch, gripping my shirt collar and steaming - literally steaming- mad.

"Who the fuck are you?" he exclaimed, and I could smell my shirt starting to burn in his hands.

"I'm not with him!" I shouted quickly, trying to focus on the whispers. "Really, I'm not. I don't know who he is, just what the whispers said! Please, all I know is that I was supposed to find you. We're tethered." I hit the center of my chest with my protein bar, sending crumbs flying. "You feel it too, right? The tug?" I asked. I was so fucking tired. When had I slept longer than a couple hours?

Cain dropped me roughly, and my water sloshed onto the couch as I landed. "You're fucking insane," he muttered, and I took the opportunity to finish my bar, in case he really did want to beat the shit out of me. "I let a crazy man into my home." He shook his head, raking his hand through his hair.

"You got the client, right?" I asked quietly, and he glared at me, his eyes flashing.

"I... did. Yes," he muttered, and I smiled triumphantly, drinking the rest of my water. My stomach ached, still not full enough to be satisfied.

"I can help you get more clients," I offered quickly, standing and walking over to the cupboard to find more bars. Helping myself to a couple, I shoved two in my pockets before opening a third. I smiled, aware that I was on a microscopically fine line right now. Cain was watching me with open mistrust and contempt, his arms folded over his chest.

"In exchange for what? I don't have money, in case it wasn't obvious," he snapped. I bit into the protein bar, nearly inhaling it now that my hunger was apparent.

"Just... don't kill me?" I offered, grinning weakly. My head was pounding, making the room shift and ripple when I looked around.

"I'm sure you'll manage that all by yourself," he muttered, shaking his head. "Just finish your food and see yourself out. I can't deal with this shit today," he announced, rubbing his face tiredly. I watched him storm off toward his room, slamming the door behind him.

Finishing my bar, I drank another glass or two of water, wishing it was something stronger. I left the glass in the sink and slipped out the front door, closing it behind me. I had no were else to go, so I curled back up in my old spot by the radiator, pulling my hood up over my greasy hair and settling back against the wall. Cain would come around eventually. I just had to be patient. Now that I'd found him, my chest wasn't hurting so much anymore, and the need to wander subsided. *I think I can finally rest, at least for a little while.*

CHAPTER FOUR

Addison

"Hey, Gwen Stacey!" I cringed, my pen slipping and leaving a wonky line through my notes from the last half-hour. I looked up to find my colleague, a bubbly young researcher named Hannah, bounding up toward me. It had been three months since we moved here, and I'd started back up in the lab last month once the transfer had been finalized. It was a great university, but smaller than the previous one, so my Arachnology study was lumped into the Entomology department's lab. I still had my own office since I was considered a senior researcher, but my subjects were housed in the main lab, which meant interacting with my colleagues.

And no offense, but entomologists were weird.

I'd managed to scare or bore most of the researchers into leaving me alone, like I preferred. All except Hannah, who was hell bent on becoming best friends, despite my aloofness. I stood up, smiling wanly as she stopped exactly three feet away, rocking on the balls of her feet. At least she respected my need for space - which I'd explained was a specific case of mysophobia- I could tell she wanted to hug me, though. She was that kind of person.

"Hannah, how's your study going?" I asked politely, and she beamed at me, adjusting her bright blue glasses further up her nose. She studied praying mantis, which had a similar stigma about them, like black widows. That was probably why she was so eager to have me here. Our studies almost overlapped in some ways.

"So good! My babies are thriving," she gushed, and I smiled, unable to help myself. Her cheer was infectious. "Listen, a few of us are going for drinks after 5 p.m. Would you like to join?" I opened my mouth to politely decline, but she held up her hand to stop me. "Before you say no," she rushed out, "it's only a couple of people, and it's only at the campus bar, so it's barely out of your way," she beamed.

Fuck, I bit my lip, struggling to come up with an excuse this time. When nothing came to mind, I sighed, and she let out a little squeal. "Yes! Yes! Yes! I knew it, I knew you'd finally cave! Oh, my gosh, it'll be so much fun. I promise you don't have to stay long, just one drink and then you can go home."

"Sounds like fun," I smiled, cringing internally. I checked my phone. At least I still had an hour to finish up my work today. I grabbed my notebook off the table and Hannah bounded away, leaving me free to skulk back to my office. I shut the door behind me and rested my head against it for a moment. What was I going to do at home, anyway? Cain was off meeting a prospective client for drinks downtown tonight, so he wouldn't be home until late. Piper was... well, he'd been pretty lucid this morning when I'd left, so he was probably wandering around somewhere getting into trouble.

I frowned and sent a text to Wyatt, letting him know I'd be home a little later today.

I didn't see him at all this morning, which was unusual for him. I was starting to worry about him. He had only had one booking in the last two months, despite setting up his website and advertising his services. He needed to work, and I could tell it was beginning to weigh on him a bit. I didn't get an answer, but I saw that he read the message, so at least someone knew where I was going after work. I'd text Austin, but he rarely had his phone on, so it wouldn't do much good, anyway.

For the next hour, I busied myself with entering my notes onto my laptop. Right at 5 p.m., there was an eager knock on my office door. Shoving my laptop into my bag and grabbing my jacket off the hook, I opened the door to find Hannah grinning on the other side. She immediately backed up to let me pass, and I smiled appreciatively, looking around us. "Oh, they're meeting us there. They left a little early to get a good table," Hannah explained.

"Oh, that was nice of them," I offered, shifting my bag up on my shoulder and heading to the door. I didn't know how to make small talk, usually I had no need for it. Thankfully, Hannah was an expert.

"We do this almost every week," she told me, leading me toward the campus bar. Although it wasn't technically on campus, it was right across the street, so everyone just called it the campus bar. It was already packed full of people, and I made sure that my sleeves were pulled down in case anyone brushed up against me. It was cold enough here that I could get away with turtleneck sweaters without looking out of place, so I'd stocked up on a few of them, hoping to avoid a repeat of the Peter situation.

I followed Hannah to a table of semi-familiar faces, leaving the end spot for me to sit in, while she took the seat next to... Vince? I smiled wanly as everyone looked at me, open shock on a few of their faces. "Everyone, you remember Addy, right? She just transferred here. She's our new Gwen Stacey," Hannah beamed, and I cringed at the embarrassing nickname. Someone had mentioned the Spider woman in front of her, meaning me, and she'd immediately latched on to that. I waved uncomfortably, feeling like a giant idiot. Everyone smiled at me for a moment before returning to their conversations, and I let out a quick breath now that I was no longer in the spotlight.

"Addy, beer?" Hannah asked, leaning over Vince to get my attention.

"Oh, uh... sure. Yes, thank you." I smiled, and she hopped up from the table, disappearing into the crowd. I should've just asked for water or something. I hadn't had beer in almost two months, not after a wicked bout of food poisoning had put me off even the smell of it. My stomach was still sensitive because of it. I swear at least once a day now I would get a wave of nausea and feel gross for a half-hour or more. I half-listened to the conversation closest to me, something about a scandal involving a professor and one of their T.A.'s. Hannah reappeared and set a bottle down in front of me, and I smiled at her again, mouthing a thank you. I held onto it like a lifeline, keeping my hand in my lap, picking invisible lint off my thigh.

"Addy, where did you transfer from again?" someone asked abruptly, and I glanced up in surprise, looking for whoever had asked. Everyone was staring at me now, and I felt my cheeks heat.

"Well, I was originally at NSU. I did my master's there," I replied, picking at the label on my beer. A few of them exchanged glances, and I knew what was coming next. Nerds loved gossip, especially when their subjects were boring insects.

"Oh my god, did you know the guy who killed himself?" one girl piped up, and Hannah frowned at her.

"Priya, that's not polite," she replied quickly, but everyone was still staring, so I sighed and nodded. The entire table erupted in titters.

"I heard his family vandalized the lab-"

"No, it wasn't his family, dumbass. It was the guy who killed him!"

"Why would someone kill him and make it look like a suicide, then trash his work?"

"Because he found something! And they wanted to cover it up!"

I let them argue theories as I held my beer, trying not to scream. No one knew the actual story except me and my guys. To the rest of the world, Peter went crazy with his obsession with me, and killed himself when he couldn't find me. *Poor Pete...*

"Guys, oh my god. This was a serious incident, and clearly it's upsetting for Addy!" Hannah interjected, hushing the entire table. Everyone stared at me again, and I fidgeted uncomfortably.

"It's alright, it's in the past," I replied quietly, and one guy at the far end of the table held out his phone, showing a news article on it.

"Holy shit, it was you, wasn't it? They said he was found in a colleague's house, in her bed." *Fuck, of course.* They'd omitted my name for privacy, but there was only one woman in that department, so it wasn't hard to figure out who it had been. *See, this is why I didn't like to go out.* I caught Hannah's eye, and she looked absolutely horrified on my behalf, her normally cheerful face twisted and drained of color.

I set my untouched beer on the table, pushing myself to stand. "I think I'll be heading home now. It's been a long day," I announced, shouldering my bag and giving Hannah a forced smile.

I could hear the conversation pick up as I walked toward the door, including Hannah's shrill voice snapping, "Trevor, you are such an insensitive jerk!" Stepping out of the bar, I took a deep, steadying breath. The sun went down earlier now, and even though it was too warm for snow, it was still cold enough to bite at my skin. I set my bag down to shrug on my coat, preparing for the walk home. At least I was only two blocks from the tattoo studio now, so it shouldn't take too long.

"Addy, wait!" a voice called out, and I turned, adjusting my bag. Hannah stopped short, rubbing her arms and shivering in the cool air. "I'm sorry, they are nasty gossips," she sighed. "I didn't know about any of that, I swear."

"I know, it's fine. People talk, it happens," I replied, shrugging. "I'll come again, once there's a fresh scandal for them to talk about." Hannah perked up a little at that, still looking at me nervously. Her gaze flitted over my shoulder and her eyes widened slightly, suddenly fearful. I turned sharply, catching movement out of the corner of my eye. Someone stepped out from under a nearby tree, stalking toward us slowly.

"Come back inside with me," Hannah murmured, taking a step closer to me. I cocked my head to the side, and the man mirrored my movements, making me smile.

"It's alright, I know him," I told her, holding out my hand. Austin approached slowly, his hood pulled low enough to obscure his eyes. He almost fooled me, partially because I didn't expected him here, and partially because he looked shockingly... different. I'd been so busy in the last few months, it hadn't really registered, but I swear, Austin had fucking grown somehow. He was definitely bulkier than he used to be, his wiry limbs replaced with defined muscles. He grabbed my hand and pulled me into his arms, leaning in to kiss me. Yeah, he had definitely gotten taller somehow. How the fuck was that even possible? Austin slipped his tongue past my parted lips, deepening the kiss, and I heard Hannah's sharp intake of breath, reminding me that I was in public right now.

I pulled away from Austin's mouth, my cheeks red, and I turned to Hannah quickly. She was staring at me, open-mouthed and shocked. "Sorry Hannah, this is Austin," I explained, grabbing his hand before he could stick it up my shirt. He smiled, his lip piercings glinting in the light from the bar.

"Oh, uh, hi!" She recovered quickly, still eyeing him uneasily.

"He does piercings in the studio, the one I live above," I explained, blushing as his arms curled around me, his chin resting on the top of my head. Hannah's smile brightened, and she tucked her hair back behind her ears, revealing nearly a half dozen piercings.

"Oh neat! I've been thinking about getting a Daith piercing, but there aren't many people nearby who will do them," she explained, and I was surprised when Austin let go of me and shifted over to Hannah, fast enough to startle her. He had no issues with personal space, and leaned down to look at her ear, ignoring her little squeak of panic.

"I do those," he rasped, stepping back. "They're tricky so most people avoid them, but I don't mind," he told her softly. Hannah looked at me for reassurance, and I nodded gently.

"I guess I'll have to make an appointment then," Hannah smiled, and Austin nodded, shifting back over to me. His hand slipped around my waist, tugging me into his chest.

"See you Monday, Hannah," I smiled, tugging on Austin's hand before he got too carried away out in the open. She smiled and bounded off back toward the bar, disappearing inside. As soon as she was gone, Austin grew bolder. His hand slid under my jacket, making me shiver as his cold skin brushed against mine.

"What are you doing here?" I asked, turning to face him. He didn't usually come to pick me up from work. In fact, he rarely stepped outside unless he was forced. Even after all the wounds had healed up, he still wouldn't leave the house, sometimes for days on end. "How did you find me?"

"Wyatt told me you were coming here, so I came to pick you up," he smiled, fangs glinting in the light. Those were definitely more defined now as well. What the hell was going on with my snaky guy?

"I'm glad you did," I smiled, and he leaned in for another kiss, his arms wrapping tightly around me, nearly lifting me off the ground. Warmth began to pool in my core, and I groaned as he pressed his hips into mine. "Austin, there are people all around us," I mumbled against his lips, and he hissed in frustration. I broke away from him reluctantly and tugged on his hand, leading him toward the main road. "Let's get home, then you can finish that thought, alright?" I smirked.

"Okay." He grinned, catching up and settling his arm over my shoulders. The walk was nice and short. You could practically see our building from campus. Austin took things very literally, so I barely had the key in the door before he was all over me once again, his hands slipping under my shirt and teasing my nipples through my bra. We tumbled inside and I quickly shut the door behind us as Austin tugged off my coat and dropped my bag on the floor. We were still on the studio level and Cain hated a mess at the front door, but Austin didn't seem to care much about that at the moment. He pulled me against him, grinding his erection into my ass, one hand slipping under the waistband of my slacks and running his fingers over the thin fabric of my panties.

"When will you let me pierce you?" Austin rasped, teasing my clit through the fabric. I arched back into him, pressing my hand against the wall for balance.

"My ears are already pierced," I replied, feeling his breath on my neck.

"I could pierce something else," he murmured, and pinched my nipple through my bra, making me whimper.

Footsteps sounded on the stairs, and I looked up to see Wyatt peering down at us. Even from here, I could see the dark circles under his eyes. Austin had just given me an idea. Maybe there was a way to cheer Wyatt up somewhat. "Hey Shades," I panted, Austin refusing to let up on his current goal. "Want to help Austin pierce my nipples?"

CHAPTER FIVE

Wyatt

I know moving was for the best, but I didn't realize how much it would fucking suck. Our new place was nice, but I now had to start from scratch building up my clientele. This was a slow, frustrating process, and in the meantime, I had way too much free time on my hands. I shouldn't be idle for long periods of time, without any distractions. I was starting to feel myself slip into a funk.

Every morning I forced myself to get out of bed, but I hated having to watch everyone else busy and driven with a purpose while I just... sat. The house was so empty some days; the loneliness was suffocating. Even Piper managed to drag himself out of the house most days, disappearing for hours at a time, doing who knows what. I touched up my tattoos just to keep myself busy, but it still didn't ease the tension building up under my skin.

I *needed to... hurt.*

Before, I'd have taken matters into my own hands. I knew it was bad, but I needed the pain to feel... something. To remind myself that I was alive. It helped me steady myself - at

least, that's how I always justified it, anyway. Cain put a stop
to that immediately, and he taught me how to channel my
self-harming tendencies into something less dangerous and
more productive - namely tattooing. *I admit, it had worked.*
It took care of the pain that would burrow under my skin
and tinge everything with shades of gray, sucking the joy
out of every corner of my life until I saw no reason to stay
conscious. Without it, I could see the colors beginning to
bleed out of everything around me.

It didn't help that I couldn't sleep anymore. I was exhausted
all the time now, but every time I closed my eyes, I was back
in that fucking warehouse. Cain didn't know this, and I didn't
think Addy would even be able to remember it. That horrible
moment was burned into my memory forever. When I ran
over to her, where she was laying on the ground and bleeding
out, I knew it was too late. Somehow, I just knew that she
didn't have enough life-force inside her to keep her alive
much longer. Cain had no idea just how reckless I truly was,
because I shouldn't have been able to save her the way I did.
If I'm being honest, I just hoped I could take her pain away in
her last moments, and then die at her side, since there was
no way I could have lived without her.

Every night, I relived the agonizing pain I pulled out of her,
each strand of burning heat dripping with terror and tinged
in death. I thought I pushed all of it out into Jake before we
escaped, but I still felt that chill of death in my bones, like
a punishment for fucking with something I shouldn't have.
In my dreams, it was never enough. My doubts from that
moment came true, and no matter how much I pulled out of
her, the blood kept pouring out of Addy's mouth, drowning
her as I held her in my arms. Every morning I woke up more

tired than when I went to bed, and I felt weaker every day, like death was slowly eating away at me from the inside. I knew I should tell Cain about it, or Addy... *someone*. But I couldn't bring myself to burden them further, not after all they've been through.

I almost turned around and ran back upstairs when I found Addy and Austin in the studio. No one needed me moping around and ruining the mood. But Addy seemed to sense what I needed, even if I couldn't vocalize it. Her voice cut through the fog in my brain, offering me some blessed relief. I felt myself getting hard just watching her, her cheeks flushed, panting as Austin pinned her against his body, his hand down her pants.

"I'll help," I croaked, stumbling down the stairs to join them. Austin guided her over to the table set up in the far corner, closest to his cabinet full of supplies. He was forced to let her go and get his needles, so I took over, lifting Addy up onto the table and sliding between her legs, my lips finding hers like two magnets being drawn together. I encouraged a little of her desire to sink into my skin, letting it burn away some of the exhaustion in my chest.

"You'll need your shirt off for this, sweetheart." I smiled against her lips, and lifted up her turtleneck, pulling it over her head and tossing it onto the counter. Addy wasn't naked much anymore. I wasn't sure if anyone else noticed. Her scars were faded, but still, Jake's damage left permanent reminders of our failings on her skin. I kissed the one on her collarbone, eliciting a shiver from Addy. I undid her bra and slid it off as well, exposing her breasts. Her nipples were already hardened into points, and I massaged her softly, trailing my lips across her scars as she whimpered, arching into my touch.

I reached down and undid her slacks, sliding them down her hips. "I don't think he's piercing anything down there," she murmured, and I chuckled.

"I'm going to keep you distracted while he's working," I told her, tugging her underwear down as well.

"Time to lie down," Austin rasped, coming around to the side of the table. He helped Addy lower her back down onto the table as I finished removing her pants, tossing them over with her sweater. I hooked her knees over my shoulders, sliding her down until her ass was nearly falling off the table, leaving her completely exposed to me.

Austin teased her nipple, and I took the opportunity to run my tongue up her slit, tasting her desire as she moaned and writhed. "Stay still," I warned her, holding her hips so she couldn't move around. I trailed kisses up her inner thigh as Austin sanitized the area and got a needle ready. I felt her tense in my arms and smiled, dragging my tongue over her clit. "Don't worry sweetheart, it won't hurt, I promise."

I was the one who liked pain, but Austin looked positively animalistic as he brought the needle down to Addy's left nipple, his fangs showing as he grinned. Now that I was paying attention, he looked... bigger? *What the hell?*

"Deep breath in, and then let it out," Austin murmured, and I felt Addy shake as she inhaled. On the exhale, I felt the sharp sting of the needle as it pierced her. I pulled all of it, every drop, moaning as it flooded me, my cock pressing painfully into my jeans. I sent most of the pleasure directly into Addy using my mouth, teasing her clit as she whimpered, desire pooling out as I stroked her with my tongue.

"You did so good," Austin hissed, setting the barbell piercing in place. "Just one more now." He kissed her deeply, and

I slipped my tongue inside her at the same time, making her moan into his mouth. She squirmed under my grip, and I didn't let up. I could feel her tensing as her orgasm neared. Austin grinned down at her as she was panting, and I held her tightly while he readied the needle. "Deep breath in," he whispered, and this time I let a little of the sting through, making her hiss before I stole the pain away, flooding her with enough pleasure to push her over the brink.

"Fuck!" Addy cried out, her orgasm shuddering through her body before she finally went limp in my arms, breathing hard. I smirked and stood up, looking down at Austin's handiwork. He was really good. I could barely feel any swelling or discomfort around the piercings. Trailing my hand up Addy's thigh, I imagined how her skin would look covered in ink. She was a beautiful blank canvas. Where would I even start?

Austin pulled off his gloves and tossed them in the trash, stalking up beside me. I was caught completely off guard when he wrapped his hand around the back of my neck and kissed me, tasting Addy on my lips. I blinked in surprise at my normally reclusive housemate, bumping against the piercing table as he pressed against me. "Austin, what's up with you, man?" I asked, feeling Addy shift up to sit behind me. "Are you fucking taller, dude?" I realized I was able to meet his eye, but I knew for a fact that he was shorter than me. Austin crowded me against the bench, his hips pressing into mine. It felt very possessive, and while I wasn't entirely opposed to the whole thing, something felt a little... *off.*

"Austin?" Addy murmured, and his gaze shifted to her. His pupils were enormous, and I felt the grip on the back of my neck tighten, his nails biting into my skin, making my cock ache.

"Mine," he hissed, eyeing her intently. Addy's hand came up, covering his and brushing the hair on the back of my head. Abruptly, his gaze shifted back to me. Before I could react, he struck out, and I felt his canines sink into my neck. Fuck, they were sharp like needles. Addy yelped, but Austin didn't move, curling around me with his teeth still buried in my neck. The pain felt so good I could've sobbed, and I was so fucking hard I couldn't stand it, my hips shifting and rubbing against Austin, who was just as turned on.

"Austin! Stop it!" Addy snapped, jumping off the table and shoving him in the shoulder. The jolt made him pull back, and I moaned as his teeth dragged across my skin. Maybe he had some sort of venom in his bite, or maybe I was just hazy with lust. I just leaned back against the table, feeling the blood drip down towards my collarbone.

"Mine," he rasped, staring at me, and I nodded dumbly as Addy hurried around, pulling on her pants and hunting through the cupboards at the same time.

"Here, we need to clean you up," she muttered, still shirtless, as she pressed an alcohol swab to my neck. I swore as it burned, and she wiped at it hurriedly, watching Austin out of the corner of her eye. He was stock-still, watching us, looking oddly satisfied. Once she was done wiping up the blood, she whirled on Austin, her face murderous. "We don't bite people!" she snapped at him. "What has gotten into you lately?" At least now he had the good sense to look chagrined.

"It's fine, Addy, everyone was a little worked up, it's no biggie," I told her, touching my neck gingerly. She turned her glare at me instead.

"It is a biggie, he bit me, too! We. Don't. Bite. People," she emphasized, swatting at his hand as he reached out for her.

"And why are you bigger?!" she exclaimed. Austin looked himself over, frowning, and shrugged.

"I didn't notice," he murmured, flexing his shoulders. Now that I was properly looking, I couldn't believe I hadn't noticed before. He packed on at least twenty pounds worth of muscle somehow. I was used to Austin being the slimmest of all of us. The only one shorter was Piper. Now, though, he might be even bigger than me.

"We're having a family meeting," Addy announced, grabbing her clothes and stalking toward the stairs, still topless. My dick ached at the sight, made worse by the throbbing in my neck. *Sadly, I think we were done with any fun times…* at least, I wasn't about to try Addy's patience at this moment. I rubbed my neck, feeling a little dizzy.

"Man, you aren't venomous or anything, are you?" I muttered, blood smearing under my fingers. Austin smirked at me, and my dick throbbed painfully against my jeans. The serpentine prick looked satisfied as he watched me adjust myself. I blinked, and he was caging me against the table again, palming my erection through my jeans. It made me jump, and I couldn't tell if he was moving unnaturally fast or if my brain was slowed somehow. I felt a little drunk…

Austin squeezed, and I groaned, my eyes closing as concerns left my brain as quickly as they arrived. My zipper was ripped open, and I felt Austin's hand wrap around my shaft, stroking it firmly. My hips jerked, and I choked out a moan. "Christ, man…" I mumbled, and my eyes flew open when his lips wrapped around the head of my cock. He was kneeling down in front of me, smirking up at me with his wild, blown out pupils. I didn't have the brainpower to consider what was happening right now. Austin took me into his mouth, and his lip piercings rubbed against my shaft as I hit the back of his throat.

My hands tangled in his hair as my hips stuttered and I thrust deeper into his mouth, another moan slipping past my lips. "God, you take me so fucking good..." I muttered, and his hands moved up to my hips, pulling me deeper as he gripped me possessively. My head was spinning, and my balls tightened as the pressure built up. My orgasm coated the back of his throat, his nails leaving grooves in my skin until I was completely spent. I nearly collapsed back onto the table, Austin grinning wickedly as he stood up. Addy was right. Something was different about our snaky friend, that was for damn sure.

I'm just not sure it was such a bad thing...

CHAPTER SIX

Cain

Jerking awake in my seat, I cursed and hunted for the phone that woke me up. I'd finished up drinks with my client an hour ago, and I'd driven home, only to stop and park a block away and sit back to watch. It's not like I was avoiding going home, not in the sense that I didn't want to be there, at least. I made a lot of excuses to Addy and to the others on why I had to leave the house lately, and often I would just... sit outside like a sentry, watching for anything or anyone weird to come around. I was getting paranoid, and so utterly fucking exhausted.

We'd been settled here for three months already, but I still couldn't bring myself to relax. While Addy had prepared for the move, I'd combed over every inch of the docks, searching for any clue about where Jake might've gotten to. For a while I hoped I would just... stumble over his body somewhere in the overgrown lots and piles of trash. Maybe he'd crawled away and ended up in the water somewhere, sinking to the bottom where his corpse could poison the nearby fish. I needed to see the body. I wouldn't be able to relax until I could kick at his bones and feel them crunch under my boot. His death had to be visible. Nothing could be left to chance this time. I'd fallen for that once before, and I'd almost lost Addy and Wyatt because of it.

Checking my phone, I saw a couple of angry-looking texts from Addy, something about a 'family meeting'. Fuck, I didn't think I could take an argument with her tonight. I dropped my phone and rubbed my eyes, patting my pockets to find a cigarette. It lit up before it even touched my lips, and I inhaled the smoke with a sigh. Addy had started to notice my absence. I was away more during the day, and some mornings I was gone before she even got up, forcing Wyatt or Piper to walk her to work. It wasn't like I was trying to avoid her. In fact, my body craved her so badly some nights I couldn't sleep. I was so desperate to hold her that I would actually climb into her ridiculous bed and curl up beside her for a couple of hours during the night, before slipping out in the early hours of the morning. I was starting to worry she would read my mind and see this secret I was keeping from her.

Finishing my cigarette, I pulled out of my current lurking spot, driving down the block and parking in the spot in front of our studio instead. I unlocked the door and walked inside, scowling when I nearly tripped over a pair of boots and Addy's purse. Annoyed, I gathered everything up and stormed inside and up the stairs, dumping the boots on the mat I'd bought and placed by the top of the stairs. I set her bag on the couch, glancing around for signs of life in our new apartment. Stomping over to my room, I slipped off my suit jacket and hung it back in my closet, shrugging out of my dress shirt and tossing it in the hamper. I grabbed a pair of sweats off the floor and dropped them immediately, swearing loudly as they started moving on their own. A ball python slithered out of them, darting for the door and slipping outside.

"Austin!" I snarled, shaking my sweats gingerly before yanking them on. What the fuck were his snakes doing out of his room? He knew better than to let them run loose. Following after the snake, I caught a rumpled-looking Wyatt wandering down the stairs. Jesus Christ, had he been in bed all day? I studied him closely as he stumbled to the fridge to grab a beer. Not working was clearly starting to affect him. He caught me staring and leveled a glare of his own as he cracked open his beer and climbed over the back of the couch to sit down in the living room.

I opened my mouth to snap at him when the door downstairs slammed closed, and Piper came up the stairs. "And where have you been?" I asked, frowning at him. Truth be told, I couldn't remember seeing him at all this week.

"Telling fortunes down at the indoor market. " He smiled, holding up a deck of weathered tarot cards. "I made $400 today." My eyebrows shot up as he traipsed past me, grabbing a beer and joining Wyatt in the living room. "Is today the family meeting?" he asked casually, and Wyatt glanced at him in surprise.

"Addy sent me a text," he explained, pulling out a rather beat-up looking smartphone. It was definitely not the one I'd originally bought for him, but I couldn't be bothered to question it right now. At least he'd come home.

"Downstairs, now!" Addy exclaimed, and I heard a door slam upstairs. I felt Addy's presence like a balm over my heart. As soon as she started down the stairs, the buzzing in my mind quieted and my shoulders loosened. She looked livid, and I just hoped I wasn't the target of her ire tonight. Her hair was loose, flowing like a waterfall of ink around her face and down her back. She was wearing an oversized tee shirt - one of mine, I realized with a jolt - and her eyes locked with mine as she reached the landing.

"You," she bit out, and I bristled at her tone. We were like oil and flame, a volatile combination when both of us were worked up.

"Little Spider!" Piper announced, catching Addy off-guard. She softened a bit and smiled at him, because of course he got the gentle treatment. "What's this about a family meeting?" he asked, and Addy headed over to him instead, leaving me a chance to grab a beer and settle in beside Wyatt, who deliberately avoided my gaze, slouching down into the cushions and picking at the tab on his can.

Austin slunk down the stairs, looking like he was trying to disappear into his hoodie, hunched over and unhappy. Addy's face hardened, and she whirled on him, her hands on her hips. Now I was truly shocked. I'd never seen her mad at Austin before. "Family meeting is officially in session," she announced, as Austin ducked around her and sat down next to Piper on the love seat. She remained standing, her body vibrating with anger.

"What's this all about, Addy?" I asked, drawing her attention. She cocked an eyebrow at me, accusingly.

"Well, Cain. It seems like some more weird shit has been happening under your roof, without your knowledge," she snapped cryptically. I eyed the room, and Austin and Wyatt cringed, while Piper just looked bored.

"Daddy Cain has been gone a lot lately," Piper noted absently, and I glared at him before looking back at Addy.

"Alright, sassy. Get to the point. What am I missing?" I snapped. She turned to Austin and grabbed him by the arm, pulling him up beside her.

"You. Hoodie off. Now," Addy ordered, and he kept his gaze on the floor as he shrugged off his hoodie, tossing it on the couch. I blinked, and then blinked again, trying to figure out what my eyes were trying to tell me. Standing, I walked up to Austin, who finally met my eyes, and I frowned.

"Did you... what the fuck?" I frowned, looking him over sharply. "Did you join a gym or something?" I asked, baffled.

"Only if the gym also provides fucking growth serum. He's taller!" Addy insisted, and Piper stood up, his interest peaked. He sidled up to Austin, grabbing his hips and pulling him around to face him. Austin smirked, looking down at Piper, who stroked a hand over his muscled arms, looking amused.

"Well then, that's different," he mused, and Austin hissed and pulled him into a rough kiss. My eyebrows shot up, not at the action itself, but at Austin's aggressive behavior. Addy clicked her tongue impatiently, and when he finally let go of Piper, Addy pushed Piper back down onto the couch.

"What the fuck is going on?" I demanded, and Addy glared at me like it was somehow my fault. And... maybe it was? I grimaced and circled around Austin, who stiffened immediately. I caught the tension in his shoulders, his hands curling into fists.

"He bit me the other day," Addy announced, pulling down her collar to show the two half-healed puncture marks on her shoulder. "And he bit Wyatt today." I glanced at Wyatt, who was very quiet during all of this, his cheeks flushing slightly as he drank his beer. I looked over at Piper, who grinned and ran a hand through his hair.

"He bit me too... a few times." Piper sighed, pulling the waistband of his jeans down to reveal several puncture marks across his hip. "It felt good. I didn't mind. " He shrugged, winking at Austin. The serpentine fucker looked proud of himself, his chin raising up with satisfaction.

"Austin, what the hell, man? We don't bite people," I growled, and he met my eye with a shocking amount of defiance.

"They are mine," he snarled, his eyes narrowing. "My nest mates. I needed to... mark them as mine." Addy gaped at him, and he pulled her into his arms, rubbing his cheek against hers, his eyes flashing as he stared at me in challenge.

Jesus Christ, was this some sort of... Discovery Channel dominance display or something? I was too goddamn tired for this. I lifted my chin, letting flames rise to the surface as I met his challenge, pulling Addy out of his arms and moving her over toward the couch. Wyatt grabbed her and pulled her down with him, leaving me with the furious cobra. "Do we have a problem, Austin?" I asked sharply, feeling the heat on my tongue as my temper began to boil over.

"You're not protecting our nest. You're gone," he rasped, his eyes narrowing at me. He shifted to the left, toward the rest of the group. I moved to block him, and he bared his teeth at me.

"Everything I do is to protect this family!" I shouted at him. I could smell burning fabric, and I grimaced. There went another shirt ruined. "If I leave here, I'm busy keeping everyone safe!" Austin was coiling, his knees bent as he watched me, so I was ready when he struck out at me. I moved right and caught him around the waist, dropping him to the floor on his back. Straddling his hips, I shoved him down, pinning him with a hand on his chest.

"You are my family. I will keep you safe. Now stop fucking biting people." I glanced over at Piper. "Unless they want it," I amended quickly. "And no more of this dominance shit. I don't have the patience for it." I waited until the rage in his face dimmed, and he stopped snarling at me. "It makes me glad that you're stronger, Austin, because I need all the help I can get. I trust you'll keep everyone safe while I'm out." He softened underneath me, the tension fading away, and I released my grip on him, standing up and offering him a hand up as well.

"Okay, are we all done with the male posturing now?" Addy asked, climbing off of Wyatt's lap. She gave Austin a sharp look, and he chewed on his lip ring sheepishly.

"Good. Now I'm going to order a pizza," she announced, glancing at me before sauntering off toward my room. I followed her, getting the not-so-subtle hint. Closing the door behind us, I listened as she placed an order for a couple of large pizzas from the chain restaurant close by. Sitting down on my bed, I wished I could just go to sleep now. My eyes felt like I'd ground sand into them and then stared into the sun.

"Hey," Addy announced, stowing her phone. "He's not wrong, you know. You're never home anymore." She frowned at me, and I sighed, closing my sore eyes so I could ignore her piercing gaze.

"I'm busy trying to build roots here, so we can stay comfortable and safe," I replied sharply, rubbing my temples. Addy's hands cupped my face, and I opened my eyes, staring at her as she straddled my legs and wrapped her arms around my neck.

"You're building roots at four in the morning?" she asked softly, cocking her head to the side. "You never met clients this much before..." My flimsy excuses weren't fooling her anymore, clearly. Her touch soothed the ache in my skull, washing over me like a drug. Addy shifted in my lap and I dropped my hands to her hips, growing hard as she rubbed herself against me.

"This is different. I have to set up new connections here," I explained softly, groaning as her lips ghosted across mine. Her hands tangled in my hair, tugging my head back.

"I miss you," she replied softly, and the guilt made my chest ache. "You don't have to keep doing this... penance for what happened. We won, he lost. We should be celebrating, not torturing ourselves over the past." She kissed me again, and I met her lips roughly, craving more of her - all of her. Addy moaned against my lips and ground her hips against mine, seeking friction. I slid my hand under her shirt, my fingers finding one of the scars my bastard of a brother had given her. Guilt threatened to drown me, twisting my stomach into knots. I gently broke off the kiss, and Addy's lips parted in frustration.

"We should get ready for dinner," I told her softly, hating the flash of hurt that crossed her face. I helped her climb off my lap and she left without a word, the buzzing behind my temples returning with a fierce vengeance.

Jake's true power was tainting everything he touched with misery, so even after we escaped, we were never truly free.

CHAPTER SEVEN

Piper

"Piper, I swear to fucking God himself -" Cain's yelling jerked me into consciousness, and I coughed as I rolled over, clenching my stomach as pain rippled through me. My door slammed open somewhere nearby, and I groaned when light hit my sensitive eyes, shivering as I pulled my comforter tighter around myself.

"What the fuck is wrong with you?" he asked, but I swear his voice was tinged with genuine concern. I had been his annoying shadow for months now, and the relationship was still... tenuous at best.

"So... fucking cold... " I mumbled, coughing again, my throat feeling like I swallowed glass. He sighed and sat down on the bed next to me, putting a hand on my shoulder. Heat poured into me, dousing the chill that had settled into the marrow of my bones. "Did you let another snake in here?" he asked sharply.

"No, I told you, it's the tug," I mumbled, my limbs turning to jelly as my shivers finally receded.

Cain sighed heavily, and his hand gripped my shoulder, rolling me over to face him. "Piper, I've told you before, I don't understand this witchy shit you're talking about. I don't care about a 'tug' or the 'pull' or whatever. What I care about is the fucking rattlesnake I found in the bathroom sink." I blinked my eyes open, frowning as his face shifted, looking like someone else entirely for a moment.

Death... my death was staring at me...

"Piper, come back," he snapped, shaking me gently. "Piper, did the snake bite you? What the fuck is going on?" he demanded. I shrugged, burrowing under my blanket.

"I'm just... so cold," I mumbled, my stomach twisting with pain. Hunger? Maybe I was hungry. It had been a while since I'd caught any food.

Wait, what?

"Fuck me, of course you'd get sick right now," Cain sighed. "Okay, listen, I called animal control for the snake again. Do not go into the main bathroom. If you have to piss, fucking hold it." He grimaced. "I'll check on you in a bit. Just sleep, okay?" I nodded, closing my eyes, feeling despair welling up in my chest. *Was it my despair?* I felt so alone but Cain was right here. It wasn't mine then, it was someone else's. Someone who needed the tug.

Cain disappeared, the door shutting behind him, and I began to shiver once more as I took hold of the tether in my chest and *yanked?* My head was spinning, and I fell asleep shivering again.

I woke later to Cain sitting beside me on the bed, typing aggressively on his laptop. "Snake's gone," he muttered, and I shifted over, groaning as my body protested the movement. Someone had beaten me to holy hell. I just couldn't remember when or who. Cain watched me, frowning, and his hand landed on my shoulder again, warming me up and soothing some of the pain. "Should I take you to the hospital?" he asked shortly, and I shook my head.

"No. We have to be here to let him in," I mumbled, coughing violently.

"Let who in?" Cain asked, setting his laptop down. I couldn't answer him, since I was busy choking on something caught in my throat. I think I passed out from the lack of oxygen. When I came to, Cain was on his feet, swearing and throwing laundry on the floor. The tug was stronger. He'd be here soon, I was sure of it. I sat up slowly, my body stiff and protesting after days in bed.

"Piper, stay put, there's a fucking snake in here!" Cain snapped at me, searching the floor wildly. I climbed out of the bed, catching a flash of red slip under the crack in the door. My legs buckled, and I fell to my knees, catching myself on the bed.

"What did I fucking say?" Cain snarled as I pulled myself up.

He was here, *he* was close. I stumbled toward the door, bracing myself on the wall as I struggled with the doorknob. Cain was still shouting at me as I made it out into the hall, following the little red-bellied snake to the stairs. Our new place was odd. I'd stumbled upon it by accident, and while Cain had no use for the shop set up on the main floor, he couldn't turn down a price that good, especially when it got us out of that tiny apartment.

I missed a step and tumbled down the stairs, rolling onto the landing in our kitchen. I saw the snake disappearing down to the main floor, and I crawled after it, hearing Cain's thundering footsteps behind me. The taste of blood filled my mouth as I licked my lip, crawling down the stairs slower to avoid falling again. The snake led me toward the front door, and I pulled myself to my feet, feeling stronger the closer I got.

"Piper, I am not chasing your feverish ass down the street at 3 a.m.," Cain snapped as I unlocked the door and swung it open. The little snake slithered out, curling up in the palm of the young man collapsed on our front steps.

"Jesus, what the fuck is this now?" Cain groaned, stepping around me to check him out. My chest felt lighter than it had in weeks, completely at odds with the scene in front of me. Cain was checking the guy's pulse when he hissed weakly at him, burrowing deeper in the oversized hoodie he was wearing. The little red-bellied snake had disappeared up his sleeve, probably trying to stay warm.

"Bring him inside. He needs to get warmed up," I told Cain, who glared at me, but did as I instructed for once. It wasn't much effort to lift him and carry him down to the basement, where we had an old leather couch and a beat up coffee table. Cain set him down carefully, and he immediately curled up into a ball on the couch, shielding his face from view.

"Hey, what happened?" Cain asked him, sitting down on top of the coffee table. "What were you doing out there?" He reached out a hand, resting it gently on his shoulder, and he flinched away from his touch. "I'm not going to hurt you, but I need answers," Cain chided, glancing up at me. I walked over until I was standing between them and sank down until my face was level with the guy on the couch.

"You felt the tug, didn't you?" I whispered, and he stirred slightly, shifting to look up. His hair might've been blond at one point, but it was so dirty and matted with blood and grime that it was hard to tell. A large, untended gash cut across his forehead and his face was a motley of bruises. I didn't care about those, though. I couldn't stop staring into his eyes. Large, yellow-green eyes with thin black slits for pupils, just like a snake. I lost myself in them, burying him deep in my soul where he'd always belonged - where he'd always been. "Austin?" I murmured.

He made a low, keening sound, pain washing over his face. I pushed the hood off his head, letting Cain see some of the damage he'd suffered. "Did you get jumped?" he asked softly, and Austin dropped his gaze to the floor, shivering as he nodded slowly.

It took Cain and me another two hours to convince Austin to have a shower and wash off the grime so we could assess the damage. The entire time, I was murmuring encouragement, explaining that he was safe with us. He wasn't much of a talker. In fact, I wasn't sure he could talk. His throat looked badly bruised under all the grime. The poor guy was emaciated, and it turned out his hoodie was full of snakes. Cain was quietly fuming as he stuck the old clothes in one of our spare rooms and shut the door quickly, trapping the snakes in there for now.

I waited outside the bathroom while Cain hunted around the kitchen for some food to give him. I was beginning to doze against the door when I heard a dull thud from behind me. Throwing open the door, I found Austin half-out of the shower, clutching the towel rod as his legs shook, refusing to hold him up. I grabbed a towel and wrapped it around his waist, helping him out of the bathroom and into my room, which was closest.

"You're okay now, it's okay," I told him, propping him up on the bed. Austin was painfully thin, and his whole body shook with a chill. I rifled through my small amount of clothes, finding a few things that would fit him. I got him dressed in a pair of sweats and another hoodie, and helped him climb under the covers of my bed, where he curled up immediately, his eyes squeezing shut.

"I found some crackers. We need to go shopping," Cain grumbled, stomping into the room. He paused, looking at the small lump in my bed, and arched an eyebrow at me. He set the crackers and a glass of water on the bedside table, running a hand through his hair in frustration. "Alright, you keep an eye on him for now. Yell if he tries to kill you or anything," he muttered, walking back out. I rolled my eyes and laid down next to Austin, exhausted from all the excitement. Austin wouldn't kill me. I knew that deep in my bones.

I jolted awake in confusion when I felt hands on my chest sometime early in the morning. My eyes opened to find Austin hovering over me, pushing me down into the bed. "Morning babe," I smiled. He often crawled into my bed during the night. *Wait... did he do that?* I blinked, and the face hovering over me lost some of its familiarity. Where were his piercings? That cocky smirk he'd learned that turned me on? Austin's face was pinched with hunger, and he flashed small, needle-thin fangs at me, bringing his face close to mine. "Hey... it's okay, you're safe here," I offered, trying to sit up. He shifted in a flash, pinning me down as he straddled me on the bed. He hissed at me, one of his hands coming up to trace over my face.

"I don't understand you," I told him gently, and his fingers grazed over my lips. I knew it wasn't *my* Austin I was talking to right now, but my body responded to him all the same, and he cocked his head to the side, frowning at me.

"Wh... Who... you..." he rasped, barely intelligible.

"I'm Piper, and the other guy is Cain," I told him, my fingers tracing up his thigh. "We're like you. You were called to us, right?" I asked. "That was me. That was the tug." I touched his chest, right over his heart, and he made a sad, keening sound. "You're safe here. This can be your home now." Cain wasn't going to be happy about that, but he'd get over it. He needed someone else to take care of. He was getting bored.

Austin leaned over, bringing his face close to mine. I inhaled sharply as his tongue darted out, tracing up the side of my neck. "H... home..." Austin hissed, and I shivered when his teeth grazed my skin. I knew what it felt like when those fangs sank into me, even though they had yet to do so. He settled back down, curled up around me and half on top of me, falling back to sleep. It felt like a missing piece of my heart had slotted itself back into place.

CHAPTER EIGHT

Addison

My eyes were squeezed shut, but the sounds of whimpering and squelching echoed around my head. I knew what was behind me, and I knew what would happen if I looked. I was frozen on the ground, shivering and aching all over, desperate for the sounds to stop. The dock worker moaned loudly, and I heard a dull thud of flesh hitting the concrete. Shuffling sounds had the blood freezing in my veins, and I rolled over, daring a glance at the horror behind me. He was standing, blood pouring from the stump as he stumbled forward toward me. No, that wasn't right.

He'd never made it through his hand, he'd never escaped. I scrambled backward, trying to get away from him, but the rope tying my hands prevented me from moving away. The dock worker lurched toward me, his bloody stump outstretched as he moaned, his face covered in blood. I screamed, hoping someone would hear me. He fell on top of me, covering me in his blood. I screamed again and thrashed, fighting him off, desperate to get away from him. He was dead. He'd never gotten through the entire hand...

"Addy!"

I screamed for Cain, for Wyatt, begging them to find me in time. He was suffocating me. I couldn't breathe, I couldn't move underneath his horrible weight.

"Addy, sweetheart! Wake up!"

My eyes popped open, and the scream died in my throat as I shot upward, Wyatt catching me in his arms. My lungs weren't working. I was trying, but the air was getting stuck. I clawed at Wyatt's back as he soothed me, murmuring reassurances in my ear. The door banged open, revealing a shirtless Austin and a confused-looking Piper. They both climbed up onto the bed and moved to my side. I sank my nails into Wyatt's back, gasping for breath as the ghost of the dock worker crushed my lungs.

"I'll take it away," Wyatt murmured, and slowly, the dead man on my chest was removed, leaving a gaping emptiness in its wake. I inhaled, and immediately sobs racked my body, leaving me shaking and limp in Wyatt's arms.

"Give me the fear. It's okay, I'm used to it," I heard Piper say, and saw a flash of jewelry as he reached out to Wyatt, clasping his hand. I heard a sharp intake of breath, and wiggled in Wyatt's arms, trying to move so I could see if Piper was okay.

"Babe, just settle down, breathe," Wyatt murmured. He let me turn around so I could see Austin and Piper, but kept me trapped in his lap, his hand stroking my hair as I took a few more shaky breaths, tears running down my face.

"I'm so sorry," I mumbled, watching Piper wrap his arms around himself, his eyes glazed over as he experienced the panic that had been coursing through my body only moments ago. "I didn't mean to wake everyone up..."

Austin tugged Piper closer as he started mumbling under his breath. His eyes began to cloud over, my fear triggering his... whatever it was. I beckoned him over, Austin helping to guide him into my arms. I ran my hands over his face, soothing him as best I could. Some of the fog seemed to lift as I stroked his bronze locks away from his face, and his eyes met mine.

"I'm not ready to die yet," he told me earnestly, a tear running down his face. His statement made my blood run cold, and I felt Wyatt shift behind me, his hand reaching out to clasp Piper's arm.

"You're not dying, man, you're okay," he assured him. They were squishing me between them now, in this awkward half hug, and my tender nipples rubbed against Piper's chest, making me wince. Wyatt groaned in response, the pain disappearing almost immediately, and I laughed hoarsely.

"You should've gotten pierced, not me," I teased, leaning back against him. Piper blinked confusedly, then his eyes dropped to my thin tank top. I yelped in surprise when he grabbed the hem and yanked my shirt up, revealing my piercings.

"Good work, Austin," he breathed, staring hungrily. Austin moved up behind him, his hand slipping down past Piper's waistband as he murmured something in his ear, and Piper tipped his head back, his fingers tracing over my breasts. Every pass over my sensitive nipples had me gasping, but Wyatt took care of it immediately. I felt him getting hard behind me, his hands gripping my hips as I ground my ass against him.

Austin was still stroking Piper, but they were both staring at me, making my skin flush with heat. Piper smirked and tweaked one of the barbells, the yelp morphing into a moan as Wyatt worked his magic. One of his hands slipped off my hip and tugged down my panties, feeling the wet heat that was growing between my thighs. "We should be gentlemen and help you take care of this," he murmured, his fingers teasing my clit. I moaned and arched my back, my chest pressing against Piper's.

"Little Spider," Piper murmured, capturing my lips with his. I closed my eyes and whimpered as his tongue slipped into my mouth. Hands were all over me, teasing me, stroking me. I heard fabric tear as my panties were shredded and removed, and someone tugged my tank top the rest of the way over my head. Piper stole the air from my lungs, kissing me so desperately I felt tears form in my eyes. He kissed like a man going off to war, knowing he would never return.

I was naked between them now, but their hands kept me warm, kneading my breasts and stroking my thighs. Wyatt's fingers continued to tease my clit, his other hand moving down off my hip to trace lower. I shivered when he circled my tight, puckered hole, his lips tickling my ear. "Can we make you feel good, sweetheart?" he whispered. "All of us?" I moaned as he teased me further, breaking away from Piper's lips with a gasp.

"Yes, please!" I begged, and Piper grinned and started trailing kisses down my neck. I felt the bed shift, and someone rifled through the side table. It must have been Austin since I was still sandwiched between Wyatt and Piper. The sound of a bottle popping open caught my attention, but then Austin's face appeared beside me. He was naked too now, and my hand moved immediately to his cock, stroking him as he kissed me. A cool liquid trickled down my ass, and Wyatt's finger returned, circling and teasing my tight hole. Austin shifted in front of me as Piper disappeared for a moment, his fingers slipping down to play with my clit.

"Just relax, I've got to get you ready for my cock," Wyatt murmured in my ear. I felt his finger slip past the ring of muscle, and fuck it felt tight.

"I can help," Austin rasped, and he smiled hungrily, flashing his fangs at me. He dropped down onto his back on the bed, grabbing my hips and pulling me over until I was kneeling on either side of his face. Piper's hands caught me as I nearly lost my balance, and he grinned cheekily. He was also completely naked, except for his copious amounts of jewelry. I noticed a new ring on his left hand, a large silver thing with a spider engraving on it. The body of the spider was a blood red jewel, and I wondered where he'd stolen it from.

"See if you can smother our serpent friend," Piper smirked, coaxing me to lower down until I was flush on Austin's mouth. He attacked my pussy like a man possessed, and Piper held me when I immediately began to tremble, my back arching as pleasure built up in my core. Wyatt's finger returned to its ministrations, but I could barely concentrate on the un-familiar stretch as Austin lapped and teased me. Piper stole my lips again, his cock pressing against my hip as I whim-pered, pressing back into Wyatt as a second finger joined in, scissoring inside me and stretching me out. The sensations were too much to bear. I cried out as I came hard, rocking my hips and riding Austin's face. I tried to sit up, but his hands gripped my thighs like a vise, forcing me to still. My first orgasm had barely faded as another started building, and I cried out, clawing down Piper's back as I came again, liquid pooling down my thighs and soaking Austin's face.

"Fuck!" I gasped, and Wyatt chuckled as Austin crawled out from underneath me, his chin glistening as he smirked. He sat up and kissed Piper greedily, who moaned against his lips.

"You're all ready for me, sweetheart," Wyatt murmured in my ear, holding me up by the waist. I could barely kneel anymore, my legs threatening to give out. Piper pulled away from Austin and smiled, dragging me over to him.

"Lay down on me, Little Spider, we're not done with you yet," he told me. I straddled his hips, gasping as the tip of his cock notched at my entrance and sank in swiftly. I collapsed onto my elbows, feeling so full already, and Wyatt hadn't even joined yet. Austin smoothed down my hair, hissing gently as I heard the bottle cap pop again, and more cool liquid trickled down onto my ass.

"Relax, I've got you," Wyatt soothed, and I felt something a lot bigger than a finger pressing into me, stretching me slowly as Wyatt slid his length inside of me. I forgot how to breathe, feeling so full I was sure something would tear. Wyatt's fingers dug into my hips, pressing into my back as he filled me completely, moaning in my ear. "Fuck, sweetheart. You're so fucking tight, it's unbelievable," he whispered. I wanted to answer him, but the only sound I could make was a breathless whimper. Any coherent thought left my brain once the guys started moving. The pressure set off fireworks of pleasure in my core, leaving me a writhing mess in their arms.

Austin gripped my chin with his hand, forcing my head up. His other hand was fisted around his cock, the tip glistening with pre-cum as he watched me hungrily. I opened my mouth immediately, licking his shaft when he thrust into my mouth, gagging me as he hit the back of my throat. I moaned, letting him fuck my mouth, feeling the pressure cresting inside of me.

Piper moaned as his thrusts became more erratic. He was close, too, and I felt him come undone as my pussy clenched around him. My orgasm was so powerful I saw stars, and I screamed around Austin's cock, my body shaking. Austin's hands tangled in my hair, and he jerked roughly as he finished in my mouth, coating the back of my throat. At the same time, Wyatt finished with a loud moan, collapsing half on top of me as I sank into Piper's chest, utterly spent.

Movement out of the corner of my eye had me looking up, and I caught Cain watching from the doorway. He looked rumpled, as if we'd woken him up - which we probably did. I wasn't quiet. My face burned under his gaze, his eyes flashing red in the darkness. I wonder how long he'd been watching, how much he'd seen. Why hadn't he joined in? My heart ached, missing his touch.

He stepped inside the room, quiet as a ghost, and I squirmed out from under Wyatt, avoiding stepping on Piper and Austin as I maneuvered out of the bed. They were all nearly asleep, curled up and sated like a pack of wolves after a hunt. I climbed off the bed gingerly, my legs still shaking from the exertion. Cain caught me as I stumbled, lifting me off my feet and carrying me against his chest out of the room. I sighed and relaxed into his arms, feeling entirely safe as he carried me down the stairs toward his room.

I thought he was taking me to his bed, but instead, he turned and brought me into his bathroom. I heard the shower turn on, and my eyes shot open when he stepped into the shower with me, appearing not to care that he was still dressed. His shirt stuck to his chest, and his gray sweatpants darkened as he held me under the hot stream, letting the water flow down my hair and pool between my breasts. I squirmed until he let me down to stand, still holding me up as I turned, letting the water wash away the sweat and other *fluids* that had accumulated on my skin. Cain grabbed a washcloth and wordlessly helped to clean me off. His touch was always exceedingly tender and completely out of character for my abrasive protector.

Once the water began to cool, Cain shut it off and wrapped me in a large towel before scooping me back up and carrying me to his bed. He laid me down on the mattress and stripped off his damp clothes before climbing in beside me. His naked skin radiated heat as he curled around me, making my bones melt and every muscle in my body relax.

"What was the nightmare tonight?" he murmured, the first words he'd spoken to me all night.

"It was the dock worker," I explained, the words catching in my throat. He stroked my hair soothingly, kissing my forehead so gently that fresh tears spilled down my cheeks.

"I'm sorry, love," he whispered, holding me as I sobbed. "I'm so, so sorry."

CHAPTER NINE

Addison

I woke up in Cain's arms, which hadn't happened for a long time. He was still naked, and I could feel his cock resting against my hip as he spooned me, his arm wrapped around my waist. I shifted under his arm, trying to roll over to face him, but his grip tightened and he nuzzled against my neck. "Stop wiggling, you kept me up all damn night and I'm tired," he muttered.

Yup, there was my surly old man. I responded by wriggling my hips, letting his erection slide between my thighs. He growled in my ear, sending shivers down my spine, and his hand moved to my hip, stilling my movement. "Aren't you tired from last night?" He asked, his breath tickling my ear. Truthfully, I was a bit sore, but the ache between my legs was nothing compared to the ache I felt from missing his touch. He'd been so goddamn distant lately. He said it was work. But... I couldn't help but wonder if he just didn't want me like that anymore. I wasn't an insecure person, so this thought made my skin prickle with rage.

"You're right," I sighed. "I had three of them last night. What could you possibly do to impress me?" My breath caught in my throat as Cain stilled behind me, and I wondered if I'd gone too far. It was so hard to tell with his mercurial moods. His fingers tightened on my hip as he rolled me onto my back, his eyes flashing like embers as he stared down at me.

"They all coddle you," he muttered, grabbing my hands and pinning them above my head. I arched my back, drawing his eyes to my new jewelry. Cuffing my wrists with one hand, he traced around my nipple with his other, arching an eyebrow. "I thought for sure that Wyatt would mark you first," he mused, and I whimpered when the metal of the barbell warmed until it was almost painful, sending a burst of need down my spine.

"You marked me first, remember?" I bit back as he teased my other nipple. The hand print he'd left on me had faded long ago, but I still felt it sometimes, like a tattoo underneath my skin. With one finger, he traced a line of heat down my stomach, making me tremble as he skirted the edge of my thigh. The heat was just shy of painful, setting all of my nerves on edge as he ghosted his finger up and down my skin.

"Fuck, you're so needy for me." He smirked as my hips bucked, his finger running achingly close to where I wanted it to go. I clenched my thighs together, aching for friction, my back arching off the bed as I tried to wiggle out of his hold. Cain chuckled, his eyes darkening as he watched me struggle. His finger trailed over my hip, and I parted my legs, granting him access. I was so pent up that the first brush of heat over my clit had me moaning his name. He barely had to touch me and I came apart in his hands, bucking my hips against his hand.

Cain released my wrists, and I sprang at him, tackling him back onto the bed before he could even think about pulling away from me again. I straddled his hips as I shoved him down, rubbing myself up and down his length. "You like to tease too much," I told him, smirking as he groaned, his hands coming to my hips. Shifting up onto my knees, I slotted him at my entrance, sinking down an inch before stopping. He growled and jerked his hips, but I simply rose up higher, refusing to let him in further than that. "Not so cocky now, are you?" I taunted him, dragging my nails down his chest. "Who's the needy one now?"

"Addison," he growled, his fingers digging into my hips as I dipped a little lower, letting him sink in another inch before pulling back up. My pussy clenched, wanting to feel him, but I needed to drive him a little crazy first. He deserved it.

"Beg me," I ordered him, digging my nails into his chest. He groaned and closed his eyes, and I smirked down at him.

"Please baby, pretty please, let me tear that pretty little cunt of yours apart," he forced out, the muscle in his jaw twitching. I smiled and sank down slowly, feeling my walls stretch to accommodate all of him. He moaned and swore as I settled fully onto his length, feeling so full I could only gasp as I rocked my hips, using him to hit the spot inside of me that felt so fucking good. Cain kept still as he watched me pleasure myself with his cock, sliding up and down his length as my orgasm built up.

"Cain," I whined, and his fingers moved to my clit, pinching it exactly the way I needed him to. My pussy spasmed around him as I came, my nails digging into his chest. While I was still coming down from my high, Cain pulled me off and tossed me facedown on the bed. "Son of a –" I began to get up, but he put a hand between my shoulder blades, pushing me back down. He moved fast, grabbing my hips and jerking them up until I was kneeling with my face still pressed against the bed. I felt him against my entrance and moaned as he thrust into me roughly, burying himself to the hilt.

My hands fisted handfuls of the comforter as he set a ruthless pace, punishing me for all my teasing earlier. "Damnit Addy, you drive me fucking crazy," Cain growled. I screamed into the bed as I came hard, and it was only Cain's hands on my hips that kept me upright. He finished with a low curse, his thrusts slowing as the last of the aftershocks ebbed out of my system. His grip loosened, letting me slide bonelessly down on the bed. He followed me down, laying with his arm thrown over my waist, his face buried in my hair.

"I guess I know how to get your attention next time," I murmured, peeking out from under my messy hair.

"You always have my attention," he replied quietly, his fingers tickling along my lower back. "Every second of the fucking day, you have me under your goddamn spell." I shivered at his unusually romantic tone.

The door burst open, and Cain lurched up, snarling. I yelped as he crashed back onto the bed, and I rolled over quickly, landing on my ass on the floor. "Austin what the FU-" I scrambled up to find Cain, still naked and pinned face down on the bed by a nearly naked Austin, who had his teeth sunk into the back of Cain's neck.

"Enough!" I screamed, and Austin jerked his mouth off of Cain, grinning triumphantly as he sat up, still straddling Cain's back. "Mine." He smirked, giving Cain a little pat on the shoulder before climbing off. Quick as a- well, as a snake - he was off the bed and at my side, wrapping his arms around me and nuzzling his face against my cheek. He was wearing a pair of baggy black sweatpants, but I could feel his interest against my hip as he cuddled into me. My eyes widened as Cain shoved himself off the bed, looking absolutely murderous. I'd never seen Austin act that way towards Cain, of all people, and I couldn't fathom why he'd chosen today to get his head ripped off his shoulders.

"What the fuck did I say?!" he exclaimed, his hands smoking as he stalked towards us. "No more of this dominance crap! I will fucking bite you back, you little shit!" Austin tipped his head to the side, grinning as he stroked my hair.

"My mark, my nest mates," he announced, and turned back to me, kissing my temple softly. "My mate," he murmured, his arms coiling around me, lifting me off the ground. "Now we will make you the perfect nest for the babies."

Cain's fury died immediately, replaced with pure, unadulterated fear. I don't think I'd ever seen him look so scared. It would've almost been comical if my heart wasn't so busy trying to jump out of my throat.

"For the fucking what now?" I squeaked, swatting at Austin's arm until he set me down. "Austin! We talked about this," I said, turning and stroking his cheek softly. "It's not a good idea for me to have a baby..." His face fell so quickly, the breath caught in my throat "- right now." I amended swiftly. "We just got here, and we're still adjusting to our new lives." I glanced over at Cain, who'd suddenly become completely absorbed in the task of finding pants, ignoring the blood that was dripping down his neck.

"So the biting thing... it was about having a baby?" I asked, still extremely confused. He nodded emphatically, and I tried my best to understand what the fuck that could possibly mean.

"I need everyone to know that they are my nest mates." Austin smiled as Cain pulled a shirt over his head, rolling his eyes. "So when you have babies, they will know they are ours." Tears pricked at my eyes when he knelt down in front of me, pressing his face into my abdomen. "We will protect the babies for you, I promise." Fuck, so he was acting so weird because he wanted a baby?

"Oh, babe..." I murmured, stroking his hair. Of course, Piper and Wyatt took this moment to walk in, but at least they were somewhat dressed. Wyatt's eyebrows shot to the ceiling, and Piper just grinned.

"Are we worshiping our spider goddess now?" he asked, dropping to his knees beside Austin. "I can get on board with that." I felt my cheeks flame, now very much naked in a room full of at least partially clothed men. Cain grabbed a shirt out of his drawer and tossed it my way, and I pulled it over my head quickly, feeling a modicum better.

"No, we are not worshiping anyone. Austin was just... well..." I waved my hands around, trying to come up with the words.

"Austin thinks that biting all of us will help Addy make little snake babies," Cain announced, and Wyatt choked out a strangled noise. Piper sighed, his hand tickling down my bare thigh.

"You look so sexy pregnant," he murmured offhandedly, and Austin hissed in approval, his face moving down lower, between my thighs. I sputtered as I pulled away from both of them, climbing back onto the bed and wrapping my arms around my knees.

"Okay, enough of the pregnancy talk, alright? That's not happening right now. I have an IUD, and I haven't even found a new doctor around here." I shuddered at the thought. The last time, I had to convince the doctor I was a panicked germaphobe until she made sure to not touch my skin without gloves. Even then, I still worried about her for weeks, but she seemed to be okay. I didn't look forward to the headache of going back for a checkup.

"You mean the little T thing?" Austin rasped, and we all turned to stare at him. Suddenly, my skin felt a little clammy, and Cain went as pale as a sheet.

"Austin, what do you know about IUDs?" Wyatt asked slowly, stepping closer to us. I knew for a fact that Austin could barely use a computer, and he wasn't leaving the house for midnight health classes, that was for sure.

"I didn't know what it was. There was a little string, and it poked me, so I tugged on it a little..." He looked between us, frowning as he caught everyone's horrified expression. "It just fell out!" he insisted, his voice cracking. "I didn't know I wasn't supposed to pull on it!"

"Oh my god." I thought about what had just happened, and last night, and nearly every day for the last... *holy fuck.* Cain dropped onto the bed beside me, his head in his hands. "When, Austin? When did it fall out?!" I was yelling, and Austin looked hurt, but I didn't care at the moment. I was too busy panicking and trying to remember the date of my last period.

"I don't know... maybe two weeks ago?" He frowned. I got up and shoved past them, slamming the bathroom door behind me and locking it. I paced up and down the small room, racking my brain. There'd been some cramping a few weeks ago. That must've been when it happened. But I hadn't bled, not since before then, before the move…

"Please go and buy a fucking pregnancy test!" I screamed. "Now!" I kicked the door to emphasize my point, wincing as my foot throbbed. I heard a lot of shuffling from behind the door, but I stayed in the bathroom, curling up on the floor and tucking my knees into my chest.

CHAPTER TEN

Austin

Addy was mad at me. I tried to get into the bathroom, but Cain grabbed me by the shoulder and dragged me out of the room. His hand stung my arm, and I jerked out of his grasp, wincing at the red handprint on my skin. He was mad too. It was evident in his face; he didn't even realize that he was burning hot. Wyatt was running his hand through his hair, his face pinched. I turned to Piper, who looked sad. He was fidgeting with his ring and leaning against the wall, ignoring the rest of us. I didn't understand why everyone was so upset. What exactly was the problem?

"I'll go out and buy a test," Wyatt mumbled, pushing his sunglasses up his nose.

"Buy a few. And cigarettes," Cain snapped, his shirt beginning to smoke as little holes formed across it. He glared at me, and I bared my teeth defensively. His eyes flashed red, and Wyatt quickly stepped between us, grabbing my arm and pulling me away.

"Austin, you're coming with me," Wyatt announced, dragging me toward the stairs. He waited while I ran up and grabbed a tee-shirt and my large blue hoodie, making sure to shake any snakes out of it. I hurried back down, following him out of the house and down the block. Wyatt was hunched as he walked, his hoodie pulled low over his face. He was in one of his moods again, where he slept all the time - but didn't really sleep. I remembered what it was like when he first came to live with us, and shivered, hurrying to keep up with him. I hoped it wouldn't get like that again. Addy needed a happy nest.

We stopped at the drugstore two blocks from the studio, and I trailed after Wyatt as he wandered down the aisles. He reached the section with babies all over everything and started pulling boxes off the shelf, grabbing one of each kind they had available. "What are those for?" I whispered, as he grimaced at the price listed underneath. He didn't answer, instead he just stalked to the front counter and dumped the boxes in front of the cashier, pointing at the cigarettes behind her as well. She raised her eyebrows but said nothing as Wyatt threw down several bills while she loaded them into a bag for us.

"Wyatt, what are the boxes for?" I asked again once we were back outside. He glared at me as he shoved the change back into his pocket.

"They're for Addy to see if she's pregnant," he replied sharply, and I grinned despite his sour mood. I was so excited the whole walk back that I even met a stranger's eye. They quickly looked away, and I lifted my chin higher. I was ready to protect Addy now. I could scare strangers away from our den and keep her safe and bring her treats. It would be perfect.

Piper and Cain were in the kitchen when we got back, an open bottle of rum on the table. Cain jerked his thumb toward his room, not bothering to look at us. We brought the bag of tests to his bathroom, where Addy was still holed up.

"I got the tests, sweetheart," Wyatt announced, knocking gently. The door cracked open, and she snatched the bag out of his hands, slamming the door again before I could try to slip inside. His hand gripped my hoodie as he dragged me back out of the room and to the kitchen once more. Wyatt let me go and dropped into one of the free chairs, and Cain handed him the rum wordlessly. I bounced on the balls of my feet anxiously, watching the hallway for Addy. The entire table was uncomfortably silent as the minutes stretched out, and I grumbled impatiently.

"How long do the tests take?" I asked Piper, since he didn't seem mad, exactly. He shrugged and took a drink of his rum, pushing his hair out of his face.

"Five minutes, I think?" he replied tiredly, and I hissed.

"Why does she need so many?" I frowned, and Wyatt groaned, resting his head on his arms.

"Sometimes the test can show a false reading. We want to be sure," Wyatt replied, his voice muffled through his hoodie.

"Oh." I nodded absently, pacing around the little kitchen. "How long has it been?" I asked Cain, who was the only one of us wearing a watch. He banged his hand on the table and turned to glare at me, his jaw clenched.

"Sit the fuck down and stop asking questions," he snapped, rubbing his temple. I scowled at him. I was too excited to sit down.

"I don't understand why everyone is mad. Is it because we won't know who the offspring belongs to?" I asked. "We're nest mates, it doesn't matter!"

Cain stood and threw his glass at the wall, and we all winced as it exploded, sending glass and rum splattering everywhere. "Of course it fucking matters!" he shouted, and I flinched away when he advanced on me. "What the fuck were you thinking?! None of us should ever reproduce! Look at us, Austin!" He gestured around the room. "We're fucking freaks! It's like a goddamn genetic nightmare in here!" I stared at him in shock and looked at the other two at the table. Wyatt didn't move, his head still resting on his arms. Piper was staring at the floor, his mouth twisted into a look of pain.

"But... you said we weren't freaks..." I rasped, hurt building up in my chest. It would've been less painful if he'd hit me. Cain's lips narrowed into a thin line, his eyes hard and cruel.

"We don't need to unleash another goddamn monster into the world," he snapped. The words sliced through my flesh. How many times have I had these words thrown at my face? Usually followed up by kicks or punches. My throat tightened painfully, and I dropped my gaze to the floor. My palms stung, and I realized that I was clenching my fists so tightly my nails were cutting into my skin.

A small noise had us all looking over. Addy was standing at the entrance to the kitchen, clutching a handful of plastic sticks against her chest. Her face reflected how I felt, furious tears glistening in her eyes as she glared at Cain. I winced, preparing for the usual fireworks of one of their arguments. Instead, she simply stalked toward him and slammed her handful of plastic into his chest, walking away without a word.

Cain dumped them on the table and we all crowded over them, trying to decipher what they meant. I didn't understand what any of the lines meant, but the one Wyatt picked up was clear enough, spelling out the word - pregnant - in the little window. I turned to Addy, but caught only a flash of ankle as she disappeared up the stairs. We all flinched when the door above us slammed, rattling the windows.

I wanted to be happy. Every atom in my body screamed in victory. We had gotten our mate pregnant! But I was the only one who felt this way evidently. Wyatt groaned and grabbed the bottle of rum, drinking straight from it. Piper looked so forlorn I swore I saw tears forming in his eyes. Cain cursed under his breath, closing his eyes and shaking his head slowly. He left without another word, storming off down the stairs, and I heard the house creak as the front door slammed shut.

Disappointed and still reeling from Cain's harsh words, I headed upstairs. I tried Addy's door, but it was locked. When I knocked, something that sounded like a lamp hit the door with a horrible crash, so I backed off. My friends hissed a greeting as I entered my room, and I sank to the floor, sliding under my bed on my stomach. I told my friends the good news, and their rustling noises grew into a chorus of joy. Slithering bodies crawled all over me, hissing and demanding. They wanted our mate here with us, where we could keep her and our offspring warm and safe.

I wanted her in my arms, too. I wanted to tell her that Cain was wrong. Our offspring wouldn't be a monster, not with her as the mother. She was perfect, so the baby would be perfect. If Cain couldn't see that, then he wouldn't stay in our den. No one would call my mate a monster.

Not even Cain.

CHAPTER ELEVEN

Piper

"Piper?" Someone was whispering my name. That *was* my name, right? I blinked my eyes open, looking around blearily. My room was dark, so I couldn't tell what time it was. Or what day it was. A hand touched my back hesitantly, so it definitely wasn't Cain. My head pounded, and my skin itched with... *need*. But what did I need?

The hand continued its path over my hip, slipping underneath the waistband of my boxers. "Mmm, hello there," I mumbled, rolling over to face Austin, who was curled up at my side, his yellow-green eyes bright in the darkness.

"Are you sick?" he rasped, stroking my dick idly as he studied me. I hardened immediately under his touch, but the need under my skin distracted me. It made me angry. I grabbed his hand and pushed it away, rolling away from him.

"I'm sleeping, Austin, leave me alone," I muttered, folding my arms across my chest and digging my nails into my arms. Everything was too much. Even the air I breathed weighed me down. I wished I could stop breathing all together, and finally be at peace.

"You've been sleeping for three days," Austin hissed. "Cain told me to get you out of bed and make you eat."

"Then lie to him and fuck off," I snapped, and he keened unhappily. I knew he wouldn't lie to Cain. He worshiped the ground he walked on. He shoved my arm roughly, and I swung at him, knocking him backward. "Fine!" I bit out, glaring at him. I got out of bed and immediately stumbled, slamming my hip into the corner of the end table. The pain sharpened my mind, dulling the ache in my chest ever so slightly.

I limped toward the door and headed down to the kitchen as Austin trailed behind me. It took the little energy I had just to make it to the kitchen, and I slumped down into one of the chairs, breathing heavily.

"I could get you a beer?" Austin offered, looking around the kitchen anxiously. He didn't eat food like we did often, and he definitely didn't cook. I nodded dully, and he wandered off to grab a beer from the basement fridge. My skin ached so badly I gritted my teeth, willing the noises in my head to shut the fuck up for just a moment. Whispers started to circle around me, too quiet to hear, but the pressure in my body was building up like a tea kettle. It needed to be released somehow, before I went insane.

Pain shot up my arm, a lancing heat that made me ache with instant relief. A dripping sound filled the room, and I searched around for the source. Looking down at my feet, I saw a small puddle of red forming next to my chair. That was odd.

More pain lanced down my other arm, like someone tore open the skin and exposed the bone. I watched as blood leaked out of my untouched skin, spreading like a dark line of fire down my forearm. The puddle underneath me grew, and I stood up, trying to get away from it. My vision flickered, and I slipped, landing on my side on the kitchen floor. I heard a door open and footsteps neared. "It wasn't me, Cain," I mumbled, sinking into the icy darkness that beckoned me with open arms.

The void of death sounded a lot more like a hospital than I'd anticipated. In fact, the beeping was really getting on my nerves. Maybe this was hell. I opened my eyes, wincing at the fluorescent lights above my head. Hell would have had bad lighting like this, that much I knew. I felt someone squeeze my hand and I looked over to find Austin staring at me, his face half-hidden in one of Cain's hoodies. "What happened?" I asked, my throat feeling like I'd swallowed a handful of sand.

"You bled all over the kitchen. Cain called an ambulance," he rasped, looking down at the floor. *Oh, right... had that been me?* I looked down at my arms, remembering the blood that had pooled out of them. They were unscathed, not a single scratch on them. The curtain pulled back abruptly, startling both of us. A large man in scrubs and holding a clipboard walked in and started looking at the IV bags I'd been hooked up to.

"Well, Mr..." He blinked down at the chart. "...Smith." He shot me an incredulous look and sighed. "Aside from missing at least a full pint of blood... you're totally fine." He frowned. "Docs couldn't find any wounds, external or otherwise, so once you're all packed full of fluids again, you're free to go." He checked the line in my hand, shaking his hand at the dried blood flaking off my skin. "It's a full moon tonight, figures," he muttered. He shot me a sharp look, his eyes narrowing. "You know, your brother, Mr. *Smith*, is in the next bed," he mused. "If you're going to have a family reunion, do it somewhere other than my ER next time."

I blinked in confusion, watching him leave. As soon as the curtain swung shut, I dragged my legs off the bed and got to my feet, grabbing the IV pole for support. Austin was at my side in a heartbeat, holding me up. "You have a brother?" he rasped, and I shook my head.

"Something's weird here..." I mumbled, and my chest ached, drawing me toward the next bed. Austin helped me shuffle past the curtain, and we came upon a lone figure curled up on a hospital bed. He looked a sight, for sure, covered in dried blood and pale as death. Unlike me, it was obvious where his injuries were. Twin bandages wrapped around his forearms, and I could still feel the ghost of the knife parting his skin, seeking relief from the pain of the world.

"Who is that?" Austin whispered, and I gripped his arm tightly, until my knuckles went white and my breath came out in sharp bursts. I saw him now, with *her*, taking her injuries into himself. He was twisted up, bent and bleeding. I felt the agony in his head. I saw the void behind his eyes.

He was ours. Our pain-eater, our healer, our purgatory.

"He's coming home with us," I murmured, and Austin grunted as I collapsed in his arms, my legs too tired to hold me up any longer. Austin dragged me back to my bed just as Cain walked in, his shirt stained with blood and his hair wild from running his hand through it.

"Insurance was a nightmare. Apparently, there's another Mr. Smith here tonight, also admitted for attempted suicide. They mixed up your charts," he grumbled, watching Austin lower me back onto the bed. "Now that you're conscious, mind telling me what the fuck happened?"

"It wasn't me," I replied automatically, and Cain's eyes darkened. "I didn't do anything. That was the tug. It brought us here for someone else." He immediately groaned, his hand going back to his hair.

"Not this again. I can't take it anymore, Piper! We've already got snakes under the floorboards. What next?! Rabbits in the shower?" He sank into the visitor chair, shaking his head mutely. "I can't do it. I can't take care of anyone else."

"Cain... he needs us," I replied softly. "He's one of us, and he tried to die tonight." Cain groaned loudly, his head in his hands.

I laid back, my head feeling too heavy to hold up anymore. I think I fell asleep, or maybe I passed out staring at the flickering light above my bed. When I woke, I heard murmuring voices on the other side of the curtain, one of which was Cain's. Austin had crawled onto the hospital bed next to me, coiling around me with his head on my chest. The bags attached to my IV were nearly empty, and I felt a little stronger now. I stayed still to avoid jostling Austin, my eyes unfocusing as I stared up at the ceiling. Whispers grew louder, swirling around my little bed. I felt the tightness in my chest increase as words filtered out of the hum. I reached up for my charms around my neck, but they weren't there. Someone had removed them.

"*Death,*" they whispered, and I wondered who was meant to die. I glanced down, ice in my veins when I saw the blood coating Austin's arms, his hair a matted mess of gore. No, *not him*, I begged the whispers, *not him*. It came unbidden, the flash of violence and pain, a nightmare of certainty that was yet to unfold.

"Piper? What's going on?" Cain lifted the curtain and walked inside, the usual pained scowl adorning his face. I blinked at him, the whispers fading as he approached, fearing him and his unbridled wrath.

"Puppets, the puppets are everywhere," I told him, grabbing his hand and jerking him toward me. "Don't trust them, Cain, please!" He stared at me for a moment, his face softening.

"Alright, Piper, I won't. It's okay now," he replied, patting my hand.

I was discharged from the hospital later that day. Cain dropped Austin and me off at home and disappeared once I was settled in Austin's room. Apparently, I was not allowed to be alone or unsupervised for the next little while. He returned later that evening, and he and Austin helped the other Mr. Smith up the stairs and into my bedroom, since the spare room didn't have a bed yet.

While I was feeling mostly better, he - Wyatt, Cain told me - was still heavily sedated and barely conscious, hardly registering the new surroundings as they helped lay him down. Cain told me he'd get some more furniture for him soon, so I could have my room back in a couple of days.

I didn't mind where I slept. It was just nice to be home, where I was supposed to be. My heart was close to whole now, just missing that one final piece. *Her*. The one the black cat would bring me.

Our Little Spider.

CHAPTER TWELVE

Cain

I t had been nearly a week, and Addy still hadn't said a word to me. Austin wasn't speaking to me either, and I didn't blame either of them. The things I'd said were pretty unforgivable - but I stood by my words. None of us should bestow the curses we'd been given onto an innocent child. *Just look at my brother, he was so evil he polluted the earth everywhere he dared to step. That* was the blood flowing in my veins, the DNA that could now be swimming in the tiny creature inside Addy. What if it came out as fractured as Piper? Could we really be that heartless? That *selfish*?

I couldn't sleep, not in the house at least. The first evening after Addy had stormed off, I'd discovered a very disgruntled asp in my bed. I stayed in my car that night, standing vigil across the street from my broken home.

Piper was the only one who deigned to talk to me, but I could only assume he just forgot the incident place. He was so morose lately, I'd catch him staring at Addy's door wistfully, twisting the rings around his fingers. Wyatt was bunking with Piper since no one was allowed into Addy's room currently. He was a ghost of his former self, and hardly even got out of bed anymore. Addy had dropped a bomb in the middle of our weird little family, and I'd shot the survivors with my cruel words.

Addy was at least going back into work again. For the first three days, she hadn't even left the room. I left food outside her door, hoping to coax her out, but she always waited until I was gone before slipping out to take it. Then one morning, I'd gone to drop off her breakfast and discovered that she had left. It must've been early, because I'd been up for hours already, pacing around the kitchen. The buzzing behind my temples was getting worse every day. I missed Addy the way my lungs missed oxygen when I held my breath. That day, I'd been a bit of a mess, knowing she'd left the house without me. I considered breaking the lock on her door, or removing the door altogether. See her trying to shut me out when she couldn't shut the door. I knew that wouldn't work, though. Addy was a crafty little spider. She'd either lock herself in the bathroom, or commit a hostile takeover of someone else's room. I'd have to dismantle this house stone by stone before she would deign to be in the same room as me once more.

So, I did what any sane person would do. I started to follow her. Every morning, I'd wait in my car until I saw her slip out the front door, and then I'd just... follow behind her as she walked to work. I'd wait until she disappeared into her building, and then I'd head home, only to return around 4 p.m. and wait for her to come out, just so I could follow her home. My sweet, stubborn Addy refused to acknowledge my presence, even though she had to know what I was doing. She was quick, and no matter how fast I parked and ran into the studio, she was always locked in her room by the time I got inside. I was exhausted. Besides stalking the love of my life, I was also now fully in charge of feeding and keeping the other members of our gang of misfits alive, and they were making things exceedingly difficult.

On Saturday, I finally snapped. I slept in my car again, afraid to find more snakes in my bed, and woke with a start when I heard our studio door slam. Addy didn't go in on Saturdays, so I was forced to pull a very illegal turn when she started walking in the opposite direction of campus. I *swear to god*, she was testing my last nerve with this shit. I nearly lost her a few times when she made an abrupt turn down a side road, and I got honked at, several times, by people I cut off as I hastily changed lanes to catch up to her.

I was sweating and looking for a cigarette by the time she stopped, entering a random building I didn't recognize. Using my phone, I tried looking it up while she was inside, but there were several offices and I couldn't begin to guess who she was there to see. She finally came out after an hour, her face an indecipherable mix of emotions. I followed her back home, shaking with barely controlled anger as I parked and did my mad dash up the steps and into the studio. I heard the door to her room slam as I reached the kitchen, and snarled, out of breath and frustrated. Raking my hand through my hair, I looked around and noticed something taped to the fridge.

Crossing the room in three strides, I crouched to study the small grainy-looking black-and-white photo she'd taped up. My heartbeat thundered in my ears, smoke curling out of my mouth as I exhaled sharply. *That's it. That's fucking it.* Enough was goddamn enough. I stormed up the stairs, bursting into the first room I came upon. Wyatt was curled up in Piper's bed, just a lump under the covers. Piper was sitting inside his closet, a half-empty bottle of rum in his hand and a glazed look in his eyes.

"Get the fuck out of bed!" I shouted, tearing the covers off. Wyatt curled up smaller, his face pinched. Okay, he was a lot worse off than I'd anticipated. I'd deal with him second. I bent over and picked up Piper by the back of his collar, jerking him to his feet and snatching the bottle out of his hand. "Downstairs, now. Family meeting!" I snapped, shoving him toward the door. He staggered, but disappeared out the door, and I heard his footsteps clomping down the stairs.

Now, for this one...

I sat down beside Wyatt on the bed and touched his arm gently. His head lifted, frowning in surprise. "We need to talk," I told him and helped him sit up. With a little support, he was on his feet and shuffling toward the living room. I left him to it, bracing myself as I turned to Austin's room. This one would be trickier. Knocking once, I opened the door, watching the floor as I stepped inside. A chorus of angry hissing met me, and I scowled, snarling back at the room until they quieted down.

"Austin!" I barked and saw his foot peeking out from under the bed. "Out, now. Family meeting." Scuffling sounded, and he appeared beside the bed, climbing to his feet. He looked sullen and defiant when he met my gaze, and I stared him down, my arms folded over my chest. "Living room," I snapped, stepping back so he could stomp past me. I followed him down the stairs, leaving Addy undisturbed for now. This was *my* meeting.

I waited until Austin sat down on the couch, joining Piper and Wyatt. God, they were a picture of defeat. It was painful to look at them, and guilt washed through me as I acknowledged my fault in all of it. I walked back into the kitchen and pulled the little picture off the fridge, bringing it with me to the living room.

"See this?" I snapped, holding it up. Austin cocked his head, frowning at me. Piper looked through me, his eyes unfocused. Only Wyatt seemed to recognize what I was holding, his mouth opening as his eyebrows rose. "This is the baby," I told them, poking my finger in the center of the photo. Truth be told, I had no clue what part of the picture was the baby, it was just a blob of cells at this stage, but the point was made. "Our baby," I emphasized.

Austin perked up at this, his eyes shining with pride. No, we had nothing to be proud of right now. I glared at him until he settled down. "We fucked up," I announced, and then cleared my throat uncomfortably. "I... I fucked up." Piper focused on me for the first time, so apparently my humility could jar him out of his comatose state. That was good to know. "I was afraid, and I hurt everyone. And I'm..." I cleared my throat again, uncomfortable with the stares I was receiving. "I'm sorry," I muttered.

"Don't pull a muscle or anything." Wyatt smirked, and I shot him a dirty look.

"Listen, smartass, you three aren't blameless either," I snapped back, leveling my glare at Austin. "You." I pointed a finger at him. "You should have told Addy the moment you pulled her IUD out. You took the choice away from her." He opened his mouth, and I waved my hand, cutting him off. "No, I know you didn't understand what you did. But that's when you ask. You owe her an apology," I told him, and he bowed his head, chagrined.

"You." I pointed at Wyatt, catching him off guard. "You need to start using your goddamn words more, and letting us know when you need help," I growled. He slouched down lower on the couch, scowling at me.

"I'm fine," he muttered, crossing his arms over his chest.

"Like fuck you are," I scoffed. "You haven't showered in god knows how long, you haven't eaten in days, and you barely get out of bed anymore. You're spiraling again, Wyatt. How are you going to be here for Addy if you're like this? How can I take care of this family if I'm busy hiding the knives from you?" I bit out. His cheeks reddened, and he looked down at the floor, chastened.

"And you." I turned to Piper, who wasn't even listening, as far as I could tell. "Piper!" I exclaimed, and he jolted like I'd woken him up. "What the fuck is going on with you?" I asked.

"I think I'm going to die..." Piper murmured, looking down at his hands. A chill rolled down my spine at his tone - he sounded so resigned, like it was inevitable.

"Well..." I grimaced, wishing my head would stop pounding. "You can't die. You need to help with this." I held up the blurry little photo. "It - er... he? Fuck." I pinched the bridge of my nose. "The baby. The baby will need your help. It's all hands on deck now, so get your shit together and start acting like grown ass men about to have a baby!"

"Babies." I turned around, catching sight of Addy on the stairs.

"What?" I asked, frowning.

"Babies, not baby. Can't you read an ultrasound?" she asked cooly, stalking toward me and snatching the little picture out of my hand. "There's two, there and there." She pointed at the picture.

"That's not possible," I announced, all the breath leaving my lungs. I actually felt dizzy.

"Look it up, it's very possible," Addy replied, rolling her eyes. "Apparently, us *freaks* are exceptionally fertile."

CHAPTER THIRTEEN

Addison

Was I still mad? You bet your ass I was. The first couple days after I had done the tests, I just... wallowed. And panicked, a lot. I couldn't have a kid. I was pretty sure I killed my own mother with the fucking curse running through my veins. How would I give birth, let alone care for a baby without touching their skin? I took a few days off work, not able to face my colleagues just yet. Just the thought of seeing anyone had made me want to puke.

Oh, I guess that was probably the morning sickness...

Most of my time off was spent raging. I was furious at Austin, who'd been so naive he'd let this happen. But I was angrier with myself for not paying attention. I'd gotten careless, and this was the result. Most of all, I wanted to hit Cain for voicing all of my fears so succinctly.

Was he right? Yes. Was he an asshole? *Also yes.*

In the dream scenario, a baby was something celebrated. But no one was celebrating this, and it hurt so badly. The rage was interspersed with a lot of tears, which made me angrier.

Whenever one of the idiot men living here tried to come in, I threw things at the door, refusing to see their faces.

Wallowing was, ultimately, a little boring. I had eventually pulled out my laptop and started researching, which was what I did best. Unfortunately, *'what do I do if I become pregnant with my snake boyfriend's baby?'* returned no useful results. Similarly, *'can I raise a child without ever holding them'* provided no answers. I stayed up all night looking for something, anything, that might give me some sort of relief.

It was so late by the time I stumbled across an obscure post on a personal blog, referencing 'strange powers'. I fell asleep with my laptop on my chest, chasing this lead down a bizarre rabbit hole. By lunch the next day, I was messaging someone by the screen name Angelsgrace23, who claimed to be cursed from birth with a unique ability.

I begrudgingly ate the food Cain left out my door, and my laptop pinged with a message just as I was finishing throwing it back up in the on-suite toilet. Apparently, the baby didn't like turkey sandwiches.

Angelsgrace23 and I went back and forth all afternoon, and well into the night. Neither of us were eager to trust a stranger on the internet, but after six hours of discussions, I had to admit – she seemed to check out. It was weird to know someone else like us, although there being only five of us (six if I counted Jake), seemed unlikely. I asked her all the questions I could think of, focusing on the issue at hand: would two "specials" - as she called us - be able to have a child safely?

After midnight, she told me she had to go, but she would try to find out more information for me. I thanked her and signed off, trying to get some sleep while I absorbed the impact of what this could mean. Sleep wouldn't come, though, no matter how hard I tried. My stupid bed was too empty, and I was far too angry to let any of those idiots inside just yet. I tossed and turned for ages before finally giving up and getting dressed, deciding to head into the lab for a bit. At least there I could distract myself for a little while.

It took a little effort to sneak out of the house without Cain noticing, but I managed it. As I'd anticipated, Hannah was bouncing with excitement when she saw me in my office. I explained away my sick time as a stomach bug – which wasn't far off the truth, really. I even had to visit the bathroom a few times during the day, after crossing 'vending machine cookies' off the list of foods I could stomach. My next step was to find a doctor, and soon. I didn't even know how... far along I was. My poor, tired mind had reeled at the thought, and I dry heaved into my office garbage. That was when I called it quits for the day.

I said goodbye to Hannah and slipped out of the lab, heading back home, my eyes refusing to stay open as I walked. Somehow, I managed to get back inside and up to my room without being seen. I locked the door behind me and collapsed into bed fully clothed, succumbing to the exhaustion at last.

Knocking had woken me up from my impromptu nap, and I snarled at the door until whoever it was went away. Crawling out of bed, I checked the door and found a little tray with supper on it waiting. The sight of chili hadn't made my stomach flip, so I decided to give it a shot. Between tentative bites, I called a doctor's office I'd seen nearby. There was an OB-GYN listed there, and she agreed to see me on Saturday morning for a scan. I warned her over the phone that I was a major germaphobe and I couldn't tolerate skin-to-skin touch. She seemed okay with this, so I agreed to come see her.

There, that was taken care of. I glanced down at my abdomen, my mouth twisting as I dared it to look different, feel different, *anything*. When nothing burst out of me like a horror movie, I settled back down with my dinner, checking my laptop while I ate. Angelsgrace23 had messaged while I'd been asleep, having compiled some info for me. I scanned through it quickly, feeling equal parts reassured and frustrated. She'd explained that she hadn't had any luck finding an instance of two specials reproducing. However, as far as she could tell, it was like a recessive gene, and regular people could be carriers. That's why specials could be born to normal parents. If they happened to both be carriers, the child would have it.

Well then, if the science behind it stayed consistent, me and... whichever of the idiots downstairs had hit the bullseye would make a special kid. Because specials affected each other... differently - this was backed up by Angelsgrace23, who'd also assured me that this was the case with her - I wouldn't kill my child by touching them. A weight was lifted off of my chest, fresh tears leaking down my face. So then, whatever sort of curse this child was born with, we could deal with that when it came up. But I could have a baby without hurting it, hypothetically at least. At some point I fell asleep, still fully dressed, my laptop beside me on the bed.

The next few days passed in a blur. My anger was slowly dissipating, but I wasn't ready to give Cain the satisfaction of forgiveness. I continued to walk into work by myself, although at some point he had started to follow me. I let him.

If he wanted to waste his time stalking me in his car, that was his problem. Ignoring him was easy, and enjoyable, knowing he was probably fuming in the car all by himself.

Saturday morning, I actually spotted him sleeping in his damn car, and that killed my enjoyment of his torture somewhat. He'd woken up as if he sensed me, and once again I had a surly shadow as I walked to my doctor's appointment. It was only a few blocks away, which was great, because I didn't think I could stomach the smells of the train right now. I slipped on a pair of gloves before I walked inside to complete the 'germaphobe' persona I was adopting. My nerves were off the charts in the quaint little doctor's office, and my palms were clammy by the time they called my name.

Dr. Priyash was a smiley young woman, and I liked her immediately. She'd been extremely respectful about my need to not be touched skin to skin, making sure to wear gloves whenever she had to come close to me. I'd explained that my IUD had fallen out - leaving Austin's role out of it - and I'd told her that I wasn't sure how long I'd even been pregnant for.

Dr. Priyash made no comment when I pulled up my shirt, revealing the faded scars on my skin. She was the picture of professionalism as she readied the ultrasound machine and pressed the wand against my abdomen. "There, see that little blob there?" She pointed at the black-and-white image floating on the screen. "That's the fetus. I'd say you're only five or six weeks from the size." She fiddled with the dials until a fast-paced thumping filled the room. She frowned, moving the wand to the other side of my abdomen.

"Is something wrong?" I asked nervously. That thumping sounded funny. It wasn't a proper heartbeat. *Oh god, was my child fucked up even before it left my body?*

"I'm just trying to get a better view," she murmured. "Ah, there it is. You've got a second little one in there." She smiled at me as my jaw dropped open.

"What? Two?" I asked, sweat breaking out across my forehead.

"Yes, it's twins! Congratulations!" she beamed. "So that makes my initial estimation wrong. I'd say that you're closer to eight or nine weeks then. Would you like a photo to show the father?" she asked. I nodded dully, and she printed a grainy little photo of my uterus and its new occupants, handing it to me with a smile.

"Alright, I want you started on a prenatal vitamin right away, and I will book you in now for your twenty-week scan. If you have any questions, or you start to feel weird, you call me directly, alright? My receptionist will put you through anytime."

I smiled wanly and used the tissue she'd handed me to wipe the jelly off my stomach. I tucked the little photo in my pocket as I headed back out in a daze, noticing Cain out of the corner of my eye, hunched over in the car. *Okay, I guess the war would have to end now.* This was fucking real, and everyone would need to adjust to it real goddamn fast. When I got home, I taped the ultrasound photo to the fridge before heading back up to my room to shower. I let the water wash away the clammy sweat I built up on the walk home, and I dry heaved a couple more times for good measure, my stomach cramping with... either hunger or nausea. I couldn't tell at this point.

When I got out of the shower, I could hear Cain yelling about something, storming around the house more loudly than normal. I got dressed in a pair of leggings and a loose tee-shirt – one of Wyatt's, I think. My lips quirked up into a small smile when I heard Cain yell 'Family Meeting'. Once the footsteps receded downstairs, I snuck out of my room and tiptoed down the hallway. I took a seat on the stairs where I could listen in to his tirade. I almost gave myself away when he actually apologized, and a gasp of shock fell past my lips. Listening to him berate everyone made me feel bad. I had been pretty hard on them this week. I should have been paying more attention to Wyatt, who clearly needed help and not just a firm scolding.

Finally, I couldn't just listen anymore. Especially when Cain clearly hadn't read the ultrasound properly. Did I take a sick amount of joy in shocking him with the concept of twins? Oh yes. My joy was short-lived when my big surly man stumbled back and dropped to sit on the coffee table, making it creak in protest. He dropped his head between his knees, and I sighed as he started to hyperventilate.

"Twins?" Austin rasped, drawing my attention back to the couch, where my men were sitting like they were in trouble in the principal's office. Austin's pupils were enormous, his face strained as he keened softly, clenching the couch cushion so hard his knuckles were turning white.

"Yup. Two babies. I guess I'm already eight and a half weeks, ish?" I explained, touching my stomach nervously. Austin slid off the couch and onto his knees. My stomach flipped as he crawled toward me, gazing on me in rapt attention.

"Are you still mad at me?" he asked softly, raising up on his knees in front of me, his fists clenched at his sides. "I'm sorry,

I didn't mean to... to... " His face screwed up as he thought it over. "To take away your choice?" he finished, glancing back at Cain, who was busy trying not to faint. My lips quirked up in a soft smile.

"I know you didn't mean to," I told him gently, "And it wasn't your fault anyway. I guess it must've gotten knocked out of position before it came out, because of the timing of it all." I watched him smile as I reached out to run my hand through his hair. The contact did it, and I saw his composure snap all at once. He rose up faster than I could blink, his arms wrapping around my waist as he captured my lips with his, kissing me with a fierceness that stole my breath away. I squeaked when he bent suddenly and scooped me up, carrying me to the empty love seat and laying me down so gently it made me laugh. My shirt was pulled up, nearly ripping in his haste, and he nuzzled his face against my stomach, the cool metal of his piercings tickling my skin.

"Gentle with her, Jesus, Austin!" Cain snapped, his face still tinged green, and he cradled his head in his hands. A hand slid across my shoulder, rings glinting in the light. I looked up to see Piper on his knees, his eyes clear and full of tears.

"Are you happy or sad?" I asked him softly, reaching out to cup his cheek with my palm.

"Both," he replied, a tear coming loose and splashing against my fingers. He bent forward, his lips ghosting across mine, unexpectedly timid for Piper.

"Have you seen them?" I asked, and he shivered against my hand. The room went so silent it was like the air was sucked out of it.

"No. There's only darkness in my dreams now," he whispered, and a chill prickled at my skin. He reached out, his hand joining Austin's as it stroked the skin of my abdomen.

"Looks like it'll be a surprise for everyone then," Wyatt chuckled weakly, shifting on the couch. "Piper can't cheat this time." His hands were twisting restlessly in his lap, and I reached out to grab one. To my surprise, he flinched away like I was poisonous. I sat up abruptly, startling Austin and Piper.

"What's wrong with you, Shades?" I snapped, a little harsher than I meant to. He looked down at the floor, running his hands through his hair.

"Everything's fine," he bit back, and Cain turned, scowling at his tone. I shifted off the couch, standing and walking toward him. He backed away from me like I was carrying the plague.

"Wyatt, what the hell? Pregnancy isn't contagious," I told him sharply, and all but leapt on him, climbing onto his lap so he couldn't run away. I straddled his hips, and he did his absolute best to not touch me, even though it was pretty much impossible at this point. "Talk to me Shades, what's wrong with you?"

"I don't... I don't want to hurt the babies," he muttered, and I raised my eyebrows at him.

"And how would touching me hurt them?" I asked, frowning. He shifted uncomfortably underneath me, looking sheepish.

"What if I... what if I give them my pain by accident? Or my..." He waved his hand, gesturing at his head. I sighed and grabbed his hand, pressing it against my face. He started to panic, and I shushed him abruptly.

"Feel. Just feel," I snapped, and he finally stilled, his face softening ever so slightly. "What do you sense?" I asked.

"Calm... happiness... excitement..." he mumbled, and dammit, a tear streaked down his cheek as well.

"I know every one of us has some... family baggage, and a baby - *babies* - bring that to the forefront of everyone's mind. But I've been doing some research. From a biological standpoint, we should pose no harm to the babies. It works in our favor for once that we're all a little fucked up." I smiled sadly, stroking Wyatt's cheek. He leaned into my hand, and I smiled at my little Eeyore. I needed to pay closer attention to these broken boys. They'd fallen apart in only a few days.

"We need a new car," Cain announced, catching my attention. He was standing again and pacing the floor in front of the couch nervously.

"Why?" Austin asked, sitting down beside Wyatt and me, his hand going to my lower back.

"We can't fit a car seat in my car!" he exclaimed, running a hand through his hair. "Oh fuck, two car seats..." He looked over at the stairwell, paling again.

"Baby gates. We'll need so many baby gates, we have too many stairs. Addy, you need to move into my room. You should be closer to the main floor in case of a fire. Oh fuck, my window doesn't open properly. I'll call a guy. We need to make sure the fire escape is up to code, too. Maybe we can convert the studio so you can just live on the main floor. But the break-in risk... I need to get an upgraded security system." He had his phone out, typing frantically. I could literally see the smoke curling off his body as small burns appeared on his shirt.

"Cain!" I snapped, and he turned, his eyes flashing red. "Could you make some more of that chili from the other night?" I asked, and he stopped in his tracks. "It was the only thing in three days that didn't make me puke." I wrinkled my nose, and Austin keened sadly, nuzzling my neck.

"I can make chili." Cain nodded quickly, smoke curling over his tongue with each exhale. "I can make it right now." He nearly ran to the kitchen, and I flinched when pots hit the floor, followed by cursing.

Okay, so overall, it could've gone worse. And we had, like, seven months to get our shit together. That wasn't so bad, was it?

It was all uphill from here.

CHAPTER FOURTEEN

Austin

Addy was having our offspring! Two! Despite Cain's worrying, I was the happiest I had ever been in my entire life. She was perfect, my Addy, absolutely perfect. I didn't need dinner, but I refused to leave her side for even a moment. When she moved into the kitchen, I was right behind her, claiming a chair at the table first. She squeaked out a protest when I pulled her down onto my lap, but I couldn't bear to have her sit so far away. My arms wrapped around her waist, my palm flat against the space on her lower belly where our offspring grew. I buried my nose in her hair, inhaling her scent. My teeth ached with the need to sink into her skin, but I was a good boy. I could behave.

"Austin..." Addy warned softly, hearing my thoughts somehow. I keened softly, kissing her neck gently.

"I'm behaving," I murmured, although parts of me weren't. That's probably what she was feeling right now. She giggled, and the others joined us as Cain dished out bowls of what he called chili. It smelled spicy and looked completely unappetizing to me. I sat very still while Addy ate her dinner, content just soaking up her presence after nearly a week without her. Cain had stopped me from climbing up the fire escape and breaking into her room, insisting that she deserved some space. That had been torture, being able to sense her but not able to touch her. My friends had been in a frenzy all week, and I know a few of them had snuck into Cain's space to punish him for upsetting her so much.

Wyatt grabbed a couple of beers out of the fridge and offered me one. Reluctantly, I removed one of my hands from Addy and took it. Cain said they were more comfortable when I pretended to enjoy meals with them, and, usually, having a beer counted. I drank idly, moving my other hand over Addy's form since she was done eating now and didn't seem annoyed anymore. Her breath hitched as I skimmed over her breast, and I felt the metal of her piercing through her thin shirt.

The beer soured in my mouth, and I hissed in rage, tossing the can at the table. Cain swore and caught it before it dumped everywhere, glaring at me. "What the hell, Austin?" he snapped.

"I need to fix it!" I rasped, making Addy yelp as I jerked out of the chair, lifting her up and setting her back down as gently as possible.

"Fix what?! Austin cut that out!" Addy shrieked, swatting at me as I tried to lift her shirt up over her head. Frustrated, I tore it down the front, parting the fabric efficiently and revealing the offensive metal. I couldn't believe I'd done that. *Stupid, stupid Austin, not thinking.* I slapped the side of my head in anger, and Wyatt was out of his chair immediately, grabbing my arms.

"Hey, calm down! What is going on?" he demanded. He was in my head. I could feel him poking, and I hissed at him. "Why are you feeling guilty?" he asked gently.

"I... I hurt Addy when I gave her the piercings. But I didn't know she had offspring when I did it. I shouldn't have..." I whispered. Addy, who'd covered herself with her arms, dropped them and looked down at her chest, her mouth opening in a small 'o' of understanding. Wyatt glanced down, frowning as he tried to catch up.

"Oh, the piercings? Oh... shit. You're right," he groaned. I lurched forward, sinking to my knees between Addy's legs.

"We can fix it. Wyatt, fix it." I looked up at him, insistent. He looked down at me, chewing the inside of his cheek. "You fixed Addy before. It's just two holes," I begged, and Cain stood, looking between us.

"Hold on now, Wyatt isn't just some pin cushion we stick our wounds in," he growled, and Addy nodded with him.

"I'll take them," I replied quickly. "My mistake, my punishment." Addy's face twisted immediately, and I regretted the words that made her upset.

"No one's getting punished, good god Austin! We were all adults, I agreed to them. You need to calm down," she told me gently, stroking my cheek. I couldn't bear it. The offensive metal that had once made me so pleased now made me feral with rage.

"Please, Wyatt? Please, fix it." My voice cracked as it rose as loud as I could manage. He nodded slowly, glancing at Addy, exchanging some sort of wordless communication with her as he slid his hands down to her shoulders. Taking this as my cue to move, I reached up, and as gently as I could, unscrewed the barbell and slid the piercing out. Wyatt groaned, and I watched as Addy's skin healed, the holes closing and leaving only a tiny scar behind. I quickly did the same on the other side, tossing the barbells on the table.

As Addy's skin healed, I grasped Wyatt's hand. Immediately the sharp sting had me catching my breath, and I felt my own piercings reopening under my shirt. I smiled at Wyatt, flashing my fangs at him, and his cheeks turned pink in response. Cain cleared his throat as he grabbed the empty bowls off the table and brought them to the sink. I grinned up from between Addy's knees.

"Alright, this has been very exciting, but now I just want to go to bed," Addy announced, yawning suddenly. I stood up at the same time as she did, and she raised an eyebrow at me. Walking over to the sink, she lifted up on her tiptoes and pressed a kiss to Cain's cheek, whispering something in his ear that nearly made him smile. She gave Wyatt a kiss on the forehead and did the same to Piper as she passed. I was her shadow, following at her heels as she headed upstairs. As she passed my bedroom door, I caught her wrist, stopping her.

"Sleep with me tonight?" I asked softly, pulling her close. She was still naked from the waist up, and I felt her nipples rub against me through my shirt.

"In your room?" Addy asked, and I nodded, opening the door and tugging her inside. She didn't come in here often. I knew my friends made her a little nervous. But they were her friends too now, and I knew they would treat my mate with respect.

I felt her hesitation as the room filled with hissing, piles of clothes moving as flashes of scales appeared all across the small space. Carefully, I guided her to the bed, pulling back the covers and making sure no one was hiding inside who might startle her.

"I don't have pajamas," she murmured, and immediately I tugged my shirt up and over my head, handing it over. Addy laughed and pulled it down over herself, and my skin practically buzzed seeing her in my clothes.

"Perfect," I rasped, tugging her down until she was laying half on top of me, her leg thrown over my thigh. As soon as we were settled, my friends started to join us, tasting the air around Addy to smell her properly. My twin vipers were the boldest of the group, twining around her calf. She shivered and her hand tightened and she clutched my chest, but my mate was fierce and didn't flinch. Even when the others began to swarm over us, coiling around our limbs and spreading across the bed like a scaly comforter.

Her body relaxed over mine, and I felt her drifting off to sleep, making my heart sing. My friends praised her strength, hissing and cuddling around her to keep her warm. My beautiful black vipers draped themselves across her hip, claiming the spot nearest to the offspring. I whispered to them, sharing the joy of the two human babies inside my mate. A cacophony of hissing spread across the room, and I quickly hushed them, worried they would wake Addy.

It felt so right to have her in my den like this. I couldn't bear to sleep and miss even a second of it. Through the night, I listened to her quiet breaths, her heartbeat steady against my side. Somehow, I ended up closing my eyes just as the sun began to peek through the window, once my friends assured me they would keep Addy safe while I slept. I'm not sure how long I dozed off for, *not long, I don't think.*

I woke when Addy shifted, her leg pressing into my thigh as she grumbled in her sleep. Her long black hair was spread around her face, and Little Red was curled up at the base of her skull, using her hair like a nest. The sight made my fangs ache and my dick harden against her thigh. I knew I shouldn't touch her because it might wake her up, but my hands moved of their own volition, ghosting a path up her thigh. Her bare skin was so tempting, it was all I could do not to sink into her. A soft whine escaped my throat, and I winced when her eyes opened, blinking at me in the dim light. She shifted further on top of me, burrowing her face against my neck.

I was being good; *I swear I was.* My hand found the bare skin of her hip and I gave it a gentle squeeze, savoring the warmth of her body in my den. A sharp sting caught me off guard - *did she just bite me?!* I nearly came undone, my grip on her hip tightening at the feeling of her teeth against my skin. In a flash, she was sitting up, a devious smirk on her face. When I tried to sit up to join her, she caught me in the chest with her hand, shoving me back down onto the bed. I laid still, obediently, keening softly as she pulled my boxers down over my hips and threw them on the floor. My hips jerked when she grasped my cock, stroking down its length with an agonizing slowness, her eyes glinting with a predatory mischief.

"Mine," she murmured, and language fled my brain entirely when she wrapped her beautiful lips around my cock and swallowed me down. My hands tangled in her long black hair, and I hissed as her tongue traced along the underside of my length, teasing me. Just when I thought I would burst, her lips slid off, making an obscene popping sound that drove me wild. Once again, I tried to get up, but she shoved me back down, baring her teeth at me. I laid still for my fierce mate as she crawled on top of me, straddling my hips to sink down onto my cock.

"You're mine. Say it," she ordered, pulling her shirt up and over her head, tossing it off onto the floor. I opened my mouth, but words fled my brain. Addy rolled her hips, her eyes closing as she used me to pleasure herself. She was perfection, every inch of her, and I reached for her, my hands gripping her hips to keep her close to me.

"Yours," I rasped, the word finally making its way out of my throat. Addy smirked and tipped her head back, riding my cock like she owned it - and she did. She owned every part of me, body and soul. Addy could tear me apart with her bare hands, and I'd worship her as she did it. I felt her clench around me, her orgasm nearing. The noises she made had me gripping her thighs possessively as her movements became stuttered. She came apart on top of me, moaning my name as her pussy spasmed, milking the orgasm out of me.

Addy laughed softly, lowering herself down to kiss me, her nose brushing against my jaw. "Was that okay?" she asked, her finger running over the bite mark she'd left on my shoulder. I grinned and rolled us over, holding myself inside of her as I nuzzled her neck.

"Always," I rasped, grazing her skin with my teeth until she shivered, and I could feel her clenching around me, needing more. I brought my hands to her breasts, rolling them in my palms as she squirmed underneath me. Her nipples looked nearly healed, but I was still careful with them, teasing them into hard points as she whimpered, arching into my hands. Unable to resist, I took one into my mouth, rolling it with my tongue. She moaned and writhed underneath me, and I could feel my cock harden inside of her. I sucked and lapped at her skin, my fangs pricking at the delicate skin of her breast. Addy moaned, her pussy clamping down around me, and I began to thrust, drawing out her orgasm with long strokes.

"Austin, please!" Addy moaned, her nails clawing into my back. I picked up my pace, driving into her until she made the noises that drove me wild with desire. I nearly collapsed on top of her when I came for the second time, her body shuddering underneath me as her own orgasm rocked through her. Using my hips, I rolled us over so I fell onto the bed, curling her up at my side. Addy felt boneless as she snuggled into my arms, warm and satiated.

Was this what happiness felt like? Because I could get used to it.

CHAPTER FIFTEEN

Wyatt

"I 'm just saying, therapy is always an option," Addy insisted, and I groaned, resting my head against the table. She and Cain had been arguing about me for the last half hour. I felt like a kid who got into trouble at school.

If I'd actually had attentive parents, that is.

Addy had been vicious this morning, storming into the bedroom and dragging me out of the bed with a strength that terrified me. After forcing me to strip, she'd pushed me into the ensuite shower. I knew I needed it. My hair had gotten pretty disgusting. She had refused to leave me alone, so I was forced to close my eyes and take my glasses off, doing everything blindly so I wouldn't trap her inside my head by accident.

As I'd fumbled for the shampoo, small hands had encircled my waist, pushing me further into the hot stream of water. "Let me help," she'd murmured, and I'd heard the sound of the shampoo bottle popping open, groaning as her hands began roaming across my scalp. She'd taken her time, letting me run my hands down her body as she'd worked the shampoo through my tangled hair, teasing out the knots I'd let develop in my near-comatose state.

I'd been so tired, I couldn't even give her the attention she deserved, my body unable to respond to her properly. Addy hadn't seemed to mind, at least. Her hands had been firm but gentle as she'd washed my body from top to bottom, her fingers running over my tattoos, tracing the fine scars underneath. My body was littered with scars. Most were mine, but some belonged to others. When her fingers had ghosted across the large gash across my stomach, my lips had twisted, tasting the guilt through her skin. Jake might've been the ultimate recipient of his own torture, but I hadn't been quite fast enough. We both had scars from that night, and they went beyond the raised skin marring our stomachs.

Addy had eventually pushed me back under the warm stream of water, letting it cascade over my head and rinse out the soap. Her nails had felt amazing against my skin, sending tingles down my otherwise numb limbs. I'd craved the feeling of them digging into me, the sting of the scratch as they tore down my back. Instead, I'd let Addy shut the water off, and a towel had been wrapped around me, leading me out of the shower and into the steamy bathroom. She'd passed me my glasses back, leaving me to dry off while she got me some fresh clothes. I'd moved like I was on auto-pilot, pulling the shirt over my damp hair and tugging the soft gray sweatpants up and over my hips.

Now I was seated in the kitchen, a cup of coffee in my hands, while Cain and Addy argued about how best to deal with me. I should be more annoyed, but I was just too tired to join the argument. I was just counting down the minutes before I could slip back upstairs and curl up in my bed once more.

"How can he go to a therapist? 'Hey doc, I absorb too much negativity sometimes and lose the will to live'?" Cain snapped back, and I glanced up at him, my brow furrowed. That felt a little on the nose. Addy glared at him, her eyes darting to me briefly. Her hair was still damp and drying in soft waves around her face, and I swear I saw it steam with the anger in her eyes.

"Cain! Jesus, be tactful," she bit back. "I just mean, he could go and see someone, and maybe they could prescribe him some medication to help."

"He opens his mouth, and they'll commit him, and then he'll be depressed and someone's lab experiment," Cain replied sharply, crossing his arms over his chest as he leaned back against the counter. Addy sputtered, her hands waving as she struggled to raise a counter argument. Cain was right, though. We'd already had this fight a couple of years ago. I couldn't talk to anyone about this but them, and honestly, it didn't help. What I needed was... more precise.

"Wyatt needs to work. That helped before, and it'll help again," Cain said, meeting my eyes. I dropped my gaze to the table, clenching the mug in my hands. It was not like I hadn't been trying, damnit. I had my website set up and running, and it included a bunch of testimonials from my old clients. I'd even dropped my prices to try to entice new customers. Not a single call or email, not even an inquiry about my services, nothing since we'd moved here.

"Well... fuck," Addy murmured, her hands dropping to her stomach. "Wyatt was going to do one for me, but now, I don't think-"

"No tattoos," Cain growled, standing up straight. "No tattoos, no more of your kinky little piercing parties, either." Addy bristled at the order, her arms folding over her chest. "I mean it, and they know better than to try it," he continued, glaring at me as if I'd dare defy him. As if I would anyway, I wouldn't risk hurting the babies just to soothe that ache under my skin.

"Who's having a kinky piercing party?" Piper asked, strolling down the stairs. Austin was at his heels, and the snake-boy slipped around him to reach Addy first, coiling his body around her and kissing her neck.

"No one," Cain growled, grabbing another mug out of the cupboard and passing it to Piper. Piper cocked his head to the side, looking surprisingly clear this morning, his hair slicked back away from his face instead of messy and wild.

"Well, that's not fair. What if I wanted a Prince Albert?" He pouted, shooting Addy a wink. She laughed and Cain rolled his eyes, shaking his head at Piper.

"We're trying to figure out how to get Wyatt some customers," Addy explained, and I grimaced. I wasn't a goddamn charity case. It was not like I was hurting for money or something. I just needed... Well, I needed the release. Somehow, that was more embarrassing.

"Oh, I could get a tattoo," Piper mused, sipping his coffee and leaning against the counter beside Cain, so close they bumped shoulders. Cain gave him an exasperated look and shifted over to give him room. I swear I saw Piper smirk into his coffee cup. He was more lucid than I'd seen him in a long time.

"I like that idea," Austin rasped, and Addy kissed his cheek, grinning happily. I raised my eyebrows. Piper didn't have

a single tattoo and had never expressed a desire for one
before.

"Really? You want a tattoo?" I asked softly, picking at a chip
on the handle of my mug. Piper nodded and set his cup down,
pulling his shirt up and over his head in one fluid motion.

"Look, I'm a blank canvas." He grinned, and Cain rolled his
eyes, but I caught the smile playing on his lips.

"Okay," I nodded, finishing my coffee in one gulp. I didn't
want to give away just how badly I needed to do this. Piper
brought his coffee with him, leaving his shirt on the kitchen
floor as he headed downstairs, Austin trailing after him. Addy
put her hand on my arm, stopping me before I followed
after them. I was so used to the feel of her by now, but still,
just the touch of her skin against mine pushed away the fog
dampening my mood. She gave me a gentle smile and kissed
me on the cheek.

"The second that these things are out, you can cover me in
ink." She smirked, and I heard Cain's scoff of protest. I left
them to that argument, trailing after the guys.

Piper was already sprawled out on the tattoo bench by the
time I got downstairs. Austin was seated on the counter next
to him, holding his mug for him.

"Any idea what you'd like?" I asked him, grabbing my tools
out of their cabinet, laying them out methodically on the tray
next to my bench.

"Mm, a spider. For our Little Spider." He grinned. "She'll love
it." His smile faded just a little, sadness filling his eyes. "Or
maybe she won't?" he murmured.

"A spider sounds perfect," I replied carefully, watching him
come back to the present. "Right over your heart?" I suggested. He nodded. I got out my sketchpad and drew out a rough

sketch of what I was thinking, showing it to both of them. That seemed to cheer him up a bit, so I got to outlining it on his skin. I quickly fell into the familiar routine, tuning out his chatter with Austin as I planned out my tattoo. Once the outline was ready, I left him to check it in the mirror while I got my gun ready. This one wouldn't be overly colorful, but I needed a few different tones ready.

Piper got comfortable back on the table, and I positioned his arm so he could relax without getting in my way. "Ready?" I asked, and he nodded, smirking at Austin, who was watching with a rapt expression. The first touch of my needle to his skin was nirvana. The pain blossomed across his pectoral and jumped into my hand when I called to it. I hissed out between my teeth slowly, trying not to groan as the pain went straight to my balls in the best way.

"What does it feel like?" Austin asked, and I focused on inking the thin line on Piper's chest, losing myself in the bittersweet discomfort blooming across my own chest.

"Like I'm being poked in the chest," Piper replied, and I chuckled. "But it doesn't hurt. I guess that's your special skill at work?" he asked me, and I nodded, wiping off the line I'd finished. Already, my chest felt a little lighter, thanks to the stinging ache left by the needle.

I heard Austin slip off the counter and step closer to the bench, his interest peaked. I did a couple more small lines before starting to work on the body, the final form slowly appearing out of the mess of my sketch. Piper's hand was resting on his stomach next to my arm, and I noticed the new ring he'd been wearing lately. I didn't know where he'd found it – or stolen it – but the spider on the back made me think of Addy, which was probably why he liked it.

I turned and nearly smacked heads with Austin, who had moved in closer while I'd been focused, leaning halfway over the table to see. I wiped off the patch of skin I'd just finished and gave him a sharp look. "Don't bump me, or I'll fuck it up," I warned him, and he grunted a noise in response. Piper looked to be napping. He had closed his eyes and fallen silent a few minutes ago already.

Already halfway done with the small design, I was sad I hadn't chosen something bigger, but that would've been a selfish move on my part. This would get me by for a while. I clenched my jaw as I went over a particularly sensitive patch of skin; the sting pulsing through my body, followed by a wash of endorphins.

"So, this helps you feel better?" Austin asked softly. I nodded, my eyes on the nearly finished spider on Piper's chest. "Why?"

I grimaced, grabbing the red ink off the tray. That was a good fucking question. Why? Why did I crave pain the way most people craved air in their lungs? Was it my fucked up biology or my lack of a childhood that caused this? Maybe the creepy priests my poor grandmother had called in were right, and I was possessed by the devil. With the amount of exorcisms they'd performed on me, you'd think they would've gotten something out. But maybe they just let whatever the hell this was in.

"I don't know," I whispered, going over the outer lines one more time, finishing the last pieces of the tattered web the little spider was perched on. After the last wipe with the cloth, I sat back and cracked my neck, bumping Piper's arm to wake him up. "Take a look," I told him hoarsely, standing up and pulling off my gloves, tossing them in the nearby bin, using this moment to adjust myself in my sweatpants.

"That's so cool..." Piper announced, and I turned back to find them both looking at it. I grabbed the wrap off the tray and brought it back over. Austin was watching me closely as I carefully covered up the newly inked skin, pulling the last bit of tenderness out of it.

"Don't get it wet, don't fuck with it. I'll check it tomorrow, alright?" I told him, smirking. Piper was watching me with a sharp look in his eyes, and it was frankly unnerving when he looked like that. I almost preferred him a little spaced out.

"Why did you never ask us for help before?" Piper asked suddenly, shifting up to sit on the bench, his eyes boring into mine.

"I had customers before, and myself," I muttered, rubbing the back of my neck. Stepping back toward the cabinets, I was forced to stop when my back hit something solid. "Fuck! Austin!" I snapped, startled. When had he even gotten behind me? Strong arms shoved me forward, closer to Piper, and I swore at the both of them. "Austin cut that shit out. You might have hulked out, but I'll still kick your ass," I snarled at him, but I stopped in my tracks when Piper pulled a pocket knife out of his jeans.

"Pain-Eater," Piper intoned, his voice taking on an odd quality that had goose-bumps breaking out over my skin. My eyes tracked the movement as he flicked the blade open, need growing in my chest. Austin wrapped his arms around my waist, pressing against my back. His lips were on my neck, and the action was nearly tender, at least until his fangs sank into my skin. I moaned as the pain seared through me, making me lightheaded. I was hyper aware of Piper and his knife, the metal glinting in the light and weaving a hypnotic spell in my brain.

"You've been starving yourself when you should've just asked for help." Piper continued, and I felt Austin's teeth retract, his lips replacing them as he kissed my neck. I squirmed in his arms, scowling at Piper as he stared at me with some kind of pity in his gaze.

"I can't ask for this from any of you," I muttered, and groaned when Austin bit me again on my shoulder. The pain was going straight to my dick, and I felt heat across my cheeks as I sagged back into Austin's arms, feeling a little drunk.

"Why not?" Piper asked, quirking his head. "Isn't that what family's for?" He brought the tip of the blade to his collarbone opposite the new tattoo, pressing down just enough to break the skin. I was reaching out to him before I knew what was happening, and Austin pushed me between Piper's legs, close enough for me to grab him as he dragged the knife down his chest, parting his own skin with a hiss. I took it all, every drop, and a whimper fell past my lips. It was like a glass of cold water after weeks of thirst. I was vaguely aware as the line slowly knitted itself back together, undoing the damage Piper had done to himself.

"It doesn't work when you do it to yourself, does it? It's not the same," Piper murmured. "Austin told me about the piercings, and how you seemed better after you helped Addy." Austin hissed in my ear, his fang dragging down the sensitive skin and making me shiver. One of his hands was sliding lower, slipping below the waistband of my sweats. I hadn't bothered with boxers earlier, so he was able to palm my rock hard cock, and blood roared in my ears.

"If you can help us, why can't we help you?" Austin rasped in my ear, giving me a rough squeeze that had my knees buckling underneath me. It was only Austin's grip that kept me standing, but I stumbled, catching myself on the table, now effectively pinned between them both.

"'s not the same thing..." I mumbled, and Piper dug the edge of the knife into his shoulder, dragging it down his arm in a flash of metal and blood. I grabbed for him, the wound healing before he'd even removed the blade from his skin. My hips jerked into Austin's hand as he gave my cock another squeeze. Every single one of my nerve endings was on fire, and I felt better than I had in months.

"You're ours, too," Austin hissed, his thumb running over the tip of my cock, smearing pre-cum around as he stroked me. "Let us help you."

I moaned and braced myself on the bench, Piper's hand on my cheek as I leaned into him, Austin still pressing into my back, caging me in. Still holding the knife, Piper dragged it down his collar, slicing recklessly, not bothering to be careful anymore. I grabbed at his throat, giving him a warning squeeze as the pain bled into me instead.

"Stop that, I can't heal everything," I growled, and he smirked at me, flipping the knife and holding it out for me to take. I grabbed it and closed the blade, realizing with a jolt that it was my switchblade, the one that was normally tucked away in my pocket, just in case. "Thief," I muttered, my hips jerking as Austin gave me another rough squeeze.

"You do it then. Give me the hurt you want so bad," he commanded, cocking an eyebrow at me. Lust was swirling around my brain, my blood hot, and charged for the first time in months. I grabbed the back of Piper's neck, dragging him close so I could capture his mouth with mine. It wasn't a gentle kiss, it was all teeth and clashing tongues. I bit down on his bottom lip hard, sucking it into my mouth as I tasted the blood and the sweet release of pain. Piper moaned against my mouth, and I could feel his cock, hard and wanting, as it pressed against my thigh. Austin hissed in approval, his hand still toying with me in my sweatpants.

"I want-" I groaned, pulling away from Piper's mouth and panting, still gripping him by the back of his neck. He hummed in approval, looking sultry with his kiss-bruised lips, tinged red with his own blood.

"Take what you need," he murmured, and fire burned through my veins, molten with desire. I grabbed the front of his jeans and yanked, tearing the button off to get them undone. I wasn't gentle as I jerked him off the bench, capturing his mouth again as I slid his pants and his boxers down. The freedom of movement caught me by surprise, I hadn't even noticed Austin disappear in my haste.

"What are you waiting for, Pain-Eater?" Piper smirked, the cocky little shit. I spun him around and slammed his chest down against the bench, forgetting all about his fresh tattoo. The wave of pain caught me off guard and I groaned, my cock leaking against my stomach. Popping my thumb in my mouth, I lubed it up before bringing my hand down to Piper's ass. I circled his tight hole, holding him down with one hand as my finger slid inside, making him moan. I teased him a bit, stretching him out, as he made sounds of approval, his hands gripping the bench.

"Here," Austin hissed, sneaking up behind me. He held out a bottle of lube, and I stared at him in surprise as he moved to the other side of the bench where he could watch, a hungry smile on his face. I removed my finger and tugged my sweats down, fisting my cock as I opened the bottle with my other hand. Pouring a bit on Piper's ass, I used some more to lube myself up. I gave him no warning before I was shoving him back down on the bench, pressing into his tight hole and burying myself until my hips slammed into his thighs.

"Fuck, you're so tight," I moaned, pulling out just enough to slam back into him. I dug my fingers into Piper's hips, and set a ruthless pace, channeling some of my pleasure back into him until he was writhing underneath me, his knuckles white as he gripped the leather of the bench. Austin, still watching, leaned up against the cabinets as he stroked himself idly, his pupils dilated so large his eyes were nearly black.

"Yes, fuck, yes!" Piper exclaimed, as I drove into him, fucking with a roughness that surprised even me. He was so responsive to it, I could feel his pleasure building, and my balls tightened as my own release neared. Piper moaned, words I didn't understand tumbling out of his mouth as he came, shooting ropes of cum onto the bench underneath him. I finished roughly, my thrusts slowing as I emptied myself into him. Loosening my grip, I smirked at the hand-prints that would be left on his hips thanks to me. I pulled out of him and tucked myself back into my sweatpants, quickly grabbing some paper towels and helping clean up the mess I'd made on him.

"You look like yourself again," Austin hissed as I helped Piper stand up, turning him around to make sure I hadn't fucked up his tattoo with my roughness. Piper looked disheveled and thoroughly satiated, grinning like a cat in cream. He caught me by surprise when he grabbed me, kissing me with a gentleness that we hadn't bothered with earlier.

"That was fun, Pain-Eater," Piper murmured, resting his forehead against mine. "Next time, don't wait so long. As long as I'm here, I'm yours," he told me, and there was that tinge of sadness again. I tried to grab for it, to see why he was so sad, but he slipped out of my grasp, a knowing look in his eye. I swear I didn't imagine it when he shook his head ever so slightly. Grabbing his now cold coffee from the cabinet, he gave me a cheeky wave and disappeared up the stairs, leaving me to clean up the mess we'd left at my workstation.

Was it just me, or was that fortune-telling weirdo hiding something from us?

CHAPTER SIXTEEN

Addison

F lashes of violence streaked past my eyes, too quickly for me to grasp. Blood, gore, someone screaming, the noise unbearable, and I covered my ears to block out the sounds. *Who is it? Who's dying? I need to save them before it's too late-*

My eyes popped open as I sat up in bed, gasping as the room spun, threatening to topple me over. I crawled to the side of the bed, hearing a grunt of pain as my elbow caught someone in the chin. I managed to get both feet on the ground and bolt unsteadily to the bathroom before the contents of my stomach made a dramatic exit.

Once the nausea subsided and I was able to stand, I quickly rinsed out my mouth with mouthwash to get rid of the lingering taste. The room was no longer spinning, but the panic was still there, burrowing in my chest and causing my heart to slam against my ribcage. I needed to find my guys. I need to see that they're safe.

Lurching back out into the room, I saw a concerned and tired-looking Cain sitting up and rubbing his jaw where I must've hit him. I grabbed the bedding and wrench it off, revealing Wyatt asleep further down. Ignoring Cain's protests, I stormed out of the room, slamming Piper's door open, only to find the bed empty. Panic ratcheted up, threatening to bring the nausea back as I practically ran to Austin's room, throwing open the door. Hisses greeted me as I entered, but the only living creatures in here were snakes.

"Austin?" I asked to the room, immediately feeling like an idiot. Of course, no one answered me, because I didn't speak fucking snake. With a disgruntled huff, I closed the door and headed downstairs, hearing Cain's shouts behind me.

The kitchen was dark, and I was trying not to cry now, my breath coming out in sharp bursts. "Piper! Austin! Goddamnit!" I shouted, slamming my foot down. My heart nearly jumped out of my chest when a head popped up from the couch. I reached over to turn on the light so I could see.

"Little Spider?" Piper's voice filled me with overwhelming relief, and I half sobbed as he rubbed his eyes, blinking at me in confusion. Austin's face appeared next to his, and this time I did sob, running over to them and grabbing them both.

"What's wrong?!" Austin demanded, alarmed. Cain's footsteps on the stairs were loud and furious, but I didn't care. Everyone was safe.

"I had this dream... I was so worried when I couldn't find you," I murmured, letting Austin pull me onto his lap. I grabbed at Piper's face, pulling him close and making sure he really was here. The scream sounded so familiar, I could still hear it echoing down my spine.

"What was your dream, Little Spider?" Piper murmured, stroking my hair as Austin nuzzled his face into my neck.

"I don't... I don't know... it was just... bad." I tried to explain, feeling more tears run down my cheeks. "Someone was in trouble, and I couldn't get to them." Piper brushed the tears from my face, and Cain held out a glass of water, glaring at me until I took it and took a few sips. "Was this you? Is this like... like the dreams before I met you?" I asked, watching Piper carefully. He shook his head, continuing to stroke my hair.

"This wasn't me," he replied softly, looking down at the floor. I frowned and forced his gaze back up to meet mine.

"Piper, do you know something?" I asked, and the whole room went deadly quiet. "Have you had a... a vision or something?" He shook his head again, a frown creasing his brow.

"I haven't seen anything," he murmured. "Nothing but darkness." The hairs on the back of my neck stood up, and I felt Austin's grip on me tighten.

"What do you mean, darkness?" I asked slowly.

"Let's discuss this in the morning. Er... later in the morning," Cain yawned, gesturing for me to get up. "You two, come to bed, so Addy doesn't flip out and storms through the house again," he snapped, taking my hand and leading me back upstairs. My eyes were threatening to close as he helped me back into the bed, tucking me underneath the blankets once more. I felt Piper and Austin climb in after me, and Piper crawled up beside me, his hand falling on my hip. I drifted back off to sleep, feeling better knowing everyone was nearby.

"Turn off that fucking alarm, please," Wyatt moaned, and I scrambled out from under Piper's arm to grab my phone. Of course, thanks to last night's panic, I overslept, and now I was late.

"Shit!" I moaned, hopping out of bed and getting dressed as fast as I could. So far, my clothes still fit, but my pants were struggling, and one good meal would have the button popping off. I wore a loose blouse so the small bump that was forming wouldn't be noticeable, and pulled my hair up into a half-assed bun as I headed downstairs. My bag was not in the chair where I'd left it, and I swore as I tore the living room apart hunting for it. Did I leave it at the lab? I frowned, trying to remember if I'd had it when I came home last night. I got so tired now. By the time Cain picked me up from work, I was basically a zombie. Did I leave my bag in the car, maybe?

I headed downstairs and growled when I saw Cain waiting by the door, my bag on his shoulder and his keys in hand. "You're late," he commented, smirking at me. I glared at him and stormed past, not bothering to hold the door for him as I headed to the car. He didn't seem to mind my silence one bit, and that made me furious. How was I supposed to give him the silent treatment if he fucking enjoyed it?

"Keep up the smirk. See what happens," I snarled at him, slamming the car door. As usual, he set my bag carefully in the backseat and waited for me to get my seatbelt on, only starting the car once I was completely secure. *The ass.* He did, in fact, keep smirking the entire way to campus, and I thought about how I could get him back the whole silent ride there.

He passed me my bag back once we were parked outside my building, and I took it from him with a sharp look. "5 p.m.?" he asked, just confirming the pickup time. I grunted an acknowledgment and climbed out of the car. Before I closed the door, I ducked back down.

"Oh, by the way, I've decided I want to have a water birth at home. So you'll need to find out where we can rent the pool from," I announced. Cain made a strangled sound as I slammed the door in his face, smirking *myself* as I headed up the steps to the building. *Let him sweat over that for the day. Serves him right.*

I was in a much better mood as I headed into the lab, but it dimmed slightly when I caught sight of Hannah hovering outside my office door, clearly waiting for me. Something was going on with her, and I couldn't put my finger on what it was, but it made me nervous. I slowed to a stop as she bounded toward me; her smile was at odds with the anxiousness behind her eyes. "Addison!" she called unnecessarily, skidding to a stop in front of me. "I've missed you! Where have you been lately?"

Avoiding you. I smiled, feeling a tad guilty. Dark circles told me that she hadn't been sleeping well lately. She looked stressed. "Sorry Hannah, just busy. You know how it is." I adjusted the strap on my shoulder, glancing toward my office door, which Hannah was now blocking. "How are you doing? Are you feeling okay?" I asked gently. Her smile brightened to a nearly unnatural level.

"Of course! I'm great! Just worried about you. Ever since the bar you've been..." She looked down at her shoes, chewing on her lip. Oh shit, she probably thought I was mad at her about what happened at the bar. Guilt washed over me. I was a suspicious jerk for no reason.

"Hannah, I'm not mad at you. The conversation at the bar wasn't your fault," I told her gently. "I've just been busy, honest. I'm not avoiding you." Her whole body lifted at my statement, like I'd re-inflated her with my words.

"Oh, I'm so relieved!" she beamed. "I don't know what I would've done if I'd lost my lab girlfriend." She winked at me, and I laughed, feeling stupid for being so suspicious. Sometimes I forgot that people actually had friends.

"I should go drop my stuff off, but I'll talk to you in a bit, okay?" I smiled, and she nodded enthusiastically, moving to let me pass.

I dropped my bag in my office and set up my laptop, yawning as I sank into my chair. I was so tired already, and it wasn't even lunch. My phone buzzed in my pocket and I frowned, checking it quickly.

> No coffee – caffeine bad
> :(

My blood boiled. Who the fuck was Cain to tell me what I could and could not drink? I'd have coffee if I wanted to! One for me, and a shot of espresso for each baby. How was that? I typed back an angry message immediately.

You know what's worse? Second-hand smoke!!

"There! Checkmate, you overbearing jerk," I har-rumphed, dropping my phone back on my desk. My stomach grumbled and I groaned out loud. In the rush, I hadn't had breakfast, and if I got too hungry, the nausea was horrible. I was already terrible at being pregnant. This sucked. I felt tears prickle in my eyes, and I groaned again. Great, now I was crying about being hungry. Fuck, I was going insane.

I went to grab my wallet out of my bag, hoping the vending machine would magically have chips with added folic acid or something. On top of my wallet was a protein bar and a container of cut-up fruit with a fork taped on top. *Dammit.* More tears formed, and I snarled out loud at my ridiculous hormones. I wasn't stubborn enough to turn up my nose at food though, so I ate my breakfast while I reviewed my notes from last week.

My mood was vastly improved by the time I went outside to check on my subjects. Hannah was still out there, sitting and looking very zoned out in front of a container with a praying mantis in it. Her notebook was on the table next to her, but it looked like she hadn't taken any notes yet today. I pulled up a chair at the table nearby, grabbing one of my spiders in their container and setting it down where I could observe it.

"Hannah?" I called out softly. She jumped as if I'd woken her up, her pen slipping out of her fingers and landing on the floor with a clatter.

"Sorry, did you say something?" she asked, her smile tight. I frowned and shook my head, watching her as she bent down to grab her pen.

"Hannah... are you alright?" I asked softly. "You look... upset. Is everything okay with your boyfriend?"

She nodded quickly, her cheeks turning a bright red. "Yes, I'm sorry. I don't know where my head is today." She laughed, waving her hand. "Everything's fine, he's great. Perfect actually." She smiled wistfully, and I nodded slowly.

"Okay, I'm glad," I replied, still not entirely convinced. But my judgment was a little... off these days, so maybe I was just imagining it.

"How's your... boyfriend?" she asked timidly, and she must have meant Austin.

"He's good." I smiled. *Actually, he was elated now that I was pregnant. Oh, and we pierced my nipples, then un-pierced them. Then I had sex in his room full of snakes that he can talk to.* I said none of this, because that would be one sure way to get committed. It was really hard to make small talk when my life was... well, fucking bizarre.

"That's nice. You have other roommates too, right? Like that guy who drives you all the time," she commented, and my eyebrows rose. I didn't make it a habit to talk about the guys, or my living arrangement, since... It prompted follow-up questions that I wasn't comfortable answering.

"Yeah, there's a few of us there. Helps with rent," I replied vaguely, watching my little test subject make adjustments to her nest.

"Do you sleep with all of them?" Now it was my turn to nearly drop my pen. I looked up at Hannah sharply, but her face was open, curious, no hint of malice, although I swear her question had a nasty undercurrent to it.

"Hannah, that's not an appropriate question," I said coolly, trying to stay professional, even when I wanted to start yelling at her.

"It's fine, honestly! Poly relationships are totally normal nowadays. Dr. Shepard lives with her two partners," she offered, smiling brightly, once again diffusing the intense rage that had been simmering in my chest. *Jesus, was I turning into Cain?* Oh my god, these babies were going to drive me to madness.

"Oh, I see..." I finally managed to reply, tapping my pen on my notepad idly. "Well, we're just friends. He gives me a ride because it's on his way," I clarified, the lie feeling uncomfortable in my chest.

Just friends was the biggest lie I'd told Hannah, and it didn't do the relationship I had with the guys justice at all. They were much more than just friends to me. That invisible wall between me and Hannah, the same one that existed between me and everyone else normal in the world, seemed to grow, and the silence in the room became weighted. I pretended to take some more notes, but my heart wasn't in it today. I put the container back in its place and headed back to my office to work on my study instead, unable to sit in that uncomfortable room any longer. This was exactly why I didn't like to make friends with my colleagues. Eventually, it became clear to them that there was a line they would never cross into my life, and it made things awkward.

I only ventured out of my office twice more that afternoon – once to make a crappy cup of decaf coffee, and then again when I caved and got a chocolate bar from the vending machine. By the time 5 p.m. rolled around, I was antsy and ready to leave. Grabbing my bag, I slipped out of my office, glancing around to see if Hannah was still lurking around. When the coast was clear, I quickly headed to the door, not stopping when I heard footsteps hurrying toward me. I let the door close behind me and bolted for the exit, feeling more than a little stupid that I was trying this hard to avoid someone.

Cain's car was missing when I got outside, and I double-checked the time, worried that I'd left too early. A low whistle caught my attention, and I saw Piper leaning against a nearby tree, his hands stuffed in his pockets. He looked... good? Like, really good. I headed over to him, my eyes wide with shock. His eyes were so clear, the blue unmarred by the clouds that normally had him half-here and half-dreaming when he was awake. He gave me a cheeky grin and caught me by the elbow as soon as I was close enough, tugging me against his chest.

"Hello, my Little Spider," he murmured, kissing my forehead. My cheeks warmed, and I sank into him, holding him in the present while I had his full attention.

"What are you doing here?" I asked, my voice muffled against his chest.

"Cain had something urgent come up, a problem with work or something." He shrugged. "I offered to pick you up instead." I smiled and finally let him go, pulling back to look him over. He was fully dressed - and in his own clothes, no less - but still covered in his usual assortment of necklaces and bracelets.

"You seem... different," I murmured, taking his hand and tracing my finger over his knuckles. He looked away briefly, his jaw clenching, and something deep inside my chest screamed at me to pay attention, because something was wrong.

"Let's go." He smiled tightly, tugging my hand and leading me toward home. I tried to talk to him about what was going on, but every time I opened my mouth he beat me to it, telling me about his day, asking about my spiders, anything he could to deter me.

"Did I ever tell you about my great-grandmother?" he asked suddenly, and I raised an eyebrow. None of us ever talk about our families because we'd need a trauma counselor and several days to unpack all of that. I tried to think about the last time Piper had mentioned his past.

"You lived with her for a while, right? And your mom?" I asked carefully, and he nodded, giving my hand a little squeeze.

"I did. She was amazing, my great-grandmother," he sighed wistfully. "She had the gift of Sight, and people would travel from all over just to have her read their tea leaves. You know, she would have been able to tell you the sex of both babies, and name them." He smiled. "She would have liked you," he continued, dropping my hand so he could wrap his arm across my shoulders as we walked. "She liked fiery women."

I smirked, elbowing him in the ribs. "Just like you," I replied, and he laughed.

"She would've liked all of you," he murmured. "Every one of you was meant to be, created for a specific purpose."

I looked up at him, frowning. "You were too, you know," I replied, but he shook his head.

"I was a mistake. A man born with the Sight is an abomination. A curse given breath," he sighed. "She told me that, you know? She loved me and couldn't bring herself to do the right thing and kill me. So she sent us away and told me to do my best and not harm anyone else with my gift." His arm tightened around me, and I stopped just in front of the steps to our studio, frowning.

"That's enough of that!" I snapped. "Why are you telling me this, Piper? What the hell is going on with you lately? You're acting weird, and you're starting to scare me!" He turned to walk away, but I grabbed his arm, digging in with my nails to stop him from pulling away. "Piper!"

"Cain is worried the babies are his, but I'm more worried that they're mine," he whispered, looking down at the ground. "Something bad is going to happen, and I don't know what it is. Everything's gone dark, Addison. My dreams, the future. All I see now is... a void. Pitch black nothing." I dropped my hand from his arm, a cold chill running through my body. He fumbled with his collar, untying one of his many charms and holding it out to me. "Put this on," he asked roughly, and when I made no move to take it, he stepped forward and tied it around my neck.

The thin cord was wrapped around a smooth, shimmering brown stone, and I touched it gingerly, frowning up at him.

"What is this for?" I asked, and his hand reached up to graze across my cheek. I couldn't help but lean into the touch, and he sighed as if the weight of the world was crashing down on his chest.

"It will protect you. And the babies," he murmured, stroking my skin with his thumb, his sad eyes tracing my face as if he was trying to memorize every piece of me. Damn him, he was cryptic even when he was fucking clear and sober. Without warning, he leaned in, brushing his lips against mine in a kiss that tasted of goodbye. My heart hammered in my chest as he pulled away, and I wrapped my hand around his wrist, holding him tightly.

"Just come inside and we can talk, okay? You're freaking me out." I insisted, tugging on his arm. Quick as a whip, he slipped out of my grasp, taking a few steps away from me so I couldn't grab him again.

"I just want to walk for a while," he replied softly, stuffing his hands in his pockets. "Go inside, Little Spider." I opened my mouth to call after him, but he was already walking away, his hands shoved in his pockets. I was rooted to my spot on the pavement, watching until he turned the corner and disappeared from view. My breath was coming out in sharp bursts, and I was beginning to feel lightheaded.

"Addy? Babe?" Hands wrapped around my elbows, catching me as my knees buckled and I started sinking to the ground. I could hear Cain cursing, but it sounded very far away. My eyes were glued to the corner Piper had just gone around, willing him to reappear, safe and sound. Something was very, very wrong, and every atom in my body was screaming at me for just... letting him walk away.

I finally dragged my attention back to the present as my legs were scooped up, and I blinked up at Cain, whose face was twisted with worry. He carried me up the steps and shoved the door open with his shoulder, snarling that it should have been locked. The dread in my stomach was leeching my strength, and I dropped my head against Cain's chest as he cradled me in his arms, bringing me upstairs.

"Austin! Get your ass down here and fucking help me!" he shouted, and I heard footsteps thundering down the stairs as he set me down on the couch.

"What happened-"

"Baby?" I closed my eyes, but all I could see was Piper rounding that corner. A cold, damp cloth was pressed against my forehead, and I pushed it away impatiently, struggling to stand up, but hands pushed me back down onto the couch.

"What's wrong Addy? What happened?" Wyatt's face appeared beside me, tight with concern.

"I'm calling the doctor. Where did we put her number? It should be on the fucking fridge!" Cain snapped, and I heard things slamming around the kitchen.

"I'm fine," I mumbled, trying to get up again. "But I need to get him back." Wyatt caught me by the shoulder, refusing to let me stand. I snarled at him, and he swore like I'd bitten him, flinching away.

"Baby, what's wrong?" Austin crawled up on the couch beside me, caging me in with his body. His nose skimmed my jaw, hissing softly as his hands stroked my hair. Tears flowed down my cheeks, and goddamn, did I ever feel crazy? I wasn't emotional like this. What the fuck was happening to me?

"Piper left," I choked out, and Austin frowned, looking towards the stairs.

"He leaves a lot, but he always comes back," Wyatt offered gently.

"Like a bad penny," Cain muttered, holding out a glass of water. "Drink this, now."

I glared at him, but took the glass, suddenly feeling parched. I gulped down the whole glass and handed it back, shaking my head. "No, I mean he left. I let him walk away and I just... something is wrong, and I need him to come back. Now!" My voice cracked, and Cain immediately had his phone out, dialing someone as he muttered under his breath. Austin was still hovering overtop of me, and his hand moved down to my chest, plucking at the charm Piper had given me.

"Why do you have this?" he rasped, and I shook my head again.

"I don't know. He put it on me and told me not to take it off," I explained, touching it gingerly. Austin glanced up at Cain, who was cursing softly and typing into his phone. He looked worried, and I didn't like that. They were the sane ones. They were supposed to tell me that I was tired and hormonal and overreacting.

"That's his special charm," Austin whispered, and Wyatt reached over to touch it, moving very carefully. "He never takes it off. He said his elder gave it to him. For protection, he said." I closed my eyes, more tears leaking out against my will.

"I shouldn't have let him walk away. Something bad is going to happen. It's... I can just feel it," I whispered, pushing to my feet. "I'm going to go look for him." Austin was right behind me, his hands on my waist, and Wyatt moved to block the stairs.

"He's not answering his phone, but that's no surprise," Cain muttered. "You are not going out and wandering around looking for that man. He's like a feral cat, he knows the streets, he's gotten around without too much trouble for years now. He always comes home, Addy. Trust me, I haven't been able to shake him yet." He was being reassuring, his hands rubbing my arms, warming me up.

"Come on sweetheart, just lay down for a while, get some rest. He'll be back before morning, I'm sure of it." Wyatt smiled, but I wasn't reassured. Still, my eyelids were so heavy, it wasn't hard for them to coax me upstairs to my bedroom, the three of them working as a team to get me undressed. Normally, this would've been a fun afternoon activity, but my mind was somewhere else, so the whole thing was quick and mechanical. Austin curled up with me on the bed, pulling me back against him and wrapping his arm around my waist. I could hear Wyatt and Cain murmuring to each other as they left us in the darkness. I felt my eyes closing, sleep coming whether I wanted it to or not.

Something - a sound or a whisper - woke me up around 3 a.m.. Carefully, so as not to wake up Austin, I slipped out of the bed and tiptoed out of the room, shutting the door behind me. I crept downstairs and found my bag by the kitchen table. Pulling out my laptop, I curled up on the couch, checking to see if my online friend was around. Knowing there was someone else out there like... *us*... gave me a faint glimmer of hope. Maybe this was normal, this... *panic*. Maybe because of our bizarre connection with each other, I was feeling Piper's panic and misinterpreting it. Could people like us even be pregnant? Safely? All of our parents were normal, as far as I knew. Although Piper's family clearly had something weird going on with them, or at least his great-grandmother. I sent Angelsgrace23 a message and waited, twisting a strand of hair around my finger as I waited.

A soft hiss made me yelp, nearly dropping my laptop as I looked up, expecting to see Austin hovering over me. Instead, I saw a small ripple along the back of the couch, black scales flashing in the dim light of my laptop screen. "Hey, what are you doing out here?" I murmured, holding out a tentative hand towards the snake. I was getting used to their boldness now, and didn't flinch as it shifted off the couch, slithering its way up my arm so it could coil itself around my neck.

This was one of the twin vipers. The black ones that Cain was always nervous about, since apparently they were the most venomous of the crew Austin had assembled. In fact, he'd looked it up, and they were illegal to own. Even the Granddaddy cobra was technically safer than this one, but I trusted Austin and I trusted my little friend here. Austin said that one was a boy and one was a girl, and I believed him, but I couldn't tell them apart.

"Are you Selene, or Helios?" I asked softly, knowing it wouldn't answer. I thought naming them after Cleopatra's twins was fitting since she'd chosen to seal her fate with an asp. Austin didn't name them, except Little Red, because he didn't understand the need for names, but I liked to. It felt weird to just call them 'snake'. As I'd expected, it didn't answer, so I stroked its body once more and turned back to my laptop, sitting up straight when I saw a new message pop-up.

Is everything okay??

I felt bad. I hadn't talked with her after all my panicked questions about pregnancy and how to deal with four emotionally stunted men.

I'm okay, sort of. I'm worried, I feel like… the babies are making me crazy.

BABIES?!!!!

Oh right, oops. I gave her the highlights, trying to be detailed but also still a little vague, because honestly I didn't know her from Adam, and who knew what this information could do in the wrong hands. I watched the little typing icon blink for what felt like ages, before her message finally popped up.

I don't think you're crazy.

Tears prickled behind my eyes, and I groaned as, once again, I was crying at the drop of a hat. Fucking useless hormones. It felt good to know that someone else believed me, though. Even the guys were acting like I was overreacting and it was starting to make me unravel.

> I found someone who had specials for parents.

My stomach clenches, noting the past tense.

> What happened to them? To the person? Are they okay??

I waited and waited, stroking Selene gently - honestly, I still didn't know who it was, I just decided it was Selene. This was a girl's night, officially.

> His dad was killed a few years ago. He was a bad guy though. Lots of enemies.

His mom died when he was born...

I flinched, and Selene squeezed my neck gently, reassuring me. *Of course, I'm sure a lot of us aren't going to the hospital on the regular.*

Does he know... was her pregnancy... odd?

I'm not sure. I can ask maybe... he doesn't like to talk about her.

I winced, go figure, we specials sure weren't much for family, it seemed. I told her not to worry about it. After all the help she'd given me, I'd hate to cause her any trouble. I chewed my lip, still fighting the anxiety clawing its way out of my chest. Piper still hadn't come home, and somewhere deep down, I knew he wouldn't. Not without our help.

CHAPTER SEVENTEEN

Cain

When I got my hands on Piper, I swear to god.

Addy was curled up on the sofa when I'd found her in the morning, her laptop on the floor next to her, and a throw blanket tucked over her shoulders. I hadn't heard her get up last night, but I hadn't been listening for her, too busy sorting through the clusterfuck my work had dumped on my lap. I left her to sleep, tiptoeing back into the kitchen to make some coffee. My eyes burned and a steady pounding thrummed between my temples, making every noise a hundred times louder. I cringed as the coffee maker started sputtering, glancing over to make sure Addy hadn't woken up.

Grabbing my coffee, I crept back to my room, shutting my door with a soft click. God, I was so fucking tired. I looked longingly at my bed before sighing and sitting back down at my desk, waking up my computer so at least it would suffer along with me. Somehow, I had fucked up. Or... something had gone wrong. I still hadn't sorted out which it was. One thing I prided myself on was my work. I didn't fuck up like this. But a client's money was missing, and of course, he was looking at me for answers since I was the asshole who was responsible for it. Unfortunately, even after working through the whole night, I still didn't have the answers. I had no clue where his fucking money went. It just up and fucking vanished, leaving me holding the bag.

I didn't have time for this crap. Wyatt barely had his shit together, Austin was... well, so far he was behaving and not biting anyone else for now, but I needed to keep an eye on him. Addy was, well, fuck. Addy had consumed my whole world, and now she was preparing to up-end everything. Babies, two babies, were going to be under this roof. I was the only one who seemed to grasp the seriousness of the situation. Addy thought she was being hilarious by joking about water births and tubs, but we really had to consider how she was going to even have these kids, considering one of them would more than likely come out with fucking scales or something. And it was not like any of us had parents we could ask for advice.

To top everything off, Piper hadn't come home. We'd done our best to reassure Addy last night, but now it looked like he really might not be coming home. I had tried his phone a couple more times this morning, but he probably didn't even have it turned on. I didn't understand what was going on with him. He always came back. That was his thing. It was impossible to get away from him once he found you. And now I didn't know where the fuck he was, and as soon as Addy woke up and saw that he was still missing... well, fuck. I leaned back in my chair, running a hand through my already messy hair. This was a shitshow. Everything was going wrong. I just couldn't catch a fucking break, it seemed.

Was it... possible? I scowled and stood up, pacing around my room. This was a lot of bad luck, all at once. I had to consider the possibility-

No. There was no way. Even if Jake was still alive, how would he have found us here? I'd been so careful this time. Everything was registered under a different name. We'd basically started from scratch here. How could he be behind this? I groaned, and my head pounded even harder, threatening to blind me with the pain. Why did I have to lie? I should have told them about Jake. I kept them in the dark, and they let their guard down. This was all my goddamn fault...

A small knock on the door startled me, and I turned to see Addy standing in the doorway, her hair a wild mess. "Now's not a good time," I muttered, pinching the bridge of my nose with my fingers. As usual, she ignored the words that came out of my mouth, crossing the bedroom until she was standing in front of me. The second her hand touched mine, the headache dulled, washing away and leaving a gentle calm in its place.

"What's wrong?" she murmured, and I wrapped my hand around hers, pulling her over to the bed so I could sit down.

"Just... work," I muttered, my legs collapsing as I reached the bed. "You should be in bed. It's still early," I told her, but I made no move to let go of her hand.

"You didn't sleep at all, did you?" she asked, her tone cutting through me like a knife. I shook my head dully, my eyes closing as she pushed me back down onto the bed. "You're too busy taking care of all of us, and you're not taking care of yourself," she admonished. I grunted at her in response, smiling as she curled up beside me, her leg thrown over mine.

"Did you like your mom?" The question caught me off guard, and I cracked one of my eyes open to look at her. She had her head resting on my shoulder, her melancholy eyes staring up at me.

"Of course, she was my mom," I replied quietly. My parents hadn't been bad people, but they'd been saddled with a couple of fucked up kids, and Jake had quickly destroyed them, like with everything else in my life. Addy reached up and smoothed down an errant curl that had fallen across my face. I needed a haircut at some point. *Add that to the ever-growing list of shit.*

"I don't remember my mom," Addy murmured, and my heart cracked at the pain in her voice. "Austin doesn't either. Did you know that? And Wyatt only remembers his grandma..." she sighed, squeezing my hand. "How am I expected to be a mother when none of us knows what a mother is supposed to be?" Well... fuck. I sighed and stroked her hair with my free hand. A small hiss erupted and a black head poked out of her hair, glaring at me. Swearing, I jerked my hand away, rubbing it over my face in exasperation.

"Clearly, we'll be an unconventional family," I muttered, and she laughed softly, the snake coiling back around her neck. "But at least we'll be together. That's more than most of us had." She nodded quietly, and I stroked my thumb across the back of her hand gently. A family of fucked-up misfits, a bunch of snakes, and a lot of love. That's another thing we'd never had growing up.

Love.

CHAPTER EIGHTEEN

Wyatt

S hoving my hands in my pockets, I stepped out of the fifth and final bar that existed within a two-block radius of our studio. I couldn't imagine Piper would have gone that far, but he'd never wandered off like this before. Addy had been sick with worry all day yesterday, and when he still hadn't shown up by this morning, Cain finally agreed that something weird was going on. He was busy putting out some sort of fire with his work, and Austin refused to let Addy out of his sight when she was this upset, so that left me to wander up and down the streets around our place. I checked alleys, behind dumpsters, inside alcoves, and every bar and bar bathroom I could find, but there was no sign of him anywhere. I didn't even have a picture of Piper to show the bartenders in case they'd seen him, or kicked him out recently.

This was beginning to feel fucking hopeless. Pushing on, I headed back, down the street I'd just come up, backtracking toward the studio again. I'd stop and grab some water, then head out in a new direction. I wasn't looking forward to facing Addy without any answers. The last time I'd popped in, she'd been calling hospitals and asking about walk-ins and John Doe's, and she'd been working herself up into a decent panic. I really didn't want to let her down again.

I stepped out of the way as a woman bustled down the sidewalk, heading right toward me with a stroller. A *stroller*. We'd need one of those. I chewed on my lip as I watched the woman push it into a nearby shop with a pile of stuffed animals in the window. Curiosity - and an unwillingness to deliver more bad news - bade me to follow her, and I entered the brightly colored shop. Everything was visually overwhelming and, for some reason, fluffy; from the blankets to the toys. Even the little clothes displayed seemed to be fluffy, or at the very least soft. I smirked when I saw a stuffed blue bunny, its eyes overly big for its head. Cain would hate that. Grabbing it off the shelf, I considered for a moment, and then grabbed a purple elephant from the same shelf.

This should bring a smile to Addy's face, and it would freak Cain out, which was a double win. I brought both the toys to the front, ignoring the double-take the girl behind the counter did when she saw me. "Um, is that, uh, everything?" she asked, gesturing at stuffed animals.

"Yeah, just these." I smiled, passing them over so she could scan them.

"You know, we do baby registries here," she told me, sticking the animals into a plastic bag.

"Sorry, what?" I frowned, fumbling to grab my wallet. Did we have to register the babies? I guess they'd have birth certificates, but didn't hospitals do that?

"Like, for gifts? Your partner can sign up and put all the stuff they'd like, and then your family can buy the right things," she explained, and I winced, taking the bag off the counter.

"I'll keep that in mind, thanks," I mumbled, leaving as quickly as I could. We didn't have anyone who'd want to buy us gifts. We were lucky we even had each other. Bag of fluffy treasures in my hand, I continued back toward the studio, keeping my eyes open for anything that could lead me to Piper's whereabouts.

I stopped at the next corner, waiting for the light to change and halt the flow of rush hour traffic currently pulsing through downtown. Even the sidewalks were crowded right now, and I bumped into more than one harried commuter racing to catch the train home. I barely dodged a boulder of a man who was huffing loudly as he hurried along, his briefcase catching me in the hip and practically knocking me off the curb.

"Asshole," I muttered, rubbing my hip as he continued on without so much as an apology. Something shiny caught my eye near my right foot, and I bent down, ignoring the flow of bodies around me, reaching for it. It was a little silver charm, with a thin leather strap attached, except the strap was broken, like it had been ripped off someone's wrist.

It was stupid, and next to impossible, but somehow I knew that this trinket belonged to Piper – one of the dozen or so he would wear every day. It was too much of a coincidence that I found this here, on a route he would've taken that afternoon. With Piper, I'd long ago realized that as improbable as it might be, most things weren't just a coincidence.

I stepped closer to the curb, getting out of the way of the other commuters as I pulled out my phone, shoving the bracelet into my pocket. Dialing quickly, I watched the traffic zip past, listening to the rings until Cain finally picked up. "Please tell me you've got something," he growled, and I could hear the strain in his voice.

"I'm not sure what I've got," I replied quickly, and he groaned. "Listen, though, I think I found one of his bracelet things," I explained, and Cain got quiet. "Near the corner of 14th and Weisling. It was next to the curb, and it looks broken, like it got ripped off." I rushed out, and I could hear his footsteps as he paced around whatever room he was in.

"Fuck... that's a start, I guess. But what the hell happened?" he muttered, mostly to himself. I stared out into traffic, waiting for him to speak again. "Listen, Wyatt, I think you should come home. I... I need to talk to you all about something," he suddenly announced.

"What? Seriously?" I frowned. "I just got a lead on this, and you want me to come home? Shouldn't I at least ask around the nearby shops?" I asked, turning to see what store I was in front of. Some kind of pawnshop. Well, Piper liked to 'find' shit and sell it, so that wasn't too crazy of a thought. He might've been in there at some point.

"No, I think you should come home. I don't think it's safe right now, I think-" I looked down to see someone standing in front of me, staring right at me.

"Can I help you?" I frowned. I tried to see their face, but it was obscured by the hood of their jacket. They cocked their head to the side as if assessing me. Quicker than I could react, hands shot out and caught me in the chest, shoving me backward. I stepped back, forgetting I was on the curb, and my foot connected with air instead of pavement.

I heard Cain shouting out of my phone as my back hit the ground, and I rolled to my hands and knees, gasping as the wind was knocked out of me. The screech of tires had me flinching, and the last thing I saw was the headlights of an SUV.

Blessed is the Lord, cleanse the evil from this boy!

The Lord compels you, demon, leave this child!

You are wrong, boy; you are all wrong.

You should be in hell where you belong.

You shouldn't exist.

Sirens blared in the distance, and gravel dug into my cheek, making it hard to sleep. *Why was I asleep?* I groaned, and my face scraped against the pavement as I tried to roll over, but my body wasn't responding properly to my commands. My hand was caught on something, and I clenched my fist, feeling the plastic against my fingers. Right, the toys.

I have to get home. I shifted, and pain blazed through my left side, the worst pain I'd ever felt. My vision swam, and I heard people shouting, footsteps crunching as they approached me. "Get the gurney over here, now!"

I need to get back to Addy. My tongue refused to move, and I felt something tugging on the bag in my hand. I clenched it harder, refusing to let it go.

No, these are for the babies. You can't take them! "Nnnn-" I groaned, and someone was shining a light in my eyes. I immediately closed them, panicking. *Where were my sunglasses?! I needed my glasses.*

"It's okay, you're going to be okay. Don't try to move, okay? We need to make sure you don't have a spinal in-jury," someone told me, and something hard and plastic wrapped around my neck.

"Hhh-hhh-" I wheezed, trying to get the words out. My chest felt like there was a car on top of it, every breath in was too shallow, I needed more air.

"Do you know where you are?" a woman asked. I could feel her hovering over me, so I kept my eyes shut.

"Ggg-glasses," I slurred, and I heard voices talking overtop of me.

"Is he blind? His pupils are concerning, they didn't react to the light," someone was saying, and hands rolled me onto my back. Immediately my lungs seized up, and I gasped for air, the car on my chest doubling in weight, crushing me.

"I think he's got a collapsed lung. We need to get him on the bus and try to stabilize him now!" I clutched the bag in my hand, feeling dizzy as they lifted me into the air, rolling me across the road. Something plastic was tugged over my face, but no matter how hard I tried, the air wouldn't inflate my lungs.

This was it. I'd finally managed to get myself killed.

CHAPTER NINETEEN

Cain

This was a nightmare, one I couldn't wake up from, no matter how hard I tried. I heard Wyatt talking to someone, interrupting me before I could warn him. I was too late, and my failure echoed through the phone as I heard Wyatt shout, and then the horrible screech of tires.

"Wyatt! Wyatt, fucking answer me!" I yelled, raking my hand through my hair. I felt so useless, standing here holding my phone while I could hear shouting on the other end of the line.

Addy burst into the room, her eyes wide. Fuck, I'd been too loud, and she'd heard me. "What's wrong?!" she demanded, and I pulled her over, keeping my ear to the phone as I sat her down on my bed. "Cain!"

"Hello?" Someone - definitely not Wyatt - picked up the phone on the other end. "Is someone there?"

"Yes, I'm here dammit. Where's my friend?" I growled, and Addy sucked in a breath. Silence on the other end went on for what felt like forever, and then another person came on.

"Hello? My name is David. I'm an EMT with Station 213. Does this phone belong to a friend of yours?" My blood ran cold, and I clenched my fingers around the screen tightly, feeling Addy's gaze burning a hole into the side of my head.

"Yes, Wyatt Collins," I replied hoarsely. "He's my room-mate." I heard some talking on the other end, and I waited, my heart pounding in my ears.

"Sir, I'm afraid your roommate was involved in an acci-dent. It appears that he fell out and into the road and was struck by a car." I shook my head, wrenching my hair with my fingers as I resumed pacing my room.

"I heard him talking. Someone fucking pushed him!" I snapped.

"... alright sir, we will be sure to mention that to the police on scene. We're taking him to East Valley General. Do you know where that is, sir?" I gritted my teeth. It was the nearest hospital, so that was lucky, I guess.

"Yes, I know where that is," I replied, my teeth grinding as I paced. Addy was watching me, her eyes wide and her lips twisted with frustration.

"We'll bring him through the ER, so if you come to the main desk, they'll let you know where to go from there. Does he have next of kin, or an emergency contact that should be notified?" I wanted to sit down. I was exhausted but buzzing with anxiety at the same time, my body refus-ing to stop moving.

"No, just me," I said roughly. There was a grunt of re-sponse on the other end, and I hung up once he'd assured me that Wyatt's phone would be left with his other belong-ings.

"Cain. What the fuck is going on?" Addy asked, her voice breaking. I couldn't bear to look at her, feeling helpless that I couldn't shield her from this pain.

"We need to go, get your coat and get Austin, okay?" I murmured, running my hand over my face. Should I change my shirt? I was still wearing the same shirt I'd put on yesterday, or was that the day before? I couldn't remember the last time I'd slept.

"Where is Wyatt? What happened? Did he find Piper?" she pressed, standing and grabbing my arm. *Fuck me, here it goes, just rip off the band-aid.* The band-aid that was super-glued to her arm.

"No, he didn't... he... there was an accident," I explained, and Addy sucked in a sharp breath. "I need you to stay calm, okay?" Grabbing her shoulders, I steadied her as her eyes went a little unfocused, the color leaching from her face. "Wyatt was hurt. He's being taken to the hospital. We need to go and meet him there, okay?"

"How bad?" she murmured, and I felt her swaying in my hands. I wrapped my arms around her, bringing her close to my chest.

"I don't know," I replied, my heart sinking. He fell out onto the road and was struck by a car. I didn't even want to think about it. I gave her a gentle squeeze before pulling away, watching her closely to make sure she was sturdy enough to let go. "Go get Austin, alright? We'll go to the hospital together." She nodded tightly and wandered out of my room, leaving me to change into something clean. I left my laptop here, because fuck them. This was more important than the dumpster fire that I'd been trying to put out.

Austin and Addy met me at the door, and from the look of pain on Austin's face, she'd clearly filled him in on what just happened. I kept a sharp eye out as we headed to the car. Austin picked up on the vibe and stuck close to Addy's side, helping her into the car before hopping in the backseat. The drive to the hospital was silent, everyone tense and unwilling to voice what I knew we were all thinking. I parked near the ER and led our silent group inside, approaching the first desk I could find with a nurse behind it.

"Wyatt Collins? He was brought by ambulance," I announced, and the nurse pursed her lips and began typing on her computer.

"Are you family?" she asked, and I bit back a snarl.

"Yes, we are!" Addy answered for me, stepping up to the desk. She nodded and continued typing for another minute.

"He's been taken directly to the ICU. You can head up there and wait. I think he's getting some scans right now," she told us. I nodded and tugged on Addy's elbow, dragging her gently away from the desk. We wandered around until we found the ICU waiting room and yet another desk to check in at. Wyatt was in fact getting scans done, as the nurse had mentioned, and we were instructed to wait here until he got back.

Addy slumped into one of the chairs, her head in her hands. Austin tried to comfort her as best he could, but I could tell he was uncomfortable being in the noisy and crowded hospital. His hood pulled low over his face as he took the seat next to Addy's, putting an arm around her. I couldn't bear to sit right now. All I wanted to do was move around, to do *something*. I paced, much to the irritation of the nurse at the desk, but I ignored the daggers she was throwing at me with her eyes. Making myself useful, I tracked down a vending machine and got a chocolate bar and a bottle of water for Addy, who was looking too pale for my liking. Her eyes briefly met mine as I handed her the treats, and the despair I saw in them froze me to my core. What I needed to do most is fix this, somehow. I couldn't let anything else hurt her. I would hunt down Piper myself if that was what it took.

We were waiting for hours in that cramped room, and I was slowly losing my mind. I probably called Piper's phone a hundred times, sending him angry messages about Wyatt because there was nothing else I could do right now. I was wearing a path on the hospital floor, pacing back and forth down the little hallway while Austin stayed close to Addy, encouraging her to sip her water and have bites of the chocolate bar. She was being obstinate, refusing to eat anything, and I was ready to fight her about it. *Why wouldn't she eat something, god dammit!* She had two tiny beings leeching all of her damn resources. She couldn't run on empty anymore.

"Collins' family?" someone called out, and my head whipped around, searching for the source of the announcement. I beelined for the doctor standing in front of the nurse's desk, and she met my eye, checking the clipboard in her hands. "Collins?" she asked as I approached, and I nodded quickly. "Mr. Collins, your..." She checked the clipboard again.

"Wyatt's my brother," I offered quickly, and she nodded, making a quick note. "Your brother is currently in serious, but stable, condition. He has a broken leg, a broken arm, several cracked ribs, and a concussion. He had a punctured lung at the scene, but paramedics were able to re-inflate it quickly. We did a CT scan and an MRI of his brain, and it looks like there is no significant brain damage or damage to his spine, but there is a fair amount of swelling in his lower vertebrae, so we will have to do a second scan to reassess once that goes down. There were also quite a number of cuts that needed to be stitched up. Two in particular were quite bad, one on his neck and another on his left temple." I nodded along, feeling Addy's presence at my side as they joined me.

"Did your brother have vision problems?" she asked cautiously, and I nodded, running my hand through my hair.

"He's blind, damage with his, uh..." I waved at my eyes vaguely. "I'm sorry. I don't know what it's called. His pupils aren't right," I sighed, and she nodded, making a note on her chart.

"That's reassuring then. We weren't sure if that was a by-product of the accident, so we did the extra scan to make sure there was no damage or bleeding in his occipital region," she explained.

"Can we see him?" Addy interjected, her face tight with worry. The doctor nodded quickly, her sharp eyes scanning over Addy with a hint of concern. She gestured for us to follow her down the hall, scribbling notes on her chart as she walked.

"He will be asleep for a while, and he will probably be groggy when he does wake up. We had to sedate him. He needed pins in his leg to set the break in his femur." Addy made a small noise, but when I glanced over, her lips were pinched together, forming a thin line. We walked into a small room, and I spotted Wyatt in the far bed, his leg propped up, a giant cast running down the length of it. "At least he should have the room to himself for a while, unless we get busy," the doctor offered.

Addy jogged over to the bed and I hurried to catch up to her, Austin at my side. I've seen Wyatt in the hospital a few times now, normally covered in blood and bandages. This... this was different. His pale skin was a patchwork of black and blue, and his face looked like he'd gone twelve rounds with a UFC world champion but had been tied to a chair for it. Fresh stitches ran along his forehead and down his temple, and there was a shaved patch in his hair where they had to continue with his stitches. It looked like his left side had taken the brunt of the damage, his arm and leg both in casts. We'd need to block off the stairs, maybe get him a wheelchair, or crutches or something.

As if she heard my thoughts, Addy turned to the doctor. "When can we bring him home?" she asked, her voice shaking.

The doctor gave her a sympathetic look and walked over to check a few of the machines Wyatt was hooked up to. "If his stats come up a bit, and the second scan is clear, he could be discharged in a couple of days." Addy bit her lip, and I could see her fighting back tears.

"Oh, the paramedics said he had some things on him. Apparently, he refused to let them go even when his lung collapsed," the doctor announced, walking over to one of the cabinets beside the bed. She pulled out a ragged-looking plastic bag and a cellphone that looked a little worse for wear. I frowned as Addy reached out to take the bag, a choked sob working its way out of her throat as she pulled out a stuffed purple elephant.

Austin was faster than I was. He saw her legs buckle and caught her before she could hit the floor. The doctor reacted just as fast. The chart was on the table and she was at Addy's side before I could stop her. "Wait!" I shouted, and the doctor turned to glare at me.

"She's got a... germ issue. She doesn't like to be touched by strangers!" I explained quickly, and she pursed her lips, but moved to the doorway where a box of gloves was available.

"Lay her down on the floor on her side," the doctor ordered, and I helped Austin lower Addy down carefully. Her eyelids fluttered, and she groaned, already coming back around.

"Does she faint a lot?" she asked, taking my place, her hands gloved as she pulled her stethoscope out of her pocket, quickly checking her heart.

"No - I mean, not before. She's done this a couple of times now. She's uh, she's pregnant. Twins," I told her quickly, running a hand through my hair. My brain was short circuiting and I couldn't fucking handle much more.

"I'd like to get some blood from her, just to be safe," the doctor said. "And get her some fluids. Can you hear me, hun?" she asked Addy, rubbing her gloved thumb over Addy's wrist. "I'll order an ultrasound too, just to be safe. Does she have an OB-GYN? How far along is she?" I scrambled to think, pulling out my phone quickly.

"Her doctor... she's on Russo street, at the women's health clinic." I frowned, trying to find the name. *I know I had the name. Damnit!* I nearly cracked my phone, gripping it so hard. "She's uh, nine... no, it would be ten now? Ten weeks?" I pinched the bridge of my nose.

"Which one of you is the father?" she asked, a hint of amusement playing on her lips. I opened my mouth at the same time as Austin, but the words didn't come out. "Relax guys, I'm no stranger to the ways of the world." She shook her head, and Addy groaned again, trying to get up.

"Ah, not so fast. When was the last time you ate, hun?" she asked, and Addy grimaced. "Mhmm, alright. Boys, let's get her over to that bed there, okay?" she ordered, pointing to the bed opposite Wyatt.

"I'm fine," Addy mumbled, and I growled at her softly as Austin scooped her up in his arms, carrying her toward the bed.

"I'm sure you are, hun, but we're just going to get some proof that you're as fine as you say so your boys here can relax a bit." The doctor smiled, grabbing a tray with tubes from a nearby cabinet and bringing them over to the bed. "Roll your sleeve up for me, okay? We're going to get a little blood so I can see what's making you so light-headed."

Austin was a statue next to the bed, his hand gripping Addy's as he watched the doctor from under his hood. I knew how he felt. Watching a stranger stick a needle into Addy's arm made my blood boil. I took a few deep breaths, distracting myself by checking out the discarded bag that Wyatt had come in with. Two stuffed animals, one of which was the creepiest little bunny I'd ever fucking seen. Of course, I bet he'd gotten these for Addy to cheer her up since he hadn't found Piper. My heart twinged, and I brought them over to the bed, setting them on Addy's lap. Her skin was still too pale, and the doctor finished up, labeling the two vials of blood and setting them on the tray, pressing a button next to the bed. Like magic, a nurse appeared in the room, and the doctor handed her the tray.

"Can you get these processed for me, please? Put a rush on them. You can have the results brought here," she instructed, and the nurse nodded, disappearing with the tray. "You lay here. I'm going to get an ultrasound machine so we can get a quick scan of those babies, and you're going to rest and have some juice while we wait for the blood test, alright?" She smiled at Addy, who opened her mouth to argue, but Austin squeezed her hand to stop her.

"Thank you, Doc," I replied for her, watching as the doctor headed back out of the room.

"This is so stupid. I'm fine," Addy muttered, and I glared at her.

"How about you let the professional with the fancy coat tell us that?" I snapped, and I could see her temper flare, more than ready to bite my head off. Luckily for both of us, the doctor reappeared, holding a juice box and rolling an ultrasound machine beside her.

"Here we go. Let's get you hydrated, and we'll see what we're working with in there," she mused, pulling on a new pair of gloves. I took the juice box and opened it for Addy, ignoring her dirty look as I jabbed the straw in and passed it over. The doctor helped her lift her shirt up, exposing her lower abdomen, and squeezed some clear goo on her skin. The three of us held a collective breath as she pressed the wand into Addy's stomach and turned on the monitor, which started making creepy whooshing sounds and formed a grainy black-and-white picture.

"I like those heartbeats, nice and strong," the doctor murmured, and Addy visibly relaxed. "There's one there. They sort of look like peanuts at this stage." She pointed out a little blob on the screen, and then moved the wand around, shifting lower. "Here's the other one, hiding a little closer to your spine." She clicked a few times, taking measurements as we all stared at the screen, watching the little blob float in and out of view.

"Okay, so I'd say you're measuring around eleven weeks, so they are right on track. I'll wait for your bloodwork, but I'd hazard a guess that you're a little anemic. I'll get you a script for some iron supplements, but in the meantime, I'd suggest you take it easy, get lots of rest, and avoid stress." She glanced over at the bed where Wyatt's machines were beeping quietly, frowning a little. "I don't know what all your OB-GYN has explained, but twin pregnancies are a slightly higher risk for preterm labor. If you aren't able to manage your stress levels, you may be forced into bed rest so you don't go into labor." Addy grimaced, and the doctor handed her a paper towel to wipe off her stomach.

"I know, easier said than done, right?" She sighed, putting the wand back onto the trolley. "You seem to have a pretty good support system around you, so my advice is to take it easy and let them do some of the work for a change." She winked and rolled the trolley back out of the room, and Addy groaned and readjusted her shirt.

"Come on, I'm taking you home," I announced, reaching out for her hand. She swatted at me, her eyes blazing.

"Fuck you, I am not leaving," she snapped. "Not until Wyatt wakes up." Austin glanced at me, then over to Wyatt's bed. We had no idea when he'd wake up. It could be at least a day before that happens. She needed to rest, not to sleep in a chair in a cold hospital room.

"Okay, how about this? You either let me take you and Austin home, or I throw you over my shoulder, carry you home, and then chain you to the bed for the next seven months," I growled. "I will come back and stay with Wyatt, and send you regular updates, I promise. But you should be home in case Piper comes back." Her face fell, and I knew that had been a low blow, but I was desperate at this point.

Gathering up the stuffed animals, Addy gave Wyatt a gentle kiss, promising to come back soon, and we headed back out to the car. The drive home was once again silent, Addy petting the little blue bunny absently as she stared out the window. Austin took her inside once we reached the studio, promising to get her something to eat and get her into bed. I didn't even get out of the car. I just waited until they went inside and then headed straight back to the hospital.

There had been no visible change to Wyatt's condition in the past thirty minutes, which I took as a good sign. I grabbed a chair and pulled it up to the side of the bed, collapsing into it. Everything was so fucked up now, I didn't even know where to start. I needed to tell them about Jake, about all the shit I've been hiding from them to keep them safe from an enemy they thought was gone. Addy was going to kill me.

And I would happily let her.

CHAPTER TWENTY

Piper

I'd always imagined it would be Cain who finally killed me. Maybe through an accident of some sort, or maybe he finally got fed up with my annoying habits. Of all the things I'd heard in the whispers, and all the events I'd fore-seen, I'd never actually bore witness to my death. It was the one great mystery left for me, and for a while I used to think it was a good sign that I hadn't, since that likely would have meant that death was imminent. But when the past and the future began to fade into darkness, leaving only the overwhelming present, I realized that maybe my death would be foreshadowed in a different way.

Because why would the whispers stop, unless they recognized the futility of telling me things that I would never live to experience?

How was I meant to accept that I would die so soon after I'd finally become... happy? My Little Spider, the shining beacon in my soul, I needed her like I needed the blood in my veins. She kept me tethered, and she made me feel valued. And now

I've deserted her and the two babies growing inside her. Not by choice, no, but I should have seen this coming.

I'd only meant to clear my head. Walk for a couple of hours, feel the wind against my face as I contemplated this foreboding silence I'd never experienced before. Addy had been so upset. I had felt her panic as she gripped my arm and, instead of staying with her like I should have, I'd selfishly walked away, hoping my talisman would ease her anxiety while I was away. The longer I walked, the more I realized that I'd need something more than a charm to beg her forgiveness. That was how I'd ended up at the little pawn shop a few blocks away.

My perfect Little Spider deserved something special, she deserved something normal. I'd gone in, no particular plan in mind, and I'd walked out an hour later with an antique ring tucked into my pocket. It was nearly dark out at that point, and I'd stopped on the curb, listening to the wind and opening my ears for whispers, an old habit I'd yet to drop. Nothing, not so much as a murmur. The silence was deafening, making my ears ring as I inhaled slowly, watching the cars pass in front of me.

The nagging feeling of eyes on the back of my head had me turning around. I half-expected to find Cain looming over me, ready with a tirade and threats of disembowelment. Instead, I found a small woman staring at me, her eyes glazed over like a sleep-walker. "Hello?" I frowned, snapping my fingers in front of her face. She didn't react at all, not even a blink. My skin prickled, and I reached for my charm that was no longer around my neck.

Fuck, well, that was bad timing. I stepped to the side, trying to move around her. The woman reached out and grabbed my wrist, and I snatched it away, the feel of her skin against mine making my teeth itch. I heard a small snap as one of my trinkets ripped off my wrist, landing on the ground between us.

Bad omen, very bad omen.

Tires screeched nearby, bouncing off the curb, and I turned to find a large van pulled up behind us. Hands caught me between my shoulder blades, shoving me toward the door, which opened and swallowed me up. I landed on my stomach and something slammed into my back, pinning me to the floor.

"Knock him out!" someone hissed, the voice rough and wrong-sounding, like a fork caught in a garbage disposal. Something pinched the back of my neck and the world around me faded into blackness.

I didn't know how much time had passed. Consciousness flitted in and out with the breeze, my head lolling on my shoulders, too out of it to wake up fully. Voices filtered in and out like a weak radio frequency, passing me snippets of information that meant nothing to me.

Did you kill him?

I pushed him into traffic.

That's not what I fucking asked.

The sound of flesh hitting flesh made my eyelids flutter, and quiet sobs filled the air. The voices faded out as the darkness enveloped me once more. I was starting to get used to the comforting emptiness. It wasn't confusing or bright. My skin didn't ache from missing Addy's touch. I just... existed, floating in nothingness. It was peaceful, if only I wasn't so lonely here.

How much did you give him? He should've woken up by now.

The full dose. He's big. I was worried it wouldn't work!

Well, wake him the fuck up. I'm bored.

The emptiness was abruptly flooded with water, and I gasped, choking as some of it went into my lungs. I opened my eyes, coughing violently as I blinked at the light invading my vision. I didn't recognize where I was, not even from my dreams. It was rare that I didn't see a place and just knew it, having experienced it someway or through someone else. I tried to wipe the water off my face, but my hands stayed where they were, and I looked down only to find them duct taped to the arms of the chair I was sitting in. My shirt was torn at the front, and my lip stung like it had been recently split open.

I glanced up at the blank-faced man – like the woman who pushed me – holding the empty bucket in front of me. His eyes were glazed over, and I shivered at the emptiness in his gaze. "So you're the pretty boy fortune-teller, eh?" someone rasped in the darkness. It was the same voice from the car, the one that sounded like rusted gears grinding together. "Didn't see this coming, I guess."

"Hello, Jake," I sighed, and he chuckled horribly, limping into view. My sweet Spider had done a number on him, and the fire had helped as well. He was now as twisted and mangled on the outside as he was on the inside. Most of his body was covered in burns, some still bandaged and trying to heal. Leaning on a cane for support, he dragged his right leg behind him as he approached, wheezing with the effort.

"Little brother tell you all about me?" He smirked, the burnt skin on his face stretching with the movement. He was grotesque to behold, but I wasn't afraid of him anymore. His face had haunted my dreams for years now.

"No," I replied, slouching down in the chair. His puppet, the man who'd woken me, was still frozen nearby, his eyes unfocused as he waited for his next command.

"Does it hurt yet? Being away from that vicious cunt of yours?" he snarled, clearly having first-hand experience with that withdrawal. It did, in fact. Every bone in my body was alert to the fact that Addy wasn't nearby, and each one was desperate to climb out of my skin and get back to her by any means necessary. Rather than answering him, I just shrugged, staring out at the small sliver of sky visible through the only window in whatever hell this was.

Something mumbled in my ear, and I turned, trying to catch the words before they disappeared. It was nearly a whisper, almost something worth listening to. It made me wistful.

"Hit him." A fist collided with my cheek, snapping my head back against the chair. I groaned and spat out a mouthful of blood, having bitten my tongue.

"Two down, and two to go," he mused, cocking his head at me. "I'd been hoping that by ruining your sad little excuse for a business, the loser in the sunglasses might off himself and make my life a little easier, but no. Oh well, he was easy enough to take care of. My little brother is next. I'm not killing him, not yet at least. I want him to suffer while all his friends die, one by one, and he's not there to save them." He sighed wistfully. "Hit him again. Hit him until your hands are broken," he ordered his puppet, taking a step back.

The blows were mechanical, completely devoid of emotion. One after the other, they rained down on me, my face, my chest, my ribs, back to my face. I felt my skin break open, bones cracking as the assault went on. I didn't know how long it lasted. There wasn't a clock down here to tell the time. A particularly nasty shot to my temple knocked me back into my quiet empty place, and I relished the peace while I could, knowing the pain would be returning soon. I wanted it to be over. *Let me dissolve into nothing, become a whisper of my own, leave me free from the agony of too much knowledge and too little understanding.*

"Wake the fuck up!" Jake snapped, and I wheezed as I fell back into my body. My vision was tinged red around the edges, bits of the world in front of me fuzzy and distorted. I tried blinking, but it didn't help remove whatever was in my eyes. He must've knocked something loose in there.

"I want you to feel every second of this, just like I had to feel my skin cooking off my bones," he snarled. "Now, you're going to help me send a little message to your fuck-buddies back home, so stay awake." I stared at the blurry shape of him as he hobbled toward me, trying to think.

"I don't have my phone on me," I coughed, blood dripping down my chin. Truthfully, I thought I lost it. I never used it anyway. Probably would have been smart to have it this time, especially because of the whole kidnapping thing. I would earn a big 'I told you so' from Cain for that one, I was sure.

"You're quick for a nut job," Jake muttered, and I felt him tugging at my hand, wrenching my fingers so they were splayed out against the arm of the chair. "I want to send something nice to Addison. Something that she'll know is from me." I blinked as the holes in my vision grew larger, hiding more and more of my surroundings from view. I guess it was nice. It meant that I couldn't see Jake anymore, at least.

"Most people would choose flowers," I offered, and he laughed humorlessly.

"No, I want a more personal touch for this," he replied coldly.

I was glad my vision was fading. It meant I didn't have to watch as Jake's knife bit into my skin, slicing down in a violent thrust until the metal reached the wood underneath. I was glad I couldn't see the crimson rivers of blood pouring down onto the floor, or the way Jake grinned as he picked up my freshly severed finger. Unfortunately, my other senses were still well intact.

The pain of every nerve ending suddenly exposed to the air.

The smell of blood invading my nose.

The sound of the splatters as the droplets formed a puddle underneath the chair.

The taste of copper as I bit my tongue to keep from screaming.

I ran for the comfort of the dark, empty place, but my screams followed me this time, echoing through the void and making my head pound. I hated that Jake was the last face I'd see, his mottled skin haunting me in the safety of the darkness. So I thought about Addy instead, trying to picture her face as best I could. Hopefully, I could die imagining her gray eyes instead.

I'm sorry, Little Spider.

CHAPTER TWENTY-ONE

Austin

Addy woke up screaming again. Her voice wrenched me out of the restless doze I'd slipped into. Hissing sounded from outside the bedroom door, joining her in her distress.

"Addy, it's okay, wake up!" I rasped, dodging her fist as she swung out blindly, her voice cracking as the screams morphed into sobs. I scrambled up onto my knees, stroking her hair gently and trying to calm her down. The doctor said she needed to relax, and this was definitely *not* relaxed.

"Please, Addy, it's me!" I insisted, flinching back as she struck out again, snarling and baring her teeth. I slipped off the bed and scrambled to the door, flicking on the bedroom light. A noise by my foot caught my attention, and Little Red slipped under the door, hissing softly. I opened it carefully, and a couple of my friends slithered into the room, ignoring me completely as they headed toward the bed. Oh boy, Cain wasn't going to like this...

Addy's chest was heaving as her eyes finally blinked open, and I hurried back to her, crawling over the bed. "He was hurting so bad!" Addy murmured, the tears continuing to spill down her cheeks. "We have to find him, Austin. He needs us!" I nodded and tugged her back until she was laying down, then I covered her up as the twins curled up next to her.

"We're looking," I murmured, kissing away the tears and stroking her hair. When we'd gotten home from the hospital, Addy had asked me to send out my friends to look for Piper, like I had with her. They had been the ones to find her, after all. Piper was a den mate, so they all knew him and his scent well. Most disappeared out through the window immediately, but to my surprise, my vipers had stayed behind. I thought it may have been some youthful stubbornness or a display of dominance, but it appeared that they just refused to leave Addy's side. I couldn't fault them for that. Nothing short of death could make me leave her side, either.

"He's dying, Austin. I can feel it. He's dying, and he's all alone!" Addy cried, and I tried to soothe her as best I could, nuzzling her face and stroking her hair. This was reminding me too much of when Piper would have his... episodes, and he'd be rambling and feel scared for hours. I finally managed to calm her down, and she fell back to sleep, the twins coiled up on her stomach and her chest. I curled up beside her, refusing to sleep in case she woke up and needed me again, so I just watched her quietly in the darkness.

Later in the morning, I heard a door open downstairs. Snarling, I slipped out of the bed and crept out of the room, heading towards the stairs. Granddaddy cobra, the oldest snake in my nest, was coiled at the top of the stairs, tracking the movement down below. I hissed a few words of thanks and left him to guard the bedrooms as I slipped downstairs to the kitchen. I relaxed immediately when I saw Cain's mess of curls pass by, heading for the kitchen. Bounding down the last few steps, I watched him quietly as he paced the kitchen floor, swearing and muttering to himself.

"Is Wyatt okay?" I rasped, catching his attention. His eyes were bloodshot, red streaking through them like hot coals burning in the wind. He nodded, his face cracking as he fought to keep his emotions in check. I didn't know why he bothered. I could feel them rippling through the air between us.

"He woke up for a minute and said he was sorry. Told me he was pushed," Cain informed me, burning hot with rage. "They had to take him for more scans, to see if... to see if he'll be able to walk after this." He raked his hand through his hair, fury rolling off his shoulders in waves. I watched anxiously, staying out of his way as his shirt began to smoke, the hem of his collar singeing as tiny licks of flame rippled across it. "Fuck!" he exclaimed, and I hissed an admonishment.

"Addy is sleeping!" I snapped. "She had another nightmare about Piper." Cain's face fell, the anguish apparent on his features. He looked so tired all of a sudden.

"I failed," he mumbled, dropping down into the kitchen chair. "I failed all of you." Footsteps creaked on the stairs, and Addy appeared, her hair a mess from sleep. I waited for Cain to set his shoulders, to bristle and huff and prepare to argue with her as they always did, but his flame had dimmed, like he'd been snuffed out. He had no fight left in him.

"You need to let us in, Cain." Addy frowned, walking toward him. "You can't keep everything bottled up inside you. I know you claim it's to protect us, but we're stronger than you think." She sat down on his lap, and he flinched away from her, his shirt still smoking from the flames licking off his skin. "A little fire never hurt me." She smirked, pressing her forehead against his.

"You should be in bed," he mumbled, and she flicked his nose lightly. "I was, but some idiot was bellowing at the top of his lungs down here." He rubbed his hand over his face. "Come on, I'll make some breakfast. You can have a shower, maybe a nap, and then we can go see Wyatt." Addy hopped off of his lap and gave me a gentle kiss as she passed, heading to the fridge.

"I can't sleep. Too much to do." Cain sighed, "But a shower sounds nice." He stood up, stretching out his arms, his shoulder popping uncomfortably. Addy pulled a carton of eggs out of the fridge, busying herself with making food. All of us fell silent when we heard a knock on the door downstairs.

"Wait!" I hissed, as Cain moved to go downstairs. I waited a moment, and a small garter snake slithered up the baseboard along the stairs. I listened as it reported in, and I hissed back, frowning. "He says... it smells like Piper by the door." Addy let out a quiet whimper, forgetting about the food on the stove. Cain was down the stairs in a shot, with Addy and me close behind.

I didn't like the look on Cain's face when he walked back inside, holding a small box wrapped in brown paper. I pulled Addy back as he walked toward us, and she protested in my arms. Something wasn't right here... I didn't like the smell, it was Piper... but it was wrong.

"Addy, go upstairs, okay?" Cain muttered, gripping the box. His face twisted.

"Fat fucking chance of that," she snapped back, but I hauled her back away from Cain, putting my body between us.

He turned it over, letting me see the creepy-looking happy face drawn on the top. Without a second thought, he tore off the paper, revealing the plain-looking box underneath. I held Addy tightly, every muscle in my body screaming 'Wrong! It's wrong!' as loudly as it could. "Don't open it," I begged Cain, but he ignored me, lifting the lid as carefully as possible to peek inside.

The color leached out of his face, his lips pressing into a thin line. "What is it?!" Addy demanded, fighting me so hard I was scared I would hurt her if I didn't let go. She jerked out of my arms and stumbled toward Cain, who pulled the box away from her, shaking his head.

"No, Addy please, don't look at this alright? You don't need to see this," Cain begged, backing away from her. A flurry of scales unfurled from Addy's neck, where they had been hiding in her long hair, and launched itself at Cain. Cain swore and dropped the box as his hands flew up to block the viper from hitting him in the face.

I watched the box fall, landing sideways on the ground. The lip popped off on impact, and a small object clattered out of the box, rolling across the floor by our feet. A glint of silver and the coppery tang of blood filled the air, and I snarled as Cain snatched Addy away from it. Her mouth dropped open in a silent wail as my viper slithered around it, cordoning it off with his body.

Den mate blood - he told me, and I stepped closer, reaching down to pick it up. A finger, hacked off at the knuckle, with a silver ring still attached. There was a dainty spider etched into the ring, with a blood red gem in the center of its body.

It smelled like Piper, and I dropped it back in the box, hissing viciously.

"What the fuck?! What the fuck!" Addy yelled, pulling away from Cain. "Who did this?! What the fuck is going on?!" I moved to comfort her, and she raised her finger to my chest, keeping me back. "I want answers and I want them now. Why the fuck was Piper's finger in a fucking box on our porch?!" She was breathing hard, her eyes lit with fury. Cain shook his head, rubbing the back of his neck tiredly.

"I don't have answers for you Addy, I'm sorry. I just... I think... I think this might be Jake." He sighed. My muscles tensed as all the air seemed to get sucked out of the room.

"Jake is dead," I rasped. "You said Wyatt killed him." Addy was glaring so hard at Cain I thought he might drop dead right on the spot.

"He did- I mean, he should have. The wounds he got, the fire, nobody could survive that!" Cain insisted. "But... when I went back to find the body... he was gone."

"Are you fucking kidding me?" Addy hissed. "This whole time, you were lying to me? To us? We thought we were safe! We thought... oh my god..." She stumbled back, dropping to sit on the stairs. "I let my guard down."

"But I didn't, Addy, not for one second!" Cain replied hoarsely. "I've been watching, waiting, for anything that could mean he'd found us. I never saw this coming, and I'm so sorry." He backed up against the wall and slid down to the floor, covering his face with his hands.

This wasn't right. Cain didn't panic. No matter what happened, he was always calm. He always had a plan.

"We have to do something," Addy whispered. "We have to find Piper. He's hurt... he needs our help." She closed her eyes, brushing away the tears that were forming.

Carefully, I picked up the box with the finger inside, replacing the lid so I wouldn't have to look at it. I turned it over in my hands, examining it slowly. There were no other markings on it, nothing that stood out. I hissed in frustration.

The three of us jumped when a loud banging erupted at the front entrance. "Police, open up!"

"Oh my fucking god," Addy groaned as Cain leapt to his feet.

"Austin, hide the finger and the snakes. Now!" he snarled, and Addy stood up, storming to the front door.

I shoved the box with the finger in the closest cabinet, leaving the door open so my viper could climb inside. I watched anxiously from around the corner as Addy jerked the door open and three officers stepped inside, forcing her to step back.

"Are you Mrs. Collins?" one of them demanded, and she frowned, nodding slowly. "Where is your husband?"

"What?" Addy blinked, looking as confused as I felt. The officer looked irritated, and Cain quickly stepped forward, his hands hanging loose at his sides. All three of them shot forward, and Addy yelped as they shoved her aside, surrounding Cain.

"What is going on?" Addy exclaimed, and Cain didn't react as they shoved him against the wall, one of them reading him his rights while another handcuffed him.

"Mrs. Collins, your husband is under arrest for fraud and embezzling funds. We are taking him in for processing, and I suggest you have his lawyer meet him at the station."

"His lawyer? Embezzling?! Cain, what the fuck?" Addy cried. Cain was staring at the ground, and I gripped the cabinet as I fought the urge to fight them off.

"Addy, listen to me. This is Jake, it's all Jake. Stay together, and don't trust anyone." Cain insisted, his eyes swirling red. "I'll fix this, okay? Please believe me. I'll fix this, I promise!" The officer who cuffed him jerked him back by his shirt collar and walked him out the door, his colleagues following behind. Addy was frozen in the doorway, and I joined her, watching as they shoved Cain into the back of the squad car and drove off.

What were we supposed to do now?

CHAPTER TWENTY-TWO

Addison

I couldn't believe this was happening. This was like a bad dream that I couldn't wake up from, no matter how hard I pinched myself. I knew that if I panicked, I would potentially hurt the tiny beings growing in my abdomen. So I took all of that panic, and I shoved it deep, deep down, locking it into a tiny box and stuffing it away for later. Was it healthy? No. But I had bigger things to concern myself with. So I decided to focus on my fucking burning rage instead.

Once again, not the healthiest way to cope.

I stormed upstairs and took a shower, leaving Austin with the finger, which I couldn't bear to look at. I seethed as I washed my hair out. Cain was goddamn lucky he was in police custody, because if he wasn't, I'd kill him with my bare hands. Wrapping a towel around my hair, I walked naked into the bedroom and into the closet that now comprised of my clothes, Wyatt's clothes, and a collection of random hoodies and tee-shirts that had made their way in here over the last couple of months. I grabbed a pair of my softest leggings and pulled those on, and one of Piper's collared polo shirts. My stomach was finally starting to look like it was housing something other than my own organs, taking on a distinctly rounded shape at the front.

It made me... uncomfortable.

I grabbed one of Wyatt's giant black hoodies and pulled it over my head, burrowing in the soft fabric and letting it obscure my shape. At some point, I would have to reconcile myself with the changes to my body, but today was not the day.

Today was for rage.

A black coil of scales shifted on the bed beside me, and I watched as... *Selene?* I thought it was her. Her tail was thinner, and she was a little shorter than Helios. She raised her head to watch me, and I smiled and scooped her up, letting her curl up in my hoodie's pouch. Stalking back out to the kitchen, my damp hair loose and wild around my face, I spotted the box on the kitchen table. My lip curled, and I stomped over to it, knocking the lid off with a flick of my wrist, staring down at the body part inside. I was so angry, I could practically feel the flames coursing through my veins. I half-expected my shirt to start smoldering, like I'd seen Cain's do when he got well and truly furious.

"Addy?" Austin appeared at the top of the stairs, looking... apprehensive. Of me? He wasn't afraid of me. I looked down and saw his King Cobra curled up by the top step, face trained at the main floor. Good, we needed all the security we could get right now.

"I'm okay Austin," I replied softly. "We are going to the police station to find out about Cain, and then we are going to get Wyatt. He needs to come home. We need to be together right now," I explained. As if we were magnetized, Austin gravitated to my side, his arms enveloping me as his lips dropped to my neck. I let out a soft sigh as his teeth grazed my skin, tempting me with a release that I sorely needed. An ache between my legs reminded me that the new hormones rushing through my system weren't all bad, some in fact were deliciously nice.

"No, not right now," I murmured, stroking the soft hairs at the back of his neck. "Not until it's safe, okay, love?" Austin stiffened in my arms, and I worried that somehow I'd offended him. He pulled back with a frown on his face, blinking at me with those eerie yellow eyes.

"Love?" he rasped, cocking his head to the side. I sputtered a laugh and stroked his cheek.

"Of course. Wasn't that obvious?" I asked. I realized, as a group, we were not the most... emotionally expressive. Should we have discussed the whole 'love' concept? Probably would've been smart, considering their kids were growing in me. But I thought that we were beyond that. How could four letters encompass this... connection we shared?

I glanced down at the ring, ignoring the appendage it was still resting on. Piper had been wearing it for months now... on his ring finger. He'd been telling me he was committed to us this whole time. And Austin, he'd marked us all as his, calling me his mate. Cain, well... that fucker had some more secrets to share with us if people were calling me his wife. I'd deal with that later.

"Oh, Wyatt." I murmured, and my traitorous eyes filled with tears once more. God help me, no one had ever warned me of the tears that pregnancy would cause. My sweet, stoic Wyatt.

Never expecting anything from me, never asking for more. I'd always assumed they all knew, and I'd never spoken the words to him that he deserved to hear.

Fuck, stick with rage, Addy. No tears right now, we can fall apart after.

I grabbed Austin's face with both hands, holding him close to me. "I love you Austin," I murmured, pressing a kiss to his lips. His pupils dilated as a sheepish grin formed on his face. For a moment, he was the shy ghost from the basement all over again, working up the nerve to talk to me.

"My mate," he rasped, nuzzling his cheek against mine and he pulled me close. "I love you too." It was almost too much, hearing him say the actual words, and my tear ducts were aching to unleash a flood of emotions. It took everything in me to reign them in, focusing on his warmth surrounding me for just a little longer, wishing I had more time to savor this moment.

Eventually I was forced to let him go and get us moving. I decided on a quick breakfast, because I knew I needed to keep my strength up, and I found containers of cut up fruit in the fridge, next to little packages of Greek yogurt that boasted a high protein content. Damn Cain, I needed to stay mad at him. I ate in silence, thinking about how furious I was that Jake was somehow still alive, while Austin watched me anxiously. Fueled and pissed off, I grabbed the keys off the end table and shoved them in my bag, gesturing for Austin to follow as I headed out to the car.

It had been a while since I'd driven. Yes, I had a license, and it wasn't expired or anything. But when I had an alphahole lover/boyfriend/husband/roommate/whatever the fuck Cain was, there wasn't much call for me to drive. Although, knowing about Jake, it made sense now why Cain had been so goddamn overbearing lately. I snarled and slapped my hand on the steering wheel, making Austin jump. I wasn't going to take it too personally that he looked so nervous with me behind the wheel. His hand gripped the door handle as I cut off a taxi going too slowly, weaving back into the lane and throwing on my signal light.

"Do you want to stay in the car with Selene while I go inside?" I asked gently, turning into the station parking lot. Austin threw up his hood as soon as the cop cars came into view, and I could feel his anxiety radiating off of him.

"Who's Selene?" he whispered, and in response, my little friend stuck her head out of my hoodie pouch, her tongue poking out to taste the air. Austin looked bewildered, and I took great pride in having smuggled a snake out right under his nose. Holding out his hands, Selene reluctantly abandoned her little cocoon and slithered up his arm, letting him tuck her into his hoodie instead. When he looked back at me, the hunger in his eyes turned my core molten, and I suddenly felt very warm. "My mate," he murmured. I leaned over and brushed my lips against his, only a hint of what I really wanted to do to him.

"I'll be right back," I smiled, drawing back to climb out of the car. I hated leaving him in the vehicle by himself, but come on, could Jake really get us at the police station? Grimacing, I hurried inside, not willing to take any chances. If he wanted to, I'm sure he could walk right in here and shoot me in the head without anyone giving a second glance. I gave Cain's name at the front desk, and a very terse older woman brought me a form to fill out, and then another officer, this one not wearing the formal uniform, came out to talk to me.

"Mrs. Collins?" the officer asked, looking me over briefly. I was sure I wasn't looking my best today, but he could get fucked. I wasn't in the mood.

"That's me." I crossed my arms over my chest, leveling him with my gaze. "Where's Cain?"

"It's a packed day today. Your husband is still being processed. We'll be holding him here until his arraignment. Have you gotten in touch with his lawyer?" I blinked, trying to follow along even though I was well and truly out of my depth.

"He's got the lawyer's information. I'd need his phone, or he could call him. Can he call him?" I asked. Was the 'one phone call' just a TV thing, or was that real?

"Well, I can't release your husband's phone. It's in evidence now. But yes, he will be able to phone his lawyer himself if that's the case," the officer replied, watching me annoyingly close.

"When can I see him? Can he come home? Is there, er, bail, or whatever?" I frowned. He shifted, a sad smile forming on his face. Oh great, I'd gone from a potential accomplice to an unwitting housewife apparently, now I got the pity.

"That depends on the judge's decision, which you won't have until the arraignment. In the meantime, I suggest you talk to his lawyer, and maybe you can schedule a phone call with him later this week," he explained. I stared at him, trying not to cry. These fucking tears. I swear I'd have my own river by the time these babies popped out.

"Alright...thank you, I guess," I replied, losing some of my bluster. Despite being absolutely furious with Cain, I also really wanted to see him and make sure he was okay. I also wanted to get some fucking answers, such as *why was I being called his wife?!*

I walked back out to the car where Austin was still slumped low in his seat. He perked up when I climbed inside, but then his face fell as he took in my expression. "I couldn't see him," I explained, and he looked down at his shoes.

"When will he get out?" Austin asked softly. I started the car, pulling out and heading to the hospital.

"I'm not sure" I replied truthfully. At this moment, I thought the better question was if he'd get out.

Austin joined me when we reached the hospital, Selene safely hidden inside his bulky hoodie. After the epic disappointment at the police station, both my expectations and my spirits were decidedly low. The room was miraculously still private, Wyatt the sole occupant, with his bed tucked into the far corner. My heart was in my throat as I approached, my breath hitching when his eye cracked open and then promptly squeezed shut. "'Lo?" he mumbled, his voice rough.

"Hey, Shades," I whispered, and he scrunched up his face, immediately trying to shift up in the bed. "Oh, for fuck's sake! Stop wiggling, you're going to hurt yourself!" I bit out, practically running to his side. I put my hand on his shoulder and he grabbed it with his good hand, his jaw clenching.

"I'm sorry," he announced, coughing and wincing. Austin found a cup of water on the end table and caught Wyatt's good hand, peeling it out of mine so he could guide the cup into it.

"Sorry for what?" I asked, my voice sounding thick. "Getting hit by a car? Well, you should be. It was very inconsiderate." I choked out a laugh, and he managed to smile back, his eyes still screwed tightly shut. I rummaged through my bag, grabbing the extra set of sunglasses I'd thankfully remembered to pack. "Here, I brought you a present." Leaning in, I slid the glasses over his face, settling them on the bridge of his bruised nose. He sighed in relief, and I caught his lips in a quick kiss, unable to help myself.

"Thank you, it's been hell remembering to keep my eyes shut, 'specially with all the drugs they've got me on," he mumbled, and I took his empty glass, setting it back down on the end table. Austin shifted around to the other side of the bed, hovering anxiously, his hands fidgeting at his sides like he wanted to climb onto the bed with Wyatt. I knew the feeling, but I was too worried about hurting him right now. "Where's Cain?"

I grimaced, wondering if now was the right time to rip off that particular band-aid. God, what to hit him with first? "Did they say when you can get out of here?" I asked instead, and he cocked his eyebrow at me.

"They said this afternoon. No lasting damage to my spine, just swelling, so I'm good to rest up at home," Wyatt replied, looking between me and Austin. "Where's Cain?" I bit my lip, catching Austin's eye. He was shifting nervously on his feet.

"Fine, alright." I sighed. "Cain's been arrested, something about embezzlement." I threw up my hands. Wyatt's eyebrows shot into his hairline.

"What?!" he exclaimed and moved to sit up. I shoved him back down gently, keeping my hand on his shoulder.

"There's more," I warned.

Once I filled Wyatt in, it was very difficult to keep him from leaping out of bed. It took Austin physically pinning him until he agreed to calm down and just... be patient. Patience, unfortunately, was none of our strong suits. I finally went and hunted down a nurse to get his discharge paperwork sorted out. Even then, it still took us over two hours to get him somewhat dressed and in a wheelchair to get him to the car. His doctor was very sweet, and helped me get his medications sorted out, even slipping in the iron prenatal pills she'd wanted me to take.

It wasn't easy, but between the two of us, we managed to get Wyatt settled into the passenger seat, with Austin sitting in the back. I drove us home, and thus began the epic journey of getting Wyatt up the steps to the studio, and then up the flight of stairs to the main floor. We might as well be scaling Everest. Wyatt had one working leg, several broken ribs, and was pretty strung out on pain meds, so he wasn't much help. Austin, thankfully, had his freakish strength and was able to hoist him up and support his bad side while I propped up the good side and kept him from pulling them both over.

The sun had set by the time we got to the kitchen, all three of us sweaty and shaking from the effort. I didn't like how pale Wyatt looked, his face shining with sweat, so we gave up and settled him on the couch for now. He took a nap while I fixed us something to eat. It wasn't anything fancy, just some boxed mac and cheese, but I was too hungry to care.

Austin prowled around the studio, checking all the windows and the front door to make sure we were locked up tight. Granddaddy cobra curled up in the entryway, acting as the official security guard. Some of Austin's other little friends had returned throughout the evening, and they all stationed themselves at windows, ready to surprise anyone stupid enough to try to break in.

After I gave Wyatt his next dose of painkillers, he passed out on the couch, and there was no way we were moving him while he was unconscious. Instead, Austin and I curled up on the love seat, his muscled body spooning mine. He let his hand rest on my stomach, and I fell asleep listening to my two men breathing in the darkness.

Chapter Twenty-Three

Austin

Addy was talking in her sleep. At least, I think she was asleep. Her eyes were shut tight, but she was frowning, whispering under her breath.

She sounded like Piper.

"Addy?" I murmured, smoothing her hair out of her face. I shifted behind her, pulling her tighter against me, trying to calm her down.

"Dark. Too dark," she mumbled, and I frowned, looking around us. It was a little dark in here, but not that bad. The sun was just starting to creep over the horizon, letting a hazy red light in through the windows.

"Puppet's coming," Addy sighed, leaning back into me. I was gazing down at her face when her eyes shot open, clouded over and white.

"Austin, *don't let her in!*"

I jumped, nearly shoving Addy off the loveseat. It had been her mouth opening, but it was Piper's voice that had come out, shouting into the silence of our studio.

"'S wrong?" Addy mumbled, rubbing her face. "Wyatt okay?" She sat up, looking over at the prone figure next to us. He was still tucked in exactly where she had left him last night, the casts making it impossible for him to move around in his sleep.

"He's fine," I rasped, watching her nervously. She seemed like herself again, snuggling into me as she tried to get comfortable, her eyes closing once more. I couldn't risk falling asleep, not after whatever that was. Instead, I held her tightly against my chest, keeping my eyes trained on the stairs. I was ready this time. Jake had stolen her from me once, but I had been weak back then, unable to protect my mate. I was stronger now. I would tear his flesh apart with my teeth if he dared to come near her. My vipers refused to leave her side. They saw her as theirs, and it made me so fiercely proud. I buried my face in her hair, breathing in her scent. She smelled a little like all of us now, with that spicy undercurrent that was all Addy. I shifted, feeling my cock harden as her ass pressed against me. I wanted to have her right here. Claim her and listen to her moans. I missed her taste on my tongue. My fangs ached with the need to sink inside of her.

No, it wasn't the time for that. I had to stay vigilant. A low whine slipped out of my throat, and I heard an answering hiss, a small head poking out of her hair, close to my face. My male viper – Helios, she called him – stared at me, eyes glinting in the darkness. I hissed a gentle reassurance that I wasn't going to wake her. He seemed content with this and laid his head back down, disappearing back into her long black tresses.

Once we were safe, my beautiful mate would stay out of clothes for an entire week, and I would do nothing but worship her that entire time. She wouldn't lift a finger, just relax and grow big with our brood. I liked this plan, and I was sure the others would too, especially Piper. He was always saying we should be naked more often, anyway.

My heart ached for my missing den mate. My friends hadn't been able to track his scent. This city was too polluted, too heavy with other scents. They weren't giving up, though. They liked the strange man who slept in our den so often, and they knew how important he was to Addy.

The sun was fully up when Wyatt began to groan, trying to shift on the couch. I carefully climbed over Addy's sleeping form and left her on the loveseat, moving over to him quietly. "What do you need?" I asked, his eyes blinking open under his glasses.

"Bathroom," he muttered, "then pills, I think." I threw his arm over my shoulder and hefted him up, my muscles sore after our climb yesterday. With my support, he was able to hobble to the bathroom, and I stayed with him, making sure he didn't fall over. I could tell he was getting frustrated at his immobility, especially his arm, which was basically useless with the cast on. I didn't mind taking care of him, because he was my den mate, and it was my job to keep him safe, too.

His face was pinched in pain by the time we got him back to the couch, and I helped him prop his leg back up as he laid back. "My pills. Addy had them, I think," he mumbled, his face pale underneath all the bruising. I looked for the container and spotted them on the kitchen table. I filled up a glass of water for him, because Addy had given him one with the pills last night, bringing both back to him.

"Thanks, Austin," he murmured, popping a couple of the pills into his mouth and chasing them with water. I crouched by his head, waiting for him to finish the water before taking the glass away, setting it on the nearby table. He heaved a heavy sigh and dropped his head back onto the pillow, turning to face me. "This is a nightmare, man."

I nodded quietly, glancing at Addy to make sure she was still asleep. "Can I help? Can I... take some of the pain?" I offered, touching his hand. Wyatt shook his head, grimacing at the movement.

"No, don't. We need one of us functional for Addy. You're the only one who can protect her right now," he replied, and my chest tightened. "S'okay, man. I've got the meds. They help some," he mumbled. I thought about it, considering what Piper had done the last time to help him.

"Do you need something else? Do you need-" I lifted my wrist to my lips, angling one of my fangs so it pressed into the sensitive skin there. I applied just enough pressure to pierce the skin, and blood welled up immediately, dripping down onto my lip.

"Austin!" Wyatt hissed, grabbing my free hand with his good one. The pain disappeared immediately, and he groaned low in his throat, the sound sending a surge of desire down my spine. He scowled at me, reaching for the arm that was still raised to my mouth. Smirking, I bit down again, this time ripping my fang down, tearing a jagged line in my flesh. He snatched my hand, wrenching it from my mouth, and I watched as the line knitted itself back together, leaving only a smear of blood behind. "Stop that, damnit!" he growled. The hand on my wrist was firm, a strength he hadn't shown five minutes ago.

"I want to help," I rasped. He didn't let go of my arm, but I could tell his resolve was wavering. Glancing down, I could see by the way his sweats had tented that he was enjoying what I was doing. He shook his head again, slower this time. "It's not... it's not a good idea," he sighed. The pain meds were starting to make him slur his words.

"Austin, what's going on?" We both looked up to see Addy sitting up on the loveseat, her hair a wild mess. Wyatt's cheeks turned pink, and she studied us for a moment, her eyes lighting up with understanding. "I heard about what Piper did, and I was furious," she announced, her voice husky with sleep. She unfurled from where she was sitting, padding over to us in her bare feet. I shifted out of the way as she took my place, grabbing Wyatt's bad leg and shifting it off the couch, propping it up on the coffee table instead. I helped him sit up, his limbs growing heavy as the painkillers kicked in.

"There are a lot of ways to cause pain that don't involve blades," she told me sharply, and I looked down at the floor, chagrined. Wyatt looked embarrassed, but his expression shifted to one of bewilderment as Addy gathered up her hoodie and carefully pulled it up and over her head, setting it gently on the floor. She wasn't wearing a shirt underneath, or a bra for that matter, her breasts naked and horribly tempting. Helios coiled tighter around her neck, glaring at me like I was the one who'd disturbed his nap. "Come here," she ordered, staring at me, and sank to her knees between Wyatt's legs. I didn't need to be asked twice. I was behind her in a flash, dropping to the floor as she tugged Wyatt's sweats down his hips, his cock bobbing free, already hard and leaking pre-cum.

"Addy, you really don't have to-" Wyatt groaned, Addy cutting him off as she grasped his cock and dragged her tongue up the length of it. She looked back at me, her pupils blown with lust.

"Austin, you're going to hurt me," she murmured, watching me under her thick lashes. I opened my mouth to argue, because absolutely not. I would never hurt her. "A little pain can be good, remember? Like the piercings," she explained, stroking Wyatt with her hand. "Wyatt will help you. He'll tell you what to do." She looked up at him. "Right, baby?"

He nodded tightly, and she smiled, taking the head of his cock into her mouth and making him moan, his eyes closing as he tangled a hand in her hair. "Austin, play with her breasts," he instructed, his voice hoarse as her head bobbed, taking him deeper into her mouth. I didn't need to be told twice. I pressed into her back, my hands wrapping around her chest to grasp her breasts. They felt bigger somehow, heavier, and I explored them with my fingers, kneading and squeezing them until she moaned around Wyatt's cock. "Fu- okay, tease her nipples. Pinch them, t- tug on them." His hips bucked, his good hand tightening his grip on her hair as she took him all the way down.

Addy's nipples were hard points under my fingers, reacting instantly to my touch. I pinched them both, feeling her shiver as Wyatt moaned, his head tipping back into the couch. I gave an experimental tug on one, and when that elicited another full body shiver, I did it to both. My own cock was rock hard as I pressed against her ass, shifting to get some friction. Addy whimpered, her thighs clenching together as she gripped

Wyatt's thighs, and he thrust into her mouth, panting hard. I continued to pinch and abuse her tender nipples, ignoring the desperate need I had to rip off her leggings and sink into her right here. Wyatt shuddered, and I gave them one last sharp tug as Addy swallowed him down. He moaned loudly as he spilled into her, his body going slack as she milked every drop from him, her chest heaving as she leaned back, pressing her body against me.

"Fuck, I need you Austin," she moaned, rubbing herself against my hard length. Wyatt was slipping his pants back up his hips, looking half asleep and pain-free, watching Addy with a satisfied smile on his face.

"What are you waiting for, Austin? Take care of our girl." He smirked, his voice hazy, as he sank back into the couch. I didn't need to be told twice. I hooked my fingers into the waistband of her leggings and pulled them down roughly, leaning down to nip at her ear.

"Climb up on his lap," I hissed, and she surged to her feet, kicking off her leggings and carefully maneuvering herself onto Wyatt's lap. He grinned as she put her elbows on either side of his face, leaning over him with her knees on the couch.

"I like this view a lot," Wyatt chuckled, cupping one of her breasts with his good hand. I shed my sweatpants and stepped up behind her, reaching my arm around her hips to cup her sex. Addy leaned down to kiss Wyatt, moaning as I began to stroke her, my erection pressing into her hip.

"That's it, sweetheart, soak my lap," Wyatt murmured as Addy's legs began to tremble against mine. I toyed with her clit until she started panting, and then I gave it a pinch just as I slid my cock inside her. Her pussy clenched around me as I bottomed out inside of her, and she cried out as she came, Wyatt swallowing her sounds in a brutal kiss. I didn't give her any kind of reprieve. Once I was inside her, I was a man possessed. I pounded into her, holding her hips in place while Wyatt continued to tease her swollen nipples, her hair draped over his chest as she held herself above him.

"Yes, oh god, fuck!" Addy screamed, and I felt her go slack under my hands as she came again, half-collapsing into Wyatt's arms. Her pussy was still spasming when my balls tightened and I spilled into her, slowing my thrusts and softening my grip as my release ebbed.

"God, you're so fucking sexy," Wyatt groaned, stroking her hair out of her face. His eyes widened when he noticed the snake coiled up around her neck, and I smirked, kissing a line of kisses down her spine. "Am I high, or did your hair turn into snakes?" he asked hazily, making Addy laugh.

I helped her climb off Wyatt's lap and scooped her up in my arms, ignoring her protests as I carried her upstairs to the master bathroom. Cain had a shower too, but this one was big enough for both of us since I had no plans to leave her alone anytime soon. Addy grumbled something about being a grown woman with functional limbs as I set her down on the tile and turned on the shower, adjusting the temperature to a heat she liked. My viper friend took a bit of convincing before I was able to remove him from Addy's neck. He even hissed a warning at me, flashing his fangs. It actually took Addy stroking his long body and murmuring encouragements before he loosened his hold and let me pull him away, setting him down on the clean towels I'd taken out.

Addy rolled her eyes at me as I ushered her under the spray, but she quickly calmed down as I began soaping up her body, gently washing her tender breasts and between her legs. Her hair was getting long and wild, and it took a lot of her fancy hair soap to untangle the mess, but the noises she made when I dragged my nails along her scalp made it worth it. We stayed in the shower until the water started to cool off, and I spent a lot of time washing along her abdomen, admiring the small bump that was forming there. It was so round and perfect already, I couldn't help but marvel at it.

Once Addy convinced me to shut the water off, I helped her out of the shower and got her towel, dislodging a now irate snake so I could wrap it around her. Addy laughed as I hissed out a reprimand to my friend, who rose up and flashed his fangs at me with a boldness I had no choice but to admire.

"Let him be," Addy scolded me, holding out her hands towards him. Helios was as smug as a snake could be as he coiled up her arm, making his way back to her neck. "Are you jealous?" She asked, smirking at me, and I glowered, following her out into the bedroom.

"No," I muttered, watching her wander into the closet, scowling as she started pulling out clothes. Why did she need clothing? I hated the fabric layers that hid her away from me. Addy caught me staring and laughed, pulling out a shirt that looked like it belonged to Piper and another oversized hoodie that had tiny burn holes peppered across it.

"I'm not walking around here naked while we are, so... out of sorts," she told me gently, and I sighed as she got dressed, carefully tucking Helios into the hoodie's front pouch. "Maybe after, when we can relax a bit," she murmured, coming over to pat my cheek. I nodded quickly, capturing her mouth in a kiss, my hands roaming underneath the hoodie. She smelled like Cain and Piper, and it made me wistful.

Since she was getting dressed, I figured I should put on some clothes too. I found my sweats where I had left them in the living room, and I dumped Selene out of Addy's discarded hoodie, pulling it over my own head. *I think it was Cain's too, or maybe Wyatt's?* But now it smelled like Addy, and I burrowed into it, feeling a touch better. Selene slithered off and found Addy, disappearing under her long hair to curl up in her hood.

I followed Addy around all morning as she made breakfast for her and Wyatt, then made a new breakfast when the eggs she had cooked made her queasy. Wyatt had dozed off on the couch where we'd left him but woke up when he smelled food, and we all sat together and ate on the couch - well, they ate, I watched - so he didn't have to get up.

Wyatt peppered Addy with questions about Cain and Jake, trying to piece together what he'd missed. She explained as best she could, but I could tell she was angry and as in the dark about it all as we were. I just couldn't understand why Cain would lie. If we had just known, we could have done something, we could've helped him.

In the early afternoon, Little Red slithered up the banister, hissing up a storm. We'd been going over a map of the city, and I'd pointed out some of the places my friends had already checked so we could cross those off our list. I frowned and looked at Addy, who paused, her hands clenched into fists. "There's a girl at the front door," I explained, and she frowned in turn.

"Let's go check it out," she replied, heading down the stairs. Wyatt shifted up in his seat, watching us leave with a grimace.

"Don't open the door," I warned, catching up to her and grabbing her arm. Addy glared at me and peeked out to see who it was, her face relaxing with a sigh.

"It's just Hannah. She's probably worried because I've called in sick so much this week." She explained, moving to unlock the door. I hesitated, glancing down at Granddaddy cobra, who was eyeing us from his spot in the corner. I hissed a gentle warning, and he slithered underneath the shoe rack, out of sight.

"Hannah!" Addy exclaimed, plastering a weird smile on her face as she cracked open the door. "What are you doing here?" She opened the door a little wider, and the tiny blond girl slipped inside, glancing at me nervously as I stared at her.

"I was worried about you! You've seemed so... off lately? And then you weren't coming to the lab. I didn't know what to do." Hannah walked toward me, stopping a few feet away, her eyes darting around the studio. Addy stepped in beside me and I put my arm around her, pulling her close.

"Sorry, I should have let you know. I just haven't been feeling very well the last few days, my stomach. Must be the bug going around," Addy lied, and I could smell Hannah's nervousness as she glanced up the stairs briefly before she looked back at Addy.

"So, everything's okay, then? You aren't... you aren't mad at me?" she asked, shoving her hands in her coat pockets. She was fidgety and anxious, and I didn't like it. My lip curled slightly, and Addy elbowed me in the side as Hannah's eyes widened in fear.

"No, of course not! I'm sorry for worrying you. Thank you for checking up on me," Addy replied gently, moving to walk Hannah back to the door. Hannah side-stepped her casually, wandering into the middle of the studio.

"It's no biggie. But hey, maybe while I'm here, I can get that piercing?" she asked brightly, her smile faltering when she met my eyes.

"Um... now's not a great time, actually. Austin caught what I had, I think. He's not feeling the best today," Addy replied, catching my eye. I nodded slowly, and Hannah's face fell.

"Oh, well, that's okay then. Hey, what if we went for a walk together? We could get a coffee and chat a little?" Hannah offered. I didn't like the whine in her voice. It was grating, but it seemed to affect Addy, who looked genuinely sad for her little friend.

"I don't know if that's a good idea. I'd hate to get you sick..." Addy replied, and Hannah took a step toward her, reaching out her hand.

"I'll be fine, come on! It'll be fine!" She smiled, and I snarled as she took another step toward Addy, who frowned and backed up again, watching her friend.

"No, not this time. We can grab coffee next week when I'm back in the lab," Addy replied firmly. Hannah's face took on a pinched look, her eyes sad.

"Please, just come with me, Addy?" she asked again, more firmly this time. Her hand went back into her pocket, and I snarled, stepping toward Addy.

"I tried the nice way," Hannah mumbled sadly and pulled out the gun, aiming it at my chest.

Addy swore, and I froze in my tracks, judging the distance between us. Hannah was a lot closer to Addy than I was to either of them, so I doubted that I could lunge and reach her from this distance. At least the gun was trained on me. I could deal with that. I just had to keep it on me, and away from Addy.

"Hannah, what the fuck?" Addy snapped, and Hannah glanced over at her, keeping the gun trained on me.

"I was supposed to get you to come with me, that's it. I didn't want to hurt anyone. But I have to hurt you if you don't listen," she explained, a pained look on her face. "You understand, right? I didn't want to hurt anyone." Addy paled and looked at me, shaking her head as I inched closer. Hannah glared at me, and pointed the gun at Addy, making me snarl.

"Don't, don't move!" she snapped. "I'll hurt her if you touch me. You need to stay away. Walk over to the stairs," she ordered, and I took a step back, hissing in rage. My shoulders tensed and my fangs ached. I flashed them at her in a threat. I couldn't risk Addy, or the babies, so I continued backward, slowly. Once I was far enough away, she turned the gun back on me and I could breathe again.

"Hannah, who told you to do this?" Addy asked, pulling her attention. Hannah's face went slack, her eyes dreamy as she smiled.

"My boyfriend, Jake. He's perfect, Addy, but you already know that." Hannah smiled dreamily, and Addy scowled.

"I wouldn't say that," she muttered. Hannah snapped back into reality, a frown on her face once more.

"Okay, now please, just come with me, yeah? I need you to come with me so you can meet him. It'll all be okay then," she told Addy, and I clenched my fists.

"Addy, no!" I rasped, seeing the decision on her face. "Don't, please!"

"I'm sorry, but if you try to stop us I'm supposed to hurt you," Hannah sighed, and Addy reached toward her, her hands outstretched as she lunged for the gun.

I shouted and leapt forward as Hannah twisted; the gun going off with a bang.

CHAPTER TWENTY-FOUR

Addison

The sound I made was inhuman, clawing its way out of my throat as I lunged forward. Austin sank to the floor, a confused expression on his face as he clutched his chest. There was a dark stain spreading out across the front of his hoodie, and I pressed my hands on his chest to stop the bleeding. "No, no, no!" I murmured, frantically.

"Shh, I'll be fine..." Austin mumbled, his eyes drifting closed. There was too much blood, it was too much blood too quickly.

"Don't close your eyes!" I snapped, freezing when I felt something metal press against the back of my head.

"Come on now, Addy. Just come with me, and I won't have to shoot anyone else," Hannah insisted. I ignored her, looking around for something to staunch the bleeding. I reached over to grab a rag Wyatt had brought down for something. It was not the cleanest, but it would have to do. Grabbing his hands,

I pressed the rag down on his chest and put his hands over it to hold it in place.

"It'll be okay, just stay awake," I told him softly, brushing my lips against his. He mumbled something, his eyelids fluttering as he fought to stay awake. I wouldn't cry, not now. I focused on my rage instead.

Standing swiftly, I charged at Hannah, and she raised the gun to stop me, her hands shaking. "Where are you taking me?" I snapped, and her face lifted in relief.

"It's not far. We can walk." She smiled, and I was tempted to rip it off her face. Risking one last glance at Austin, I stormed through the door, letting Hannah run after. I heard her scream, and she slammed into the door behind me, clutching her ankle. I smirked. *Granddaddy still had it in him, I guess.* "You have snakes in your house? What kind of freaks are you?!" she yelled, and I waited for her to stumble down the steps, the gun held tightly in her hand.

"You have no fucking idea," I muttered, and she waved me forward, shoving the gun into her pocket and pointing it at me like some sort of movie robber.

"I didn't want to shoot anyone," she told me blankly, limping beside me as we walked down the sidewalk. The same route Piper had taken the day he'd disappeared, I realized, bristling. "If you had just listened to me in the first place, we would have been fine."

I turned to her, vividly aware of the gun still in her hand. "If you knew what Jake had done to me, you'd understand why Austin reacted the way he did," I snapped, and she sighed.

"He said you might be difficult, but I don't understand how one little fight could make you so angry with him," she replied, shrugging. I blinked at her, my mouth opening in confusion.

"A little fight?" I repeated incredulously. "What did he– oh whatever. I don't give a fuck about the lies he told you. He could've told you I was an international spy, and you'd believe him," I muttered, rolling my eyes. She chose to ignore that comment, wincing as we continued to walk, turning the corner and heading down a street I'd never visited before. The buildings on this block were older, some of them worn down and condemned, judging from the signs on the doors. A couple were already in states of demolition, new condos being advertised on the nearby billboard. She stopped in front of one that looked ready to be torn down, but clearly they hadn't gotten to it yet. I raised an eyebrow, staring at the dilapidated entryway.

"Well, go!" she snapped, pulling out the gun and waving it at my face. Jesus, where was the fun little scientist who liked bugs? I stomped up the stairs, staring at the door that looked like it should've been locked. Hannah sighed like I was the problem here and limped past me, wrenching the door open and waiting for me to go inside. My skin prickled with nerves as I walked into what used to be an office of some kind. Faded blue carpeting and cracked gray tiles covered the floor, and there was a front desk that sat empty in the middle of the foyer, covered in dust and mouse crap.

"Move!" she demanded, limping toward a closed door at the far end of the abandoned room. I trailed along beside her, my heart hammering in my chest as I looked around, watching for movement. Hannah ushered me into a different room, shoving me in the back when I slowed in the doorway. I didn't like this place. Something about it was... wrong.

My breath caught in my throat when I noticed a figure off to one side, slumped over in a chair. His hair was matted with blood, and his shirt was in tatters on the floor around him, blood and cuts littering his chest. I couldn't see the man's face, but I would recognize the necklaces he was wearing anywhere. "You fucking bitch," I whispered, stumbling toward him, panic flooding my veins. He wasn't moving, was he breathing?! *Please... please, let him be breathing.*

"What, no hello for me?" I froze halfway across the room as men materialized from the shadows all around me. All of them had expressionless faces and guns, much to my dismay. They stood like sentries around the room, staring at nothing, like robots. The source of the gravelly voice emerged last, the dramatic fucking prick. I was happy to see that, despite not being dead like he was supposed to be, he was at least as fucked up on the outside as he was on the inside.

Cain's fire had done a number on him, and honestly, I wasn't sure how he'd survived at all. Still-healing burns covered a large portion of his body, and his hair and eyebrows appeared to have burnt off. One of his eyes was cloudy, and his leg dragged as he walked, clearly causing him a lot of pain. Despite the fear churning in my gut, I couldn't help but smile. He met my gaze, his face twisting into what I assume was a scowl, but it wasn't easy to tell with the burns. "Jake, looking well," I told him, crossing my arms over my chest.

"Still have a mouth on you, even now that you're a married woman? My little brother needs to learn how to train his bitches to behave." Ugh, his vocal chords must've been damaged, because every sound he made was like nails on a chalkboard to my ears.

"And that's why you weren't invited to the wedding," I replied drily, my eyes flicking back to Piper. I needed something, anything, just to know he was alive. He looked so... broken. I clenched my fists, my nails biting into my skin.

"Did you get your present? I thought it was funny, the nut job wears a ring and your husba-"

"Don't fucking talk about him," I snapped, and Jake's jaw clenched, clearly not used to being interrupted.

"Little Spider... making friends... are we?"

Oh, thank god! I jerked like I'd been slapped, watching Piper's head tilt up, clearly alive, although how, I wasn't sure. His face was minced meat, and I couldn't even tell if he was meeting my gaze, his eyes swollen and bruised.

"You're the people person, not me, love." I smiled, and he coughed out a dry laugh, blood dripping down his lip. I was going to kill Jake for what he'd done to him.

"I'm glad you got here in time. I was just about to put your dreamboat out of his misery. You know how I hate to witness suffering, don't you?" Jake rasped out a chuckle, and I shifted closer to Piper, biting back a snarl.

"You won't touch him again," I told him coolly.

"No, I won't. But one of my friends will," he mused, gesturing around the room. "See, even though you ruined some of my appeal, I can still make friends anywhere. And they are much better equipped than your friends, as you can see."

"Are they? They seem pretty human to me," I replied, glancing at Hannah. Her face was ashen, and she was leaning against the wall, unable to put weight on her bad leg anymore. He followed my gaze and scowled.

"Sorry Jakey, did I break your favorite toy?" I bit out, inching closer to Piper. His head had dropped back down against his chest, and his breathing was too shallow for my liking. Jake was too busy studying Hannah to notice me, so I gently slid my hand over Piper's, hating how cold and clammy it felt against my skin. He inhaled sharply, and his fingers flexed under mine. "I'm going to get you out of here," I murmured.

"Where're the others?" he whispered, flinching as Jake started yelling at Hannah, who was slumping to the floor.

"He..." a lump formed in my throat. "They aren't coming. It's just us," I whispered back, giving his hand a gentle squeeze.

"Mhmm, I heard Austin," he frowned, "he's calling you. Answer, Lil' Spider." His head sagged forward, and I whimpered, squeezing his hand again.

"No, stay with me, please! Not you, too," I gasped, tears burning in my eyes. "Come back to me, Piper!" I grabbed his shoulder and shook him gently, but I couldn't see his chest rising anymore.

A thud made me jump, and I spun around to see Hannah slumped over on the floor, Jake grimacing over her. "I liked her," he sighed. "She was so responsive." Turning back to me, I noticed a bloody knife in his hand. My blood froze in my veins, seeing the same knife from my nightmares.

Not again. He would not take that from me again. Rage that would have made Cain proud boiled up inside my chest, and I squeezed Piper's hand so tightly I worried I might crush his fingers. With every ounce of my soul, I took that pain that was crushing my heart and tugged.

CHAPTER TWENTY-FIVE

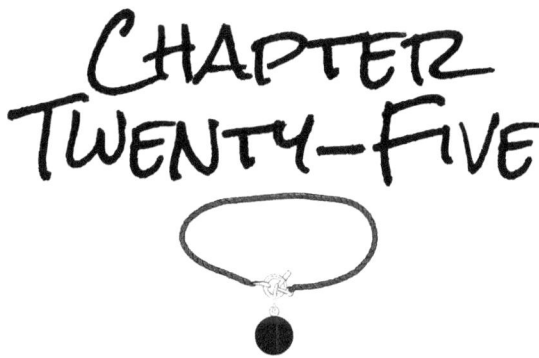

Piper

I'd been content in my safe place, enveloped in the pillowy darkness, hiding from the pain, from the cruelty out in the world. The whispers had crept back, offering comfort as best they could, sharing little pieces with me, little bits of knowledge. I could concentrate on them more easily here. Maybe it was because I was closer to death myself? I could pick up on individual whispers, listening to one at a time instead of trying to decipher the jumble all together.

The Little Spider is coming.

They told me this, and I wept. I didn't want Addy anywhere near this place. Not here, in this tainted, evil place. Her voice had drifted through the darkness, calling to me like a siren's song. I'd reluctantly emerged, the pain hitting me all over again, making my chest spasm as I struggled to breathe again.

Of course, she was mouthing off to that twisted mass of evil, her power shining so brightly I could almost see it. The moment she had touched me, my entire body sparkled back to life. And fuck, did it ever hurt. The whispers immediately intensified, but the strongest voice... Austin? I felt him. I felt the raw pain in his voice as he called out for his mates. We needed him. He was strong enough. He just needed to find us.

The noises were too much, so I retreated into my safe place, the pain receding and letting me concentrate. With Addy's hand in mine, I felt more. The whispers were clear as day, and I could sense the... tether attached to my chest, the one that drew me to everyone. If I thought hard enough, I could put my hands on it, feeling the ripple travel down toward the others. I needed Austin, his friends, all of them. I put him in my mind, concentrating on his voice calling out to us. As hard as I could, I wrenched the tether toward me, tugging him closer, willing him to follow it here.

Find us...

The effort left me tired, so tired. All I wanted to do was curl up in my safe place and rest. But Addy was here. Addy needed me. I wasn't done yet. I could rest when Austin came. Reluctantly, I emerged from the darkness, gasping at the assault of sounds, the pulse of pain across my entire body. Addy's hand was crushing mine, and I could taste her fear. I wiggled my fingers, letting her know I was here, and she gasped in relief.

"'m still here," I mumbled, my tongue heavy in my mouth.

"You're much more effort than you're worth," the twisted man - Jake? - snapped, and I heard Addy chuckle.

"If I had a nickel..." she murmured, and I smirked, my lip splitting open. The whispers had decided to join us, maybe because Addy was still holding onto me, or maybe because they pitied me. I listened, focusing on them, knowing what I needed to do now.

"You're just jealous," I announced, and Addy squeezed my hand in warning. I couldn't tell where Jake was, but I could tell that I had his attention now. "You were more handsome, more charming, but still, everyone always chose Cain. Your parents, teachers, Addy. Even with your abilities, you were no one's choice. This is all about jealousy."

"What the fuck did you just say?" Jake wheezed, and I heard his shuffling footsteps. Addy brushed against my leg as she moved in front of me. No, I needed her out of the way, where it was safe. I jerked my hand, tugging her back, leaving me open, vulnerable. The whispers surrounded me, cocooning me in their safety. "You play with people because you're bored, but you feel nothing. You are fueled with hate, but still, somehow, empty. All you are is a shell, and your cracks are beginning to show. Jacob Virgil Morgan, we find you lacking!" My voice didn't sound like mine anymore. The whispers were lending me their tongues now that mine was growing too weak.

"You stupid hippy freak!" Jake snarled. "You think I'm nothing?! I'll make you watch while every one of my puppets takes their turn with your precious little whore. I'll gut you and let you bleed out while she writhes on the floor beside you!" Addy snarled and tensed under my fingers, and I gripped her tightly.

"Do you wish to know your future, Jacob Virgil Morgan?" I intoned, the words flowing through me unbidden, a mind of their own. "The walls you've built are torn down around you, and the ground opens up and swallows you down. Hell will rise up to claim you, bleeding you out with a thousand cuts.

You've always been too brazen, and that will be your demise. The strings will be cut and you will die alone and forgotten. Your name will die in this room." My lungs filled with air that wasn't drawn from this world. "You lose, you nasty piece of shit." The last part was me, and my mouth quirked up in a smile as I sagged into the chair, my energy spent.

"No, you don't get to die yet!" Jake snarled, and Addy cursed as her hand was wrenched out of mine, the world upending as my chair fell backward, tumbling me back into the darkness.

CHAPTER TWENTY-SIX

Addison

The man who grabbed me would be the first to die. One of Jake's puppets wrapped his arms around my chest, dragging me away from Piper as Jake advanced on him, looking like the devil himself. I'd never heard Piper sound so... possessed before. It wasn't right, and it sent chills down my spine as he taunted Jake. I struggled against the man who held me, sending an elbow into his gut and jerking my head back until I heard a satisfying crunch, and he howled in pain. He stumbled back as Jake kicked over Piper's chair, sending him tumbling to the floor.

"Piper!" I screamed, and he twisted, pulling against his bindings as he laughed, blood dripping down his cheek.

Selene hissed, her tongue brushing against my ear. I wish I could speak to her like Austin could, because it felt like she was trying to tell me something. My heart was pounding, adrenaline pulsing through me so hard it felt like the floor was shaking. Wait... *was it actually shaking?* The puppet barreled toward me, one hand clutching his bloody nose, but something dropped onto his head from above, and he screamed, collapsing to the floor in front of me.

I heard a thud and whirled around, snarling as Jake aimed another kick at Piper. "Don't fucking touch him!" I yelled, running at him. Shouts of panic erupted around me as the room descended into chaos, and a cacophony of hissing filled the room. I cocked my fist back and caught Jake in the chin, forcing him to stumble back. His good eye turned towards me, his pupil dilated with... *ew, lust? What a fucking creep.*

"I forgot how good you felt," he growled, and I raised my fists, stepping between him and Piper. The door to the room slammed open, and the guard nearest to the door went down to his knees, blood spurting out of a gaping hole in his throat. "Shoot it!" Jake exclaimed, but the other guards were a little distracted at the moment, and I smirked. Two of them were grappling with pythons that had wrapped themselves around their throats, their guns forgotten at their sides. The one nearest to me was wailing and stumbling around as a rattlesnake sank its fangs into his hand. More snakes poured into the room, hissing and coiling as they surrounded us.

Another scream of pain erupted, and one of the men fighting the pythons was face down on the ground, a shadowy figure perched on top of him. I winced as the figure wrapped his hands around the guard's head and wrenched, twisting it at an unnatural angle. Jake swore as the figure leapt at the next man, his thumbs slamming into his eye-sockets as he brought him to the ground. The screams made my stomach churn, but they were silenced quickly, and the figure rose up, blood dripping off him.

He smoothed his hair back away from his face, and I smiled, my arms relaxing at my sides as palpable relief washed over me. Austin stalked towards us, his eyes focused on me, looking absolutely deadly.

"Fucking shoot him, you useless piece of shit!" Jake snarled, and the man with the rattlesnake hanging off of him swung his gun around, his eyes unfocused as he tried to aim. Austin was a blur as he struck, taking the man down before he could pull the trigger, blood spraying the nearby wall as he tore his throat out.

Jake's hand closed around my arm and I jerked away from him, freezing when a familiar prick of cold metal pressed against my neck. I let him wrench me backward, grimacing as he wrapped a hand around my waist. This time, the crazy man wielding the knife didn't scare me, because I was more powerful than he knew and his time was already up.

Austin advanced on us, blood dripping down his face as he hissed, his fangs flashing. The smile tugged at the corners of my mouth, even as Jake tugged me back, the metal biting into my skin. "I was so worried about you," I told Austin, and his pupils dilated. He'd shed the bloodstained hoodie I'd last seen him wearing, leaving a tight black tee-shirt with one of the sleeves missing, as if it had been torn off by hand. The place where I knew the bullet had hit him was scarred and angry, but clearly healing over. His patches of scales glistened under the light. He looked like a predator right now, and my face flushed with heat at the sight.

"I heard you calling," he hissed, his voice rough and barely audible.

"Shut the fuck up!" Jake snarled. "Stop moving, or I'll slit her throat!"

Austin froze, his hands clenched into fists. I shook my head, giving him a reassuring smile.

"It's okay baby," I murmured. The blade pressed against my skin, and Jake's hand tightened against my stomach.

"You ruin everything!" he snarled in my ear, and I laughed bitterly, the sound echoing across the room.

"Jake, this time, I'm going to make sure you're well and truly dead," I murmured. "Selene, Helios, take care of him for me, would you, please?" I felt Helios shift in my hoodie's pouch, his body coiling tight before he struck out, latching onto Jake's hand. Selene struck in tandem, and Jake reeled back, the knife dropping to the ground as his hands went to his face. I turned and smiled as Selene extracted her fangs from his cheek, dropping to the floor and slithering away. Helios, my brave boy, coiled his body around Jake's arm, biting him several more times as Jake screamed in agony.

"You shouldn't have touched me, Jake," I sighed, stepping away as he writhed in pain. "You should have just left us alone." Austin grabbed my arms and spun me around, pulling me tightly against his chest. I breathed in his scent, melting into his arms.

"Did he hurt you?" Austin rasped, his fingers raking through my hair, tugging it back until I tipped my face up to look at him. He looked like a monster, with the blood streaking down his face, and his fangs bared as he snarled at Jake's twisting body. He was my monster, and I rose up on my tiptoes to press a kiss to his cheek.

"No, but he hurt Piper," I whispered, looking over my shoulder, and Austin's face darkened with rage. As his hands slid off my back, I stepped aside, leaving him to finish the business with Jake. Hurrying over toward Piper, I found Selene curled up on his chest, watching me. I looked around and spotted Jake's discarded knife on the floor. I used it to cut the duct tape on Piper's wrists and ankles, and then I grabbed him carefully under the shoulders and dragged him off the chair, laying him gently on the ground. He was a mess. I could barely see his skin underneath all the bruising and blood.

"Piper, can you hear me?" I murmured, wincing as Jake screamed in agony. Not really sure what I was doing, I pressed my fingers to Piper's neck and managed to find his heartbeat, faint but steady. "I need you to wake up. We need to get you out of here," I told him, stroking his cheek. He let out a soft groan, but his eyes didn't open, and I started to panic.

Another crack, like a gunshot, echoed across the room, and Jake screamed, his voice breaking. "Austin, we need to go. Piper needs a hospital," I announced, and he hissed in response. Another snap, and Jake's screaming stopped abruptly. I exhaled in relief. It was finally done. Austin dropped down beside me and I picked Selene up off Piper's chest as Austin lifted his limp body up awkwardly in his arms. We walked out of the room, leaving the cluster of bodies behind.

I glanced down at Hannah, a shiver of remorse rippling through me. She didn't deserve to die. She was just another victim in Jake's horrific reign of terror. I shut the door behind us, entombing them together, and made a mental note to come back here tonight and set a well-placed fire to destroy the evidence we left.

The next part wasn't fun. I had to convince Austin to leave Piper in an alley a block down from the building. It felt all kinds of wrong, but it would be too suspicious if we brought him in looking like this. I called an ambulance, stating that someone had been mugged and where he was located, hanging up before they could ask questions. Austin and I waited in a doorway nearby until the ambulance arrived and gathered him up, rushing him off to the nearby hospital.

We got back home, and I discovered Wyatt passed out in the studio, propped up on one of the benches. He had fresh blood on his chest and all over his cast, but no visible wounds, thank god. To my utter devastation, I found Granddaddy cobra coiled next to him on the floor, belly up.

Apparently after I'd left, Wyatt had crawled down the stairs by himself to find Austin on the floor, bleeding out. Not knowing what else to do, he'd healed Austin, but it had been too much for him to take on himself. The old snake had made the ultimate sacrifice for them, letting Wyatt push the injury into him instead.

There was no time to mourn him, not today, at least. Tears stained my cheeks as Austin and I found him a shoebox and tucked him inside, and he brought him up to his room for his other friends to watch over our fallen. Then I helped Austin strip out of his bloodied clothes, setting them in a pile to burn later, and pushed him into the shower to get cleaned up. I set Selene and Helios in with the others to rest and dropped my clothes into the pile with Austin's, checking myself over for blood. Just Piper's and Austin's, which coated my hands. I scrubbed in the sink for ten minutes, trying to get my skin clean, but I could still see the stain on my fingers even though the water ran clear.

Austin stepped out of the shower and pulled me away from the sink as my hands began to turn pink from the hot water. I was so tired; I wished we were a normal family who could just nap the afternoon away. Instead, we got dressed in silence, checked on Wyatt to make sure he was breathing, and then headed back, out into the world like we hadn't just massacred a room full of brainwashed people.

When we reached the hospital, I had to think up a decent lie to explain how we knew Piper was there since he'd been brought in as a John Doe. In reality, I'd taken his wallet and phone myself since a mugging wouldn't make sense if he had all his valuables still on him. The nurse didn't seem to care either way, and pointed out his bed in the ER bay.

He looked even worse under the ugly fluorescent lights. The few patches of unbruised skin were tinged a sickly gray. I collapsed into a chair next to the bed, trying to figure out where to even hold him without hurting him. Austin hovered behind me, for once not hiding underneath his hood. He stood proudly, his shoulders firm, with a hand on the back of my neck.

We waited, listening to the machines beeping quietly, for nearly an hour before the doctor came by to check on him. His amputated finger was a priority, because it had been poorly done and left untreated for a long time, leaving him wide open for infections. Another concern was head trauma. The EMTs had reported that his pupillary response wasn't what it should be, and clearly he'd taken several blows to the head. They had me remove all of his jewelry and gave me the scraps of his clothes, which they'd had to cut off of him to assess his injuries on the way here.

I busied myself with storing all of his necklaces, bracelets, and assorted rings into my bag so I wouldn't lose any of them. A pair of nurses joined us in the little curtained room and prepped Piper to take him up for his scans. There was no reason to keep the scraps of his clothes, not even for rags, so

I brought them to the nearby garbage bin. A small clatter had me pausing, and I looked down to see something glinting on the floor, whatever it was having fallen from my pile of fabric. I dumped the handful of clothes in the bin and bent to pick it up, wondering how one of Piper's trinkets had ended up in the clothes.

At a closer glance, I realized that it wasn't one of his; it was much too small. It was jewelry though. In fact, it was a beautiful antique ring with a blood red gemstone. It looked so similar to his own spider ring that tears pricked in my eyes. Maybe it was a little presumptuous, but I couldn't help but slip it onto my finger, admiring how perfectly it fit without being sized.

"Addy?" Austin murmured, coming up behind me. "What's wrong?" I shook my head, brushing the tears away quickly. Not yet. I couldn't cry just yet.

"Just tired," I whispered, and let him pull me back towards the chair, dropping down into it with a sigh. Somehow, I managed to doze off in that uncomfortable little chair, waking only when a loud ringing went off in our small space, startling me violently. Austin hissed as I dug through my bag, trying to find the source of the ringing underneath all the crap I had stuffed in there.

I finally unearthed my cell phone, and we both stared at it for a minute, confused about who would bother to call me.

"Hello?" I asked tentatively, as Austin crouched to listen in.

"Mrs. Collins?" a man asked, and I glanced at Austin.

"Yes, who is this?" I frowned.

"I'm Harold Leonberg, your husband's lawyer," he offered, and I opened and closed my mouth several times, trying to figure out the proper response to that, other than, *huh?!*

"What, um... can I do for you?" I asked, at a loss for anything else to say.

"Well... do you know, uh, where your husband is?" Harold asked, sounding a little sheepish. For fuck's sake, Cain may have lied about a lot of things these last few months, but I would be pretty dumb to not notice he'd been carted off to jail.

"Yes, trust me, I'm well aware. I actually was supposed to talk to you about how to visit him? They wouldn't let me see him when I went to the police station." I grimaced.

"Mrs. Collins, your husband isn't at the police station, or jail, for that matter. In fact, I'm here right now and I cannot find him," Harold told me, and I let out a string of very *ladylike* curses that had him clearing his throat uncomfortably. "I'm sorry to have upset you. I was hoping to speak to him, but he's not answering his cell phone either. You were the only other listed contact, I'm afraid," He explained gently.

"I swear to god, if that dumbass broke out of jail somehow, I will-" I hung up on Harold, who let out a strangled yelp at my mention of a prison break. "Cain is missing," I told Austin, blinking away tears of frustration. At least when he was locked in jail, he could stay out of fucking trouble. Could we please just go twenty-four hours without one of my men going missing or getting injured?!

I realized I was clenching my phone and took a deep breath, quickly dialing Cain's number. It went straight to voicemail, and I let it beep, fuming at this point. "You son of a bitch! You'd better call me back and explain what the *fuck* is going on, because if I find out you've done something stupid, I swear I will tear you apart limb from limb. Piper is in the goddamn hospital and you'd better not have broken out of jail. So help me god, Cain..." I sighed and hung up before I said anything else too nasty.

CHAPTER TWENTY-SEVEN

Cain

For the first time in my pathetic life, I was considering a vacation. I'd think I'd fucking earned one at this point. My presence caused an absolute shitshow at the police station, and it became apparent as I watched the back and forth of the officers who'd arrested me with their supervisors, and then with each other, that Jake hadn't done a thorough job this time. He'd fucked with my clients' money somehow, and then he'd tricked the officers into arresting me, that much I could figure. He hadn't covered his bases, though. There was no fake paper trail, or actual evidence that I'd done anything but try to help my client find the money that had gone missing. So nobody knew what to do with me.

I waited, growing more and more irritated as I sat on my ass in the musty little cage, shooting glares at the drunk sleeping it off next to me. Sleep was never going to happen for me, and I must've been up for close to forty-eight hours straight at this point. There had been two shift changes since

I'd gotten here and still, I hadn't been processed or even told what was happening. I'd called my lawyer, Harold, with my allotted phone call, but he was stuck in court today and wouldn't be by until later. Meanwhile, my family was being targeted by a psychopath and I was just sitting and doing nothing. I clenched my fists and took a deep, calming breath. No, I couldn't get mad. There were cameras, and people who would ask questions if I randomly started a fire in here.

I saw one of the arresting officers walk past the cage and I stood up, shoving my hands in my pockets to look less... I don't know, murderous? "Excuse me?" I called, and he stopped, shooting me a dirty look. "Can you please tell me what's going on? How long am I going to be held here?" I asked, trying to keep the irritation out of my voice.

This is not the time for anger. They will fucking Taser you.

"Just sit and wait for your damn lawyer, alright?" he snapped back in response, and I raised my eyebrows.

"I just... I've been sitting and waiting for nearly twenty-four hours. My wife is pregnant, and I'm worried about her. Can I call her at least? I haven't been processed or anything yet, and I don't know what's going on." I tried appealing to his humanity, as Addy routinely encouraged. He scowled at me, stepping up to the bars.

"Listen, I know what you did, alright? You're a fucking swindler, and you aren't getting out of here." He spat at my feet and stalked off, leaving me stuck in the cage. So clearly, he was the one Jake had talked to. That was good to know. I sighed and sat back down, resting my head against the brick wall behind me.

"Gonna be a dad?" the drunk across the room piped up, still sprawled across the bench. I closed my eyes, blocking him out. This was my hell. Stuck in here, forced to make small talk. I was officially in hell.

Hell, it seemed, had stale ham sandwiches for its inmates at least. I begrudgingly ate the thing, desperate for a cigarette or a cup of coffee. My drunk friend was clearly sobering up, and he tore into the sandwich like it was a four-course meal. He kept trying to talk to me, and I just gave him grunts and one-word answers, trying to dissuade his friendliness.

"Do you know what you're having yet?" Grunt.

"Are you and the missus doing birthing classes? My girl-friend wants to do one, but I ain't needing to see no pictures of afterbirth." Angrier grunt.

"Think you'll circumcise if it's a boy? If you do, make sure to get someone legit. My cousin had a botched one and it loo-" I raised my eyebrow at him, scowling and standing abruptly. He trailed off, eyeing me wearily, and I raked my hand through my hair, looking out into the bullpen and trying to find someone I could flag down and talk to. My blood was burning hot, making me feel restless. I needed to get the fuck out of here, right fucking now.

I paced up and down the length of the cell like a tiger in the zoo, clenching and unclenching my hands to try to dispel the feeling in my gut. Something was wrong, I just knew it. I was mid-step when it felt like someone hooked a fishing line into my heart and just... yanked. I stumbled and dropped to my knees, clutching my chest as a groan bubbled out of my throat. *Oh my god, was this a heart attack? Had they poisoned that awful sandwich?* Just my luck, of course I'd die in a cage thanks to tainted sandwich meat.

"Hey, what's wrong with you, man? Are you having a heart attack?" My ears were ringing, every atom in my body shifting with the need to run, and in only one direction. I was tethered to something, and it was calling to me. The whole room spun around me, and my drunk friend started yelling about something. I swear, if I had to listen to one more story about circumcisions, I would turn this building to ash around me.

"Mr. Collins? Are you with me? Mr. Collins?" The fishing line in my heart relaxed, and I gasped for air as it resumed beating as normal. Fuck, I was dizzy. I grabbed the bars next to me for support as my chest heaved, and people were still yelling around me.

"Did you touch him?"

"No, honest, he just dropped!"

"How long has he been here? Who is this man exactly?"

"Someone get Officer Hendrix on the phone, right fucking now."

Addy, I needed to find Addy. There was a hand on my shoulder, and someone flashed a penlight in my eyes, making me wince. "Sir, can you hear me?" I blinked as spots filled my vision, nodding grimly. "Get me some water, now," they snapped, and a dixie cup of water was suddenly thrust into my hands. "Drink this." I nodded again, draining the little cup in one shot. "Come on now, let's get you sitting up here." Small hands hooked under my armpits and pulled, guiding me up onto the nearby bench. I blinked and saw a short, fierce-looking plain-clothes officer staring at me, her brows pulled together as she studied my face.

"Alright, Mr. Collins, can you tell me what you're in for today?" she asked.

I shook my head. "Honestly, I don't know," I replied hoarsely.

She scowled and put her hands on her hips. "Andrew, did you get a hold of Hendrix? I don't give a shit if he's sleeping. He left a guy in my cell with no fucking paperwork!" She looked back at me, studying me carefully. "I don't know what you did to piss my colleague off, but we're going to get to the bottom of this, alright? Now you just stay here, take some deep breaths, and I'll come back with some answers in a few minutes." She patted my shoulder, and I gave her a weak smile, feeling drained after... whatever the hell that just was.

Officer plain-clothes wasn't fucking around. She tracked down my friend Hendrix, who apparently woke up from a nap with no recollection of who I was or why he'd arrested me. Since I hadn't been processed or even admitted properly, they just... opened the cell door and let me walk out. I didn't wait around for them to change their minds. I just grabbed my stuff and bolted, heading in the direction that the tether had been pulling me toward. My phone was dead, of course, so I had no way to get ahold of Addy or the others and make sure they were alright.

The tug I'd felt took me close to home, and I paused at a corner a few blocks away, conflicted. I wanted to go straight to the studio, but there was some invisible destination plotted out in my brain, pushing me to turn and walk down a different street instead. Instead of fighting it, I just let it pull me because this witchy bullshit smelt too much like Piper to safely ignore, and I ended up in front of an abandoned building. I had a nagging sense of dread as I wrenched open the front door and walked inside, following a path of footsteps in the dirt that led to a door.

The smell of blood hit me like a kick to the teeth when I walked inside, but nothing could have prepared me for the bloodbath I walked into. Body parts were strewn across the room, and blood was everywhere, even the fucking ceiling somehow. Corpses of people I didn't recognize were scattered in a circle, guns on the floor beside them, and there was an upturned chair in the corner with duct-tape still stuck to the arms. The last body I found was Jake's, somehow recognizable even with all the burns and lacerations. Someone had jammed him through a wood-chipper, or something similar, the way he was mangled and left in a heap. I guess in death, the lies he'd told no longer held true, it would explain why officer Hendrix had woken up with no memory of my supposed crime.

I checked his pulse this time, but there was no way he could be breathing in this condition. I wasn't even sure his heart was still intact enough to beat. With my hand still pressed to his neck, I let out the anger that I'd been keeping at bay for these long months. His skin began to crackle and twist, turning black as he burned underneath my hand. The fire grew, eating away at his remains, turning them to ash before the heat began to spread outwards, the carpet igniting under my feet. I backed toward the door, letting my fingers drag across the drywall, paint bubbling as flames licked up to the ceiling. By the time I reached the door, the whole room was ablaze, and I watched for another moment before I made my exit, letting the blaze clear away the rest of Jake's evil.

Fresh out of jail and now having committed arson, I quickly headed back to the studio to find a phone charger, or better yet, someone who could explain the pile of bodies I just incinerated.

The door, unsurprisingly, was unlocked when I got home, because even with a murderous psychopath hunting us down, no one bothered to lock a damn door. I burst inside, locking it behind me, and spotted Wyatt sitting at the bottom of the stairs looking, well, like he'd been hit by a car. There was a dried puddle of blood next to him, which had smeared all over the place.

"How the hell did you get out?" Wyatt asked, hooking his hand onto the railing and lifting himself up until he could sit on the step. I crossed my arms over my chest and watched him do it again, and then again, slowly climbing up the stairs on his ass.

"This is painful to watch. Let me help you, for fuck's sake," I snapped, and followed after him, hoisting him over my shoulder. We managed to get up the stairs in only a fraction of the time, and I got him settled on the couch, taking note of all the blood on his clothes.

"Well? Did you make a jailbreak?" he asked, wincing as he settled into the cushions. I helped him get his leg propped up so he could rest, rolling my eyes at him.

"Of course not! They let me go," I replied, locating his meds on the kitchen table. I handed him a couple and grabbed him a glass of water, which he gulped down immediately. "What the fuck happened here? Why is there blood all over the place?" Wyatt rubbed his face tiredly, flecks of blood flaking off and floating to the ground.

"Austin got shot, and Addy was taken," he explained, and I started to swear and head for the stairs. "Wait! Jesus. It's fine, well, sort of." He explained how Austin had massacred the room full of people and how Addy and Austin had taken Piper to the hospital, while I sank down onto one of the kitchen chairs, resting my head in my hands.

"So... it's done then," I muttered. "It's actually done. He's gone, and it's over now." I shook my head, the buzzing behind my eyes amplifying until I thought I'd pass out from the pain. Wyatt stayed quiet while I processed everything and, when I looked back up, I found him passed out asleep. With a heavy sigh, I dragged myself up and headed off to my room, plugging in my phone to get it charging while I changed. I was just going to throw on some new clothes, but after almost two days in a cell, I smelled pretty ripe, so I had the quickest shower I could manage. My phone was back on when I came out, and I winced when I saw it lit up like a beacon, full of missed messages and texts. Harold had tried to reach me several times, as had Addy.

I listened to her voicemail and winced, guilt settling in my stomach. I tried to call her back, but she didn't answer, either out of spite or because her phone was dead now. She still had my car, but I figured she was probably at the hospital with Piper, so I'd try there first. At least if she ripped my limbs off in a room surrounded by doctors, I might have a chance at survival.

CHAPTER TWENTY-EIGHT

Piper

I was floating in the darkness, my body weightless as I basked in the peace it provided. There was no pain, no screaming, and no hunger, just me and the whispers. They were less urgent here, showing me things one at a time, giving me a chance to contemplate what it all meant.

"Piper? Can you hear me?"

A voice filtered into my safe place, and they sounded decidedly pissed off. One of my whispers told me it was Cain, and they led me down his path. I followed him as he walked from the jail, watching him burn the bodies, and felt a glimmer of satisfaction that Jake was truly gone.

"You disappear from jail, duck my calls, and then show up here out of the blue?! Are you fucking kidding me?! Oh, and can you please explain to me why everyone is calling me your WIFE?!"

My Little Spider was pissed, and it made me want to smile. I didn't want to leave my safe place, but I would for a chance to have her in my arms again. When I tried to blink, my eyelids felt weighed down. I tried to move my hand, but it felt wrong, like it wasn't quite there. The more I came back into the present, the more awareness flooded back into my cells. And fuck, was it awful.

"Li... Spid..." My tongue didn't want to work, and my lips cracked when I opened my mouth to talk. Everything hurt, every inch of my skin, every bone, every nerve. All I felt was pain.

"I'm here! Piper, I'm here! Oh, thank fuck you're awake!" Addy sounded sad. I hated that I'd made her sad. Her hand found my cheek, and I groaned, leaning into her touch. It was like a beam of sunshine. I wanted to curl up in it and nap for hours. I forced my eyes to open, but nothing happened, even when I blinked. I reached up with my right hand, trying to grab the bandage or whatever was covering them. Addy caught my hand in hers and held it tightly. "Don't, Piper," she murmured, and I frowned, turning toward the sound of her voice. I could see an outline of her, glowing in the darkness like a star.

"'s wrong with m'eyes?" I mumbled, and she squeezed my hand.

"The doctors are going to run some tests, but you got hit really hard in the head, and it damaged something. I'm not sure... oh Piper. I'm so sorry."

Everything was darkness now. It finally made sense. Someone touched my shoulder, and I flinched, trying to see them, but there was only a faint glow there, nothing like the light Addy emitted.

"It's me," Austin rasped, and I sighed, feeling his hand smoothing down my hair. "You're safe now. I killed them all."

Addy shushed him quickly, but I smiled, feeling my lip split open.

"I'm so sorry, Piper. This is all my fault." Cain's voice was faint, as though he was standing far away. I looked toward his voice and saw a flickering outline in front of me.

"It's not... didn't see it," I mumbled, and Addy squeezed my hand. "Should've seen it."

"It's nobody's fault," Addy replied sharply. "Well, it's Jake's, but that's it," she amended, making me smile.

"I found them, by the way," Cain offered, and I nodded, remembering what I'd seen. "The building was still on fire when my taxi went past on the way here."

"For the love of god, could we wait until we get home to discuss this?" Addy groaned. "You just got out of jail. You should know better!"

The bickering was comforting, and I felt myself drifting off as I listened to them talk around me, my body too weak to stay conscious.

I'd drifted in and out of consciousness a lot over the next few days, or at least, that was what Addy told me. It was hard to tell, now that the passage of time was even less apparent to me than it used to be. They'd run their tests as promised, but apparently the damage had been left untreated for too long, so it was unlikely that there'd be anything they could do to restore my sight. The doctors had given me daily doses of antibiotics to treat the swamp of infections currently hosted in my body. They made me nauseous and groggy, and more than once, Cain had to hold a bucket while I'd puked up the sad excuses for meals they provided in the hospital. Addy told me it had only been five days since I arrived here, but it honestly felt like months.

At least one of them stayed with me during the day, except Wyatt, who was stuck at home thanks to his own injuries. Addy read to me when she visited, or just talked with me, telling me about the foods making her nauseous or how her colleagues reacted to the death of the girl at work. Austin was quiet when he stayed, but he touched me more, his hands traveling up and down every inch of my skin that he could reach. He got in trouble once already for climbing onto the bed and curling up at my side, but the nurses were too scared of him now to say anything.

Cain camped out in the room with me at night, refusing to leave even after the visitor hours were over. During the day, he forced me out of the bed and got me walking around, bullying me to use the cane they provided to keep me from walking into a wall. I held on to his arm as we shuffled down the hallways, back and forth for hours, until I was exhausted and frustrated. It was torture, being inside this long. I was not used to being this aware of... everything. The whispers didn't overlap with my vision anymore, so the past and the future didn't bleed together like they used to. If I saw something, it was clearly a vision from the whispers, so I didn't get as confused anymore.

But the present was exhausting, painful, and overwhelming at times, and the hospital was stifling. I needed to go back home and heal in my own way. Cain could tell I was struggling here, so he convinced the doctors to discharge me as soon as the infections were cleared out and I was off the antibiotics.

Addy took the day off to help me get home. She brought me a comfortable pair of sweats and a tee-shirt to change into, and I already began to feel better once I was out of the stupid hospital gown. I held onto Addy's arm tightly as we walked outside, the cool fresh air filling my lungs like a soothing balm. She hopped in the backseat with me and Cain drove us home, leaving the windows rolled down so I could experience the wind on my face. The city felt so loud now, like someone had turned the volume up on the world.

I had a low, thrumming headache by the time we reached the studio, and Addy and Cain steadied me on either side as we made our way up the stairs. I heard Austin's foot-steps approaching as we reached the top of the stairs, Cain cursing for a moment as he banged on something metallic-sounding. "We put in the baby gates early," Addy explained, her hair tickling my cheek. "My *husband* was worried you might fall. But now he can't get the damn things open." I heard the laughter in her voice, and Cain cursed louder, slamming his hand on the gate.

"I said I was sorry. It's just a piece of paper, it's not a big deal," Cain muttered as the metal gate rattled.

"It's just a lift and pull, for god's sake," Addy sighed, exasperated, jostling me as she pushed past. I heard a metallic creak as she pushed the gate open and pulled me up with her. "Austin, be gentle!" was the only warning I got before arms wrapped around my waist, pulling me into a fierce hug. It felt so good to be home where I belonged. I melted into him, wrapping my arms around his shoulders. Austin smelled like

Addy's favorite honey and oat shampoo, but underneath it was the earthy and wild scent I always associated with him.

"Excuse me, you assholes have seen him all week," Wyatt interrupted, and I heard soft thumps on the floor approaching us. "Let the cripple through, please."

Austin hissed and let me go, his hands lingering briefly on my hips in a silent promise. Wyatt smelled like clean linens mixed with the coppery tang of old blood as he wrapped his arms around me, his cast brushing up against my neck. Immediately, the pain in my body lost its edge, my headache receding into nothing.

"You look worse than I do, and I was hit by a fucking car," he murmured in my ear, and I laughed, the tightness in my chest lightening.

"Speaking of which, you need a bath," Addy announced. "The doc said water is fine as long as you don't get your bandages wet." Her hand was on my arm again, pulling me along. She showed me how to tug the gate upward to have it swing open, and then counted the number of stairs until we reached the top floor. She must've been reading about how to adjust to blindness or something, but it did make me feel more confident.

"You'll sleep in the bedroom with me until I..." she trailed off, her voice getting a bit echo-y. We must've walked into the bathroom. "Until I feel like you won't disappear on me again." She pulled away from me, leaving me stranded in an ocean of darkness. I heard the water turn on nearby, filling the tub.

"I won't be going anywhere for a while, trust me," I murmured, taking a tentative step toward her, shuffling my feet so I wouldn't trip. I could still see her outline. That hadn't been a weird by-product of my medications, after all. But it seemed to be reserved for just my family, or maybe people with... weird abilities. It was hard to say. Hands gripped my arms, steadying me, and Addy's outline grew a little stronger before I felt her lips on mine.

"Not without me you won't," she replied, her lips still ghosting mine. "My heart couldn't take it.

"Are you saying you can't live without me?" I teased, but my throat felt thick with emotion. Addy kissed me again, more insistently this time, and I could feel the tears on her cheeks dampening my skin.

"I'm saying I love you, you idiot. So no more vanishing acts. And keep your damn cellphone on you from now on!" She smacked me in the chest, and I nodded solemnly, my fingers trailing up her sides.

"I'm sure those baby gates will keep me contained for a while at least," I murmured, earning myself a choked-up laugh. "I love you too, Little Spider. Your name was written on my heart back before we even met."

Addy helped me underdress, laughing when she uncovered the tattoo Wyatt had given me, a beautiful little black widow spider sitting on a tattered web over my heart. She stroked her fingertips across it for a moment before helping me into the tub. I lowered myself down to sit while she rummaged around, muttering under her breath about someone using her shampoo.

"Nope, I'll do it. I've been eyeing this patch of blood all week and today it's gone," Addy announced. I flinched a little as water poured suddenly onto my head, but I quickly relaxed as she began working the shampoo into my scalp. Her nails felt like sin as she worked her way over my hair, careful to avoid the stitches in my temple. She warned me before she began washing it out, and I let my eyes close as the water poured down my face and neck, humming quietly as she did it all over again. Once she was finally satisfied with my hair, she took a gentle washcloth and went over every cut and bruise on my face and my chest, making sure they were all clean and healing.

I was getting sleepy by the time she deemed me properly clean and helped me out of the tub, wrapping me carefully in a clean towel before walking me into the bedroom. "You can sleep closest to the bathroom, and you can wake one of us up if you need to get up during the night," she told me gently, sitting me down on the bed. I was still naked, but I didn't care. I slid under the covers and pulled them up to my chest. They smelled like earth and smoke, honey and safety, my family. My eyes started to close before Addy had finished talking.

I dozed for a while before the bed shifted, and Austin's muscular frame tucked in behind me. He was also naked, and I heard his hum of approval as his hands slid down my body, pulling me tightly against him. I could feel the roughness of his patches of scales as his chest rubbed against my back. I was half-asleep, but he knew I didn't mind if he woke me up like this, so I laid still and enjoyed the feel of his body against mine as he kissed my neck. "I missed you," he hissed, nipping at my earlobe. A groan worked its way out of my throat when his hand wrapped around my cock, his own already hard and pressing against my thigh.

"I missed you too," I told him earnestly, my hips jerking into his hand, seeking friction. He was playing coy tonight, and he squeezed down at the base of my cock, making me swear. "Please, Austin?" I begged, rolling over onto my back, my hand seeking out his face so I could touch him, draw him in for a kiss.

"No, this is a punishment tonight," Austin replied, stroking me once before squeezing the base, sending a jolt of need down my spine. "You should never have left us," he murmured, and I could hear the hurt in his voice. His touch had a bite to it, a stinging edge that left me feeling as raw as he sounded.

"I'm sorry, I wasn't thinking... I didn't mean to leave. I was coming back," I insisted, and was rewarded with a tongue swirling over my head, his hand still firm and unmoving. "All I wanted was some time to think. I wanted to buy Addy a gift," I mumbled, and his tongue swiped across the tip once more, making me groan.

"You scared her, she was crying," he hissed, capturing my lips before I could apologize again. He nipped lightly at my bottom lip, making me moan. The door opened and Austin pulled away from me, but his hand never let go of my cock.

"Austin, what the hell! I told you to let him sleep," Addy bit out, her footsteps approaching. "What are you doing? He looks like you're torturing him!"

"Just a little..." Austin replied, giving me another squeeze. I groaned and thrust into his hand, gripping the sheets beside my head. "But he likes it, obviously." I swear I could hear the smirk in that husky voice of his.

I heard something soft hit the floor, and the bed dipped as Addy whispered something in a low voice. Austin's hold on my cock loosened as he pulled away, and I groaned in frustration. "It's okay baby, I've got you," Addy murmured, and her thigh slid over mine to straddle my lap. "I won't let him torture you like that." She situated herself over me, and

I reached for her, but Austin caught my arms, pulling them up over my head and pinning them down.

"But you are going to make it up to both of us," Austin hissed, as Addy sank down onto my cock, the walls of her pussy squeezing me like a vise. I nodded as he pressed my arms into the bed, and I felt the tip of his cock nudge against my lips.

"Yes," I murmured, opening my mouth so he could slide his length across my tongue. Addy was gentle, her hands teasing my sides as she clenched her thighs around mine, rocking her hips, using me to hit that spot that made her moan. Austin was still punishing me, holding me still underneath him as he thrust into my mouth, gagging me when he buried himself in my throat.

The two of them overwhelmed my senses, setting my nerves on fire as pleasure began to trickle down my spine. Without my sight, every sound was more clear, every feeling intensified. Addy's soft whimpers as she pleasured herself with my cock, the gentle sting as Austin buried his fingers in my hair and gripped it tight.

"You'd better make her come," Austin rasped, pulling out to let me breathe only for a moment before his pubic bone pressed into my nose once more. "I want to hear her scream before you think about marking her." I shuddered around his cock, a line of drool trailing out of my mouth as I swallowed him down.

Addy moaned and shifted her hips, and I felt her pussy flutter around me. "God, yes!" My balls tightened when she clamped down around me, crying out as her orgasm hit her, her voice thick with tears. Austin hissed in warning before he thrust one more time and spilled out over my tongue.

I sucked him down, swallowing every drop until he finally pulled out of my mouth, releasing my arms.

"I forgive you," he murmured, kissing me roughly, and I whimpered as Addy shifted on my lap, leaning forward and taking me deeper inside of her.

"Can I..." I swallowed, reaching out for Addy. I found her face, and cupped it with my good hand, cleaning the tears off her cheek. She clasped my hand gently and moved it lower to her breast. She took up my entire palm now, and I pinched her nipple, reveling in the sound she made when I did. "That's my Little Spider, so fucking responsive," I groaned, flicking it with my thumb as she writhed on my lap. I moved my hand lower, trailing down her stomach, feeling the bump that hadn't been there before. I felt her orgasm starting to build, so I moved toward her clit. Austin helped me, dragging my fingers through the wet folds. I had her body memorized in a heartbeat, and she arched as I circled her clit with my fingers, teasing her until she clamped down around me once more, screaming my name as I spilled into her with a moan. My hands dropped to the bed, and I was utterly spent, barely feeling as Addy climbed off of me.

Someone – maybe Austin? – took a damp cloth and cleaned me off before tucking me back into bed. It wasn't long before the mattress dipped and Addy slipped in beside me, wrapping herself in my arms. I felt another arm curl around my waist from behind and Austin's lips pressed against my ear. Twice more, the bed shifted as everyone climbed in. Addy had to get up once or twice, but she always came back to snuggle into my arms. I held my Little Spider close, refusing to let her go again.

Epilogue
Wyatt

I 've never been so scared in my entire life. The entire house was on eggshells. No one, not even the damn snakes, was making a sound. I crept into the kitchen, trying to find something to eat. I'd had a particularly exhausting session today and my arm throbbed, but I'd be willing to tattoo someone else for a few hours just to hide in the studio a while longer.

I found an apple in the fridge and grabbed it, freezing when I heard loud footsteps sound behind me.

"Are you kidding me right now?" the voice growled, and I cringed, rising up slowly from behind the fridge door.

"What? I'm hungry," I grumbled, holding the apple protectively.

"What if Addy needs that apple? It's the last one, and we won't have time to go buy more before the babies come!" Cain snapped.

Addy was due any second, and Cain was going insane with worry over it. He'd been insufferable for weeks now, snapping over every little thing. We'd turned Piper's room into the nursery since it was the closest to Addy's room, but then Cain had insisted on bassinets in the master bedroom because of night feedings.

Piper had offered to kill him last week, and I was mad at myself for rejecting the offer so quickly.

"Cain, leave him alone. I don't need a fucking apple," Addy snapped, coming down the stairs. She was huge. It looked physically painful. Her stomach was so stretched it stuck out from under her shirts, even the special maternity ones we'd bought her.

Cain ran to her, offering an arm, which she swatted away in annoyance. She'd started maternity leave only last week, much to Cain's distress. Addy had told me she'd stopped going in only because Cain had started to scare her coworkers with his obsessiveness about lurking outside the lab door.

"You're only supposed to walk around small areas! No stairs!" Cain snapped, and Addy bared her teeth at him, causing him to back away immediately.

"I love you, dear *husband*, but if you don't calm down, you'll burn through your last good shirt, and they won't let you into the hospital shirtless." Addy replied, rolling her eyes, waddling up to pat his cheek. Ever since she'd found out that Cain had gone ahead and forged a marriage certificate for them when we moved here, the word *husband* was thrown around a lot - and not usually in a nice way.

It was almost comical to see the struggle on Cain's face, his body at war with itself as he tried to relax while still on high alert. "Babe, I love you, but I'm *begging you-*"

"I'm only three centimeters dilated, it's not even that big of a deal!" she huffed.

"You're nearly halfway dilated?! You could go into active labor any minute!" Cain insisted, his eyes wide.

"Want to help speed it along? Orgasms are supposed to help speed up labor," she smiled, batting her eyelashes at him. Cain's face went from stormy to white as a sheet, and he shook his head, mumbling about warming up the car and heading downstairs.

"That was mean," I told her, smirking. She smiled back, but then her face creased with pain and she gripped her waist, panting quietly.

"What? Are the contractions worse?" I asked, moving to her side immediately. The moment I touched her hand, I doubled over, swearing so violently Cain would've been proud.

"I told you not to do that," she snapped. "I need to know how far apart they are."

"Oh my god, please, go to the hospital now," I groaned, clutching my stomach, the apple laying forgotten on the floor.

"I'll be fine. Piper says I've got another hour until we need to leave," she replied primly, resuming her pacing around the living room.

"Piper wanted you to have a home birth. Are you really going to trust him on this?" I asked, giving her a sharp look. Her face blanched, and I raised my eyebrows in alarm.

"Oh fuck," she murmured, glancing at the stairs.

"Okay, it's fine. Don't panic!" I exclaimed, thanking the gods that Cain had been sleeping in the car for the last two weeks, just in case this happened.

I helped her down the stairs, and just as we reached the bottom, something just... came out of her.

"Oh no," she murmured, glancing down at the puddle on the floor.

"Please tell me you just peed," I begged. She shook her head grimly, grinding the bones of my hand in a death grip.

"Don't panic." I smiled wanly, turning to shout up the stairs. "ASSHOLES! Get down to the fucking car *now!*" I held Addy around the waist and we walked down to the car, footsteps thudding down the stairs behind us.

Cain was white knuckled in the driver's seat, and I avoided his gaze as I helped Addy into the passenger seat. "Um, no worries... but drive fast," I told him gently. Austin all but threw Piper into the back seat, piling in on top of him as Cain peeled away from the studio, breaking several laws as he sped to the hospital.

Addy's doctor handled the four of us crowding the birthing room pretty well, only commenting when a black snake stuck its head out of Austin's hoodie, scaring one of the nurses half to death.

One hour and a lot of screaming later, Cain was fast asleep in the hospital chair, mainly thanks to the mild tranquilizers the doctor had given him. Cain had reacted... poorly when they'd approached Addy with the epidural needle.

Addy was sitting up in the bed, going to town on a giant sandwich that Piper had ordered to the room, full of all the lunch meats that Cain had banned from the house months ago.

Austin was holding our baby girl with Piper at his side, looking at her like she was the only thing that existed in the world. She'd been the first one out and screamed so loud my eyes had watered. Meanwhile, I held our little boy, who'd followed his sister only ten minutes later and had let out one gentle cry before settling down immediately. I'd watched in awe as he'd opened his eyes and had looked around the room, taking in the freaks surrounding him with a stoicism few ever managed. We'd all checked the babies carefully, looking for scales, or freaky eyes, but so far they looked like normal, healthy, slightly potato-y newborns.

I walked over to Addy, careful not to jostle the little King I held in my arms. She smiled up at me, her hair still damp with sweat. "Feeling okay?" I asked softly, and she nodded, her face pinched with exhaustion. "You did good, sweetheart. Even when Cain threatened to kill the anesthesiologist for trying to see your pussy." I smirked, and she rolled her eyes, holding out her arms for our son. I passed him over gently, trying not to disturb him. They both had dark hair like their mom, and I was excited to see who they'd take after in terms of special abilities.

"Hey Shades?" she whispered, as the little man's eyes started to close. "You know I love you, right?" Her eyes looked pained, almost guilty, and it made me smile.

"Of course I do. I feel it every time I touch you," I reminded her, and she gave me a relieved little smile. "I love you too, sweetheart. I'd die for you." She opened her mouth, a frown creasing her forehead, and I stopped her with a kiss. "But I'd much rather live for you," I clarified, grinning.

I looked around at the five of us, now seven with the little ones. We didn't have a good set of parents between the lot of us, but I knew for a fact that these kids would be the most loved and protected little weirdos in the world.

Acknowledgments

I 've never considered writing an acknowledgements page before, mostly because it's still a bit unbelievable that these stories are out there in the world! To anyone reading this, know that you've made my day by picking up this book, and you're playing a part in making my dreams come true (it sounds sappy but it's true!).

I think first and foremost, I owe a huge thanks to **my partner.** I appreciate all your patience as I asked you insane questions and taught you terms like why-choose and 'knotting'. Thank you for all of your unwavering support (as well as your spreadsheet prowess and math skills).

The next person I'd like to thank is **Alina**, whose steady guidance and thorough understanding of proper grammar saved my ass more than once. I have a tendency to set the bar low for myself, because that way, it's harder to fail and risk disappointing anyone. You made me raise that bar with your constant encouragement and your thorough, grounding advice. I hope that you realize how much I look up to you as an author, and how much I appreciate you as a friend.

Jamanda, you dazzle me constantly with your kindness and your glowing words. You've made it impossible for me to doubt myself, and if we could bottle up some of that power you have to make something as silly as a why-choose romance novel feel amazing, we could make millions! I'm so thankful that our paths crossed.

I also want to thank the wonderful and extraordinarily helpful **Bec (on insta as @bookishspiceandeverythingnice)** who not only read and supported BWB, but also volunteered her time and energy to Beta read Dreaming of Darkness! I'm so lucky to have you in my corner, and I sincerely appreciate all of your support!

And of course, a super special shoutout to my **Team of Misfits**! I never thought anyone would love my guys as much as I did, and you proved me so wrong! Your kind words and excitement to read my stories are overwhelming, and I will never adequately express my gratitude toward you all for supporting a tiny indie author and her dreams.

Also by Bella Reves

Standalones

The Bodyguard

Monsters in the Darkness Series

Black Widow's Bite - Book 1

Dreaming of Darkness - Book 2

www.ingramcontent.com/pod-product-compliance
Lightning Source LLC
Chambersburg PA
CBHW070441120726
47910CB00003B/878